THE PURSUIT OF
MARY BENNET

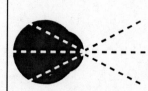

This Large Print Book carries the
Seal of Approval of N.A.V.H.

THE PURSUIT OF MARY BENNET

A PRIDE AND PREJUDICE NOVEL

PAMELA MINGLE

KENNEBEC LARGE PRINT
A part of Gale, Cengage Learning

GALE
CENGAGE Learning

Detroit • New York • San Francisco • New Haven, Conn • Waterville, Maine • London

GALE
CENGAGE Learning®

Copyright © 2013 by Pamela Mingle.
Kennebec Large Print, a part of Gale, Cengage Learning.

LIBRARY OF CONGRESS CATALOGING-IN-PUBLICATION DATA

Mingle, Pamela.
    The pursuit of Mary Bennet : a Pride and prejudice novel / by Pamela Mingle. — Large print edition.
        pages ; cm. — (Kennebec Large Print superior collection)
    ISBN-13: 978-1-4104-6455-2 (softcover)
    ISBN-10: 1-4104-6455-5 (softcover)
    1. Large type books. I. Austen, Jane, 1775-1817. Pride and prejudice.
II. Title.
PS3613.I599P87 2013b
813'.6—dc23   2013037859

Published in 2013 by arrangement with William Morrow, an imprint of HarperCollins Publishers

Printed in the United States of America
1 2 3 4 5   17 16 15 14 13

For Katie, with all my love

CHAPTER 1

Sometimes anger is a living thing. It rose up in my chest and made me want to chew thorns. They would tear at the tender flesh on the roof of my mouth, at my cheeks and tongue. When I swallowed, the sweet, salty taste of blood would linger on my palate, along with pointy bits of thorn. I squeezed my eyes shut, contemplating the pain.

Why was I loitering outside the upstairs sitting room, eavesdropping on a conversation between my parents? Especially since it aroused such ire in me. That couldn't be healthy. I leaned closer.

"To see all my girls but one settled. Such joy!" Mama said.

"Is Kitty engaged, then?" my father asked.

"She soon will be, mark my words. We will have another wedding by Michaelmas."

We had already celebrated three weddings in the family. My two elder sisters, Jane and Elizabeth, had wed wealthy and propertied gentlemen three years ago, Mr. Bingley and Mr. Darcy. Lydia, my youngest sister, formed a rather disastrous union with one Mr. Wickham, formerly of the militia, and went off to live in Newcastle, as he was currently attached to a regiment quartered there. Only Kitty and I remained at home.

"Ah, you refer to Mr. Walsh, I presume," Papa said. "Jane describes him as a reserved sort of fellow. Not at all the kind I thought Kitty would have chosen. Perhaps she is too eager to be wed."

I nearly choked on the irony. Kitty's foremost preoccupation was with finding a husband. And success at last! She had lately acquired a beau, a friend of Mr. Bingley's, whom she met during a lengthy stay with Jane and my brother-in-law. The very man my parents were now discussing.

"What do you mean? He's a handsome man, and has six thousand pounds a year! You only met him the once, Mr. Bennet, and cannot have formed a correct impression. And anyway, who cares if he is reserved?"

"Kitty, perhaps?"

I pressed my lips together to quell a laugh. I pictured Mama casting my father a severe look and knew his gaze in return would not waver. "Walsh has made his intentions clear, then. Shall I expect a visit from him soon?"

"Not yet, but it won't be long." Assured for some time of the matrimonial nature of the relationship, she had, I was quite certain, already spread the idea around the neighborhood.

"What of Mary? Does she wish to wed?" Why was he inquiring about me? No one ever thought of me when marriage was discussed. I was a person of no consequence. I'd never had suitors, nor did I desire any.

"Mary will make an excellent governess for Jane's or Lizzy's children someday," Mama said. "Marriage is not for her. I cannot think of any man who would have her."

I imagined dashing into the room and pouring the contents of the teapot over her head. She was wrong, in any case, about one thing. Neither Jane nor Lizzy would want me as a governess for her children. They didn't think well enough of me.

"Perhaps Mary should have some say in the matter," said my father.

"Bah!" she said dismissively. "When you are dead and Mr. Collins takes possession of our home, dear Jane or Lizzy will take us in, depend upon it. And her sisters will welcome Mary's help." Mr. Collins was our unctuous cousin, upon whom my father's property was entailed. My mother believed his intention was to swoop down upon us grieving females to claim his inheritance before Papa was lowered into his grave. I cringed every time she mentioned Papa's death, seemingly unconcerned about his feelings on the matter.

She continued. "Of course, she may be called upon soon enough to Newcastle to help Lydia and Wickham when their child is born."

And that was what infuriated me and made me wish to chew thorns. Sharp, spiky thorns. It was time to make my presence known. I knocked.

"Mary," my father said. "Sit down and have your tea. Tell us your opinion of Kitty's lover."

He has two heads and is only three feet tall. I grant you, both countenances are fine looking. And Mama is correct; he does have six thousand pounds a year, from his appearances at country fairs and exhibitions.

"I hardly know him, sir."

"Of course you do. You've met him at High Tor, have you not?"

"On a few occasions. But I've never had a conversation with him." In my mind's eye, Henry Walsh stood in the doorway of the salon at High Tor, Jane and Mr. Bingley's home, while I played the pianoforte. A few years ago during a visit to Elizabeth at Pemberley, my sister had persuaded Mr. Darcy that I would benefit from instruction on that instrument. To my surprise, he arranged it and bore the expense, and my playing had improved dramatically. Since then, I'd had to amend my opinion of the man. He was not the insufferable snob I once thought him to be. Unfortunately, no one suggested voice lessons, and so my singing continued to make people squirm. I refrained from forcing anybody, family or friends, to listen to my off-pitch performances.

On the evening in question, Mr. Walsh, who was far too handsome and fine figured to entertain locals at a country fair, leaned into the door frame watching me and presumably listening. Perhaps he was carried away by the music. I felt all the self-consciousness — and irritation — one would expect from such attention but managed to maintain my composure. After a few moments, the rest of the party arrived, and I rose, surrendering the instrument to Georgiana Darcy. Mr. Walsh had seated himself next to Kitty. A few furtive glances in his direction assured me of his indifference to me. Excellent, since *I* did not desire his attention.

"But you've observed him and Kitty together. What do you think of the match?"

My father's insistent questions caught me off guard. Was he teasing? My opinion usually counted for nothing. "I-I confess, I have never noticed them speaking much to each other, aside from the usual courtesies."

"Oh, what nonsense!" Mama said. "What good is talking, anyway? It only leads to quarrels and misunderstandings. I wouldn't place too much importance on it. I am certain they have a great regard for each other."

"You're right, my dear. Why should any lady desire to converse with the person she may be spending the rest of her life with?" His gaze shifted to me, and I noticed the thinly concealed mockery it held. "And what about you, Mary?"

Settled on one end of the sofa, I'd been pouring my tea and pondering what to say to Mama regarding Lydia's lying-in. I had not expected all these questions. "What do you mean, sir?"

"A man, of course. Any prospective suitors at Pemberley or High Tor who have captured your interest?"

My mother snorted. "Men don't notice Mary."

Her words burned, as though she'd slapped me. I wished I were bold enough to invent a suitor, a handsome, elegantly dressed gentleman with £15,000 a year, who had declared his undying love and devotion to me. But I'd have been found out soon enough.

"Of course not, sir." Resentment, so entrenched, rose in my chest against them both.

But when I raised my eyes and peered at him over my teacup, my father's look held no hint of disdain. Since my elder sisters had married, Papa paid me more attention than he used to do. I believed he missed Lizzy's sharp wit and intelligence, and I hoped I might someday take her place, if not in his heart, at least intellectually. Though I was foolish in so many ways, I harbored no improbable dreams of replacing Elizabeth in his affections.

I added milk to my tea and thought back to the morning Papa had first summoned me to his library and suggested a volume for me to read. "Mary," he said, "I set out some books for you. If you would be so good as to read them, perhaps we may, from time to time, discuss them. You might begin with Marcus Aurelius."

I recalled how reverently I'd run my

13

fingers over the books before picking up *The Meditations* and, after a quick curtsy and murmured thank-you, scurrying from the room, fearing my father would change his mind. Thus, over the course of the last few years, I had studied the Romans and Greeks, English history and literature, and whatever of Shakespeare I hadn't already read. John Donne, John Milton, Samuel Pepys, Dr. Johnson, and James Boswell. A whole new world had opened up to me, a world far beyond Fordyce's *Sermons* and Chapone's *Letters on the Improvement of the Mind.*

Papa left me to my own reflections, for the most part, although on a few occasions he asked my opinion of one of the works. Once we had a lively discussion of Pepys's diary entries about the Great Fire. For the briefest moment, his eyes danced with excitement, just as they used to do with Lizzy, right before he returned to the volume in his lap. He reminded me to shut the door on my way out, which I often forgot to do.

I smiled at the memory and sipped at my lukewarm tea, reflecting on my current situation. With Lydia gone, Kitty was kinder to me, inviting me to sit with her and Mama while they sewed, netted reticules, and shared whatever gossip was currently circulating around the neighborhood. Mama pestered me to take up my own work, but I preferred reading. The best days were those on which my mother and sister visited Lady Lucas or my aunt Philips. I welcomed the quiet while they were from home. As did my father, I was quite certain.

Even better, Mama and Kitty often spent a fortnight or more with Jane or Lizzy. I also made brief visits to my elder sisters when invited. Although they and their husbands extended every courtesy to me while I stayed with them, I was painfully conscious of their invitations to me bearing the weight of obligation.

If I were to raise an objection to a sojourn in Newcastle, now was the time. I bit into a scone to fortify myself. "Mama, I believe I heard you mention my attending Lydia when her child is born."

"You were listening at the door. Wicked girl! How many times have I admonished you not to do so?" Mama herself was an inveterate eavesdropper, but I was to be labeled wicked on account of it. I ignored her remark, and at last she said, "Yes, and so what of it?"

"I think it would be far better if you or Jane or Lizzy were to go. I know nothing of births or taking care of babies."

She gave me her most formidable glare. "Such cheek! Look at you, Mary, you have crumbs on your bosom."

I brushed at the crumbs, my face flushing with embarrassment. "I don't believe I would be very helpful in the circumstances." That was not the chief of it. The thought of passing any time with Lydia and the husband who'd been forced to marry her turned my stomach. *Mama couldn't make me go.*

She continued her rant. "*I* could not withstand the rigors of the trip. My nerves would never allow it. And your elder sisters are busy with their own families. It is your duty to go, Mary, as the only unmarried sister."

"But, Mama, I am *not* the only unmarried sister!"

"Before long, you will be!"

"Kitty should go. You know how close she and Lydia are."

"We dare not remove Kitty from High Tor at this time. No, that wouldn't do at all. It must be you. You've nothing to do besides embroider seat cushions and trim bonnets."

Two of the most odious tasks I was sometimes forced to undertake. My mother made it sound as though these were activities I chose to do. The truth was, she herself insisted these were skills all young ladies must possess. Quite satisfied with last season's bonnets given to me by Jane and Lizzy, I desired no others. Why should I? And in my view, none of the seat cushions appeared worn. Mrs. Hill had taken the utmost care of them over the years.

Just then, that lady appeared in the doorway with a stunned look upon her face. "What is it, Hill?" Mama asked, a sharp edge to her voice.

"Miss Lydia — I mean Mrs. Wickham — is here, ma'am."

None of us made a response. We were too stunned.

With her usual shrill laughter, Lydia flounced her way into the parlor. She was great with child, her time fast approaching. "You needn't look so shocked!" she said, untying her bonnet strings and dropping her reticule on the nearest table.

My mother hastened to the side of her youngest and favorite daughter. Clapping her hands in unrestrained delight, she said, "Lydia, dear, what a joy to see you. But you should not be traveling so close to your confinement."

I stared at my sister, who seemed grotesquely large. *A cow about to calf.*

Papa caught my eye, his brows quizzical. "What is the reason for your visit, Lydia?"

"I've left Wickham," she announced as she pulled off her gloves. "I am moving back to Longbourn."

CHAPTER 2

Something akin to laughter gurgled up from my diaphragm and burst out as a mixture of snort and giggle. I clapped my hand over my mouth to prevent it from happening again.

"Oh!" Mama said, collapsing upon the chaise.

"Lydia, what is the meaning of this?" My father's stern look revealed exactly how he felt about Lydia's unexpected arrival. Ever since she'd disgraced the family by running off with Mr. Wickham, while Papa and my uncle Gardiner searched the whole of London trying to find them, he had not been kindly disposed toward my sister or her husband.

"The drinking and gambling I can tolerate, although I don't like him squandering our money. But I do not think I can bear to live with a man who prefers the company of other women!" She began to cry, her carefree guise crumbling along with her countenance.

I softened. "Do sit down, sister," I said, leading Lydia to the nearest chair. "This turmoil cannot be good for you or your child."

Papa asked Mrs. Hill to bring refreshments for Lydia, and when her crying let up, she explained the details of her situation. "There is a certain lady who, in recent months, began to appear at assemblies, and at private balls and parties as well. A Miss Susan Bradford. She is a particular friend of the general's wife, and indeed, since I've been in this condition" — at this she gave a smart slap to her bulging belly — "she has replaced me in that lady's affections. In Wickham's affections, too, I fear. He spends all his time by her side at any party or dinner and dances with her at the balls. When I called his attention to it, he made a show of waiting only on me the next time we were in company. But he soon returned to his old ways. He said I shouldn't begrudge him a little fun when I'm with child and cannot dance."

"This is scandalous, Lydia!" Mama said. "Mr. Bennet, you must speak to Wickham immediately!"

"Does your husband know you are here?"

Papa asked.

"I left him a note."

"Shouldn't you have spoken to him before rushing off?" I inquired. When Lydia eloped with Wickham, she had informed her chaperones by means of a note, and now, in leaving him, she had done the same. Rash decisions followed by hastily penned notes seemed to be her preferred way of managing difficult situations.

"Oh, hush, Mary. You're only a spinster. What do you know of dealings between men and women? I am sure it will be a great relief to him to have me gone."

Indeed, and who would fault him for that?

"Dear Wickham loves you, Lydia! I am sure you are wrong to have done this. Oh, what shall I do when news of this gets out? Mr. Bennet, you must leave for Newcastle immediately."

"I shall do no such thing." He strode out of the room, shaking his head and muttering to himself. I fully expected him to remain sequestered in his library for the rest of the day, and he did not disappoint.

My mother put it about to friends and neighbors that Lydia had come to Longbourn to await the birth of her child. Since Mr. Wickham was busy with military duties

21

and didn't know when he might be called away to defend the English coast against a French attack, this seemed a reasonable way to explain her presence. After all, there was a war with France going on. With a good deal of cajoling from both Mama and myself, Papa agreed to write to Wickham and demand an explanation. I, because my mother's nerves caused her to take to her bed, wrote to both Jane and Elizabeth.

If Lydia was disturbed that her husband had not communicated with her, she hid it well. While penning my missives to my sisters, I pondered this. Was Lydia simply putting on a brave face? I sniggered and continued writing. Bravery wasn't a characteristic one associated with my youngest sister.

Out of sorts because Kitty was at High Tor, Lydia spent the next several days lying on the chaise and bemoaning her fate, grumbling about everything. "Oh, la, this baby is kicking me all the time. I cannot sleep for it," she said one afternoon.

My mother had gone to Lucas Lodge and Papa to his library, leaving the two of us alone. I was reading, or trying to. "That is what babies do, is it not?"

"What do you know about it? Nothing! Nor will you ever."

I tossed my book aside, realizing I couldn't give it sufficient attention while Lydia prattled on. I was eager to read it — Mr. Southey's *Life of Nelson.* My father had recommended it. But it would have to wait while I dealt with my sister's grievances.

Lydia continued with her complaints. "Kitty's having all the fun while I wither away with boredom. And she has a man! Henry . . . Walker, is it?"

"Walsh," I said, correcting her, ducking my head so Lydia would not notice the rapid coloring of my face.

"Oh, you've met him then? Do tell me all about him, Mary! Does he return Kitty's affection?"

I remembered Lydia's barb, that I knew nothing about dealings between men and women. "As I am such a poor judge of these things, perhaps you would be better off asking Kitty."

Lydia's mind had already fluttered back to her own state, so my words had no effect. "Can we not walk to Meryton?"

"In your condition, you shouldn't be walking anywhere. And I'm quite certain you would not want to be seen in public right now."

"Since when have you become such a know-it-all?"

I chose not to answer. "Would you like to sew some clothing for the babe?" I asked instead. "I could walk to town and purchase fabric. Or wool, if you would rather knit. You need only tell me what is required." This was something of no interest whatsoever to me, but if I walked to Meryton, I would be spared Lydia's company.

"Lord, no! The regiment wives who breed one child after the other forced me to sew every day. I have enough clothes for a dozen babies. Not that I expect to have another one. Depend upon it, I don't intend to let Wickham anywhere near my bed."

Hearing of Lydia and Mr. Wickham's intimate life made me wince with embarrassment. "Lydia, please don't speak of such things."

Just then, Mrs. Hill shadowed the threshold and I looked up. "Mr. Bennet wishes to see you in the library, miss." *What now?*

"Come back when you're done with Papa!" Lydia said. "I crave company, and must make do with you."

Visions of biting her head off and throwing it to the pig danced through my mind as I left the room.

"Close the door, Mary, please," Papa said as I entered his library. "I received this by special messenger." With a pale counte-

24

nance, he held out a letter and asked me to read it. I couldn't account for his serious demeanor and felt a twinge of fear in my stomach. Had something happened to Jane or Lizzy? But when I glanced at him, he said, "It's from Wickham."

2 March

My dear Mr. Bennet,

Allow me to express my great regret at what has transpired. That my wife chose to leave my home proves to me what I have long suspected. I am sorry to tell you what I know will cause you and all of the family pain, but I have no choice but to come out with it. I do not believe I am the father of the child Lydia carries. As it grieves me to mention this disturbing turn of events, perhaps Lydia can be prevailed upon to give you the particulars.

For now, I think it best that Lydia remain at Longbourn. I wish only the best for my wife and the child.

Yours, etc.
George Wickham

To say I was stunned could not be over-stating my feelings. Indeed, I didn't know what to say to Papa. *"I am sorry to hear Lydia has added adultery to her other sins"?* *"Unforgivable of Lydia to give you a grandchild of questionable paternity"?* After what seemed like a very long time, I said softly, "Can this be true, Papa?"

"When it comes to Lydia's behavior, there is little I cannot believe. But we know Wickham's character, and I am not fool enough to accept his version of the matter without questioning Lydia."

"Have you told Mama?"

"No. I will see Lydia first. Now, before your mother returns from her calls. Perhaps she need not be told, at least for the present. But I harbor no illusions, Mary. This will not be a pretty business no matter who is at fault."

"What do you wish me to do, sir?"

"Because this is a matter of such . . . *sensitivity,* I would like you to be present at my interview with Lydia."

"She won't like it."

"I am not inclined to worry about offending her. She has shown such a want of good judgment and manners, she can have no say in the matter."

"Shall I summon her now?"

He nodded, and I left the room in some agitation. To think that Lydia had returned to Longbourn and laid all the blame at her husband's feet! Did she not know she would soon be found out? As always, she thought of nobody but herself. Apparently she had not considered how this would hurt my parents, or me and my sisters. They, who had hoped that marriage, even to Wickham, would force her to behave with more decorum. What a mistaken notion that had been.

She was still reclined on the chaise, dozing. "Lydia," I said. "Papa wishes to speak with us in the library."

"La! What for? I'm resting."

"He received a letter from Wickham this morning. Perhaps —"

The blood drained from Lydia's face. "Never mind, I shall go. But there's no need for you to be present, Mary." She pulled herself up with great effort. When I tried to assist her, she waved me away.

I followed her down the stairs, and when we reached the bottom, she repeated her admonition. "I'm sorry, Lydia, but Papa requested my presence."

"Why does *she* have to be here?" Lydia asked as we entered the library.

My father, brows pulled together, looked very grave. Ignoring her question, he motioned to the two chairs in front of his desk, and my sister and I sat. After handing her the letter, he said, "I received this from your husband this morning. I would like you to read it."

She read, and tossed the missive onto the desk when she was finished.

"Well, Lydia, what have you to say?" Papa asked.

She started. She stammered and sputtered. Papa waited, and after a long while, she began to speak.

"You will take his part. I knew it would be that way."

"I've taken nobody's part. I am trying to get at the truth. Does Wickham have reason to believe you are carrying another man's child?" I lowered my head, not wishing to see the shame on my father's face. How it must have embarrassed him to be forced to confront his daughter about such a flagrant breech of conduct!

"No!" Her mouth snapped shut, but after prolonged glowering by my father, it opened again. "That is to say, maybe."

"Lydia!" I said. I realized then I had hoped it wasn't true. That my sister would deny it. That even she could not have committed such an egregious sin.

"Explain yourself, daughter," Papa demanded.

Lydia's expression looked unsettled and,

with some effort, she half rose from her chair, then sat again, her demeanor rapidly changing as she prepared to defend herself. "Why shouldn't I have a little fun, when my own husband was bedding another woman? If Wickham could ignore me and be seen about town with *her* on his arm, why should I not please myself?"

I interrupted. "You said — implied — that his association with Miss Bradford occurred *after* you knew you were with child."

Lydia gave me a disgusted look. "Well, I may have done, but that was not precisely the case."

Papa shot up from his chair. "What, then, *was* precisely the case? Answer me now, Lydia. Is your husband the father of your child or not?"

"I don't know," Lydia said defiantly. "That is the truth."

I took in a sharp breath. Papa leaned into his desk, propping himself up with his hands. "You foolish, foolish girl," he said. "Get out of my sight."

Lydia hauled herself up the rest of the way and left the room, just as the rumble of carriage wheels sounded out front.

CHAPTER 3

I heard Jane's voice in the entryway. "Don't bother announcing us," she said. Then someone else called, "Lydia!"

Kitty. She must have come with Jane from High Tor, and Lydia had brushed past them in her flight.

Papa hadn't moved; it was as though his hands were stuck to the desk. But at the sound of Jane's voice, he rose. "I never thought Lydia could cause the family any more harm or disgrace herself more than she already has. I see I was wrong. Apparently there is no end to her folly."

"Papa?" Jane entered the room while Kitty, presumably, ran after Lydia. "What has happened? You look as if you've seen ghost."

"Believe me, my dear, a ghost would be preferable. It would likely mean I was having a nightmare from which I could awake. Leave me, please, girls."

"Some brandy would help, perhaps?"

"No, Jane. I desire nothing but to be left alone."

"At least sit down, sir."

He glared, and Jane and I hurried out of the library and into the downstairs sitting room. My sister removed her bonnet and gloves, and when she was seated, said, "What could Wickham have been thinking? How could he hurt Lydia in this way?"

"You don't know the half of it." *Nor the worst of it,* I thought.

"You had better tell me, then."

And so I did, revealing to her the contents of Wickham's letter and Lydia's shocking response to Papa's question. Tears glistened in Jane's eyes. She bowed her head and when she looked up asked, "Does my mother know?"

I shook my head. "But she's due home directly. There is no way to keep it from her, although before Papa had the truth from Lydia, I think he thought of doing so." I gave my sister a questioning look. "Why have you come, Jane?" I asked.

She half-smiled. "I thought to be of some help. And I intended to swap Kitty for you."

"I beg your pardon?"

"Kitty was to stay here with Lydia, and you were to return to High Tor with me.

Those two have always been thick as a pair of conniving thieves, and I daresay if anyone were to hear the whole tale from Lydia, it would be Kitty. But now I think you both must leave."

"Oh," I said softly. But I did not wish to go to High Tor, where I would be separated from my books and my solitude. Although, truth to tell, my solitude had been shattered by Lydia's presence. Always demanding I sit with her, and then abusing me when I did.

"What news from Elizabeth?" Jane asked.

"None so far."

"I can only imagine what Mr. Darcy will say about this. After all he did for Wickham and Lydia, this is how he is repaid."

When Lydia ran off with Wickham, there was some question as to whether or not marriage was intended. Our family had been thrown into hopelessness and near panic. Mr. Darcy, the closest thing to a relative Wickham could claim, located the couple and arranged for their wedding. He settled an additional thousand pounds on Lydia, apart from what she was to receive from Papa, and also made good on Wickham's debts. To secure their future — or perhaps that of our sister — he purchased a commission for Wickham. In doing so, he received all the respect and gratitude due him from our family. And if Elizabeth still harbored doubts about loving him, Mr. Darcy's discreet handling of the matter had banished them.

Jane leaned back and rested her head on the chair. "What is to be done?"

Clearly she did not expect an answer, but I made one anyway. "Lydia will remain here until her child is born. We can keep up the lie Mama has already put about, that Mr. Wickham's military duties prevent him from being at her side. In the meantime, Mr. Darcy can pay a visit to Newcastle and try to talk some sense into him, and perhaps ascertain more accurately the circumstances."

Jane stared at me. "Why, Mary, I believe you are right. If Mr. Darcy will agree, that would be just the thing. Although we have no right to expect it of him, he will most likely feel it his duty. I do not envy Lizzy having to be the one to tell him all of this."

"Nor I. Jane, I —" As I was about to raise objections to staying at High Tor, we heard a commotion from the entryway — Mama arriving home from her visit to Lady Lucas.

"Jane is here?" she asked the butler. "And Kitty, too, you say?" She swept into the room and embraced my sister. "Oh, dear

Jane, I should have known you would come. My poor Lydia! What Wickham has done is unspeakable." She shed her wrap and rang the bell for tea. "But where are the other girls?"

Neither Jane nor I answered, and she looked about her, as though they were hiding and would soon pop out and surprise her. I glanced pointedly at Jane, who said, "There is more bad news, Mama. You'd better be seated."

"More bad news? Is someone sick or injured? Is your David all right? Lizzy's twins? Oh, do not keep me in suspense!" She flopped down on the chaise, her face having turned quite pale.

"No, be assured the children are all well." She hesitated a moment.

"What then?"

"It concerns Lydia and Wickham, Mama. Mr. Wickham wrote to Papa and . . . and accused Lydia of being unfaithful to him. He does not believe himself to be the father of her child."

"Good heaven!" Mama slumped the length of the chaise, and I hurried over to make sure she hadn't truly swooned. "That blackguard! Such a falsehood! He has never told the truth in his life!" She hoisted herself up and said, "What's the matter with you,

Mary? Why are you staring at me?"

I jumped back. "I was only making sure you were well."

Mrs. Hill entered the room with the tea and Jane poured. I handed Mama a cup and said, "When Papa asked Lydia directly, she confessed that she didn't know who the father of her child was." There. It was said. Mama would simply have to accept it.

A long, pitiful wail escaped her lips. It sounded quite similar to the baying of a hound scenting his prey. "How could this be happening to me? Don't my own children care about the condition of my nerves? And my dear Lydia, how could she have behaved so shamefully?"

The familiar sounds of giggling and chattering from my two younger sisters emanated from the stairway, and very shortly afterward they entered the room.

"Jane! You *would* come," Lydia said. "I'm only surprised Lizzy is not with you. And Mama, see who Jane has brought home! Now I shall not be so bored."

"What is wrong, Mama?" Kitty asked. "Are you ill?"

"How can you ask such a thing, you stupid girl?"

From the dumbfounded look on Kitty's face and the question she put to my mother,

I deduced that Lydia hadn't informed Kitty of her latest indiscretion.

"Lydia, I would never have thought this of you," Mama said. "How could you?"

"What is she talking about?" Kitty asked, looking from one of us to the other.

"To think that I believed you happily married and settled! How could you have deceived me in this way?"

"Good God, would someone please tell me what has happened?" Kitty shouted.

"Lydia does not know who the father of her child is," I said bluntly. That quieted everybody.

"Mary, you need not state it in that way," Mama said.

"What other way is there? Lydia herself owned to it; I was merely repeating it for Kitty's benefit."

Kitty jerked around to face Lydia. "Who else if not Wickham? He is your husband."

Will Lydia now catalog all her lovers? Could there be more than one?

"Lord above! As if I didn't know that," Lydia said. "He's the one who seems to have forgotten."

Jane rose. "Everyone, hush! This is not a fit subject for discussion in front of Mary and Kitty. The last thing we need to hear about is . . . well, never mind." She folded her hands in front of her and paced the room for a moment, during which time no one broke the silence, not even Mama.

"Kitty, you must return to High Tor with me, and Mary, you as well. It's not proper for either of you to stay here at present, while Lydia's . . . *situation* is under discussion."

Kitty looked horrified. "But I don't want to! Mr. Walsh has gone away."

"You cannot leave me here by myself," Lydia protested. "It would be unbearable. Kitty must stay."

"Yes, please," Kitty said, Lydia's little echo.

"*I* will not permit both Mary and Kitty to leave, and therefore, neither will Mr. Bennet. Not one of you selfish girls has considered my feelings in the matter," Mama said.

"Dear Mama, both Lydia and my father will be here, and you have the servants to look after you," replied Jane.

"This is not to be borne! Mr. Bennet is useless in these situations! And what if the babe should come? I'm no midwife."

No, more a fishwife, I thought unkindly.

"We must engage a midwife for the birth. You have about a month left until your lying-in, do you not, Lydia? When the babe's birth is imminent, either Elizabeth or I will come and attend you as well," Jane said.

"I shall come to High Tor, too," Lydia announced. "I would like it above all things."

"You most certainly shall not," Jane said through clenched teeth. "Now, Mary and I will go and have a talk with Papa and inform him of our decision. I'm sure he will agree we are doing what's best for all concerned."

Jane's authority was something to behold. Indeed, I believed she was the only daughter from whom my mother would countenance such talk. Marriage and motherhood had bestowed a new dignity upon her. "Come, Mary," she said, and I followed, although I didn't relish speaking to Papa when such a dark mood was on him. And if he adopted his usual indifferent manner in such affairs, I was not at all certain he would exert himself enough to go against Mama's wishes.

As we took our leave, I heard my mother say, when she believed we were out of hearing, "Lydia, you sly thing, tell us about the other man."

Jane stopped in her tracks, her face blanching. She pressed her lips together tightly, and for a moment I thought she would turn back. But then she grasped my hand and together we sought out my father.

She knocked lightly before opening the door. In a few minutes, she had explained everything. To my surprise, Papa agreed with the plan in its entirety.

"You've heard nothing from Elizabeth today?" Jane asked him.

"I have not. I suppose I should write and inform her of the latest . . . developments," he said wryly. "Darcy will be furious."

"He has every right to be," Jane replied.

"Just so."

"Sir, can you speak with my mother?"

"Concerning what?"

Jane slid her eyes toward me, as if to confirm that I, too, heard Mama's remark. I gave her a slight nod. "We informed her of Lydia's indiscretion, and as Mary and I left the sitting room, she was overheard asking Lydia to tell her about 'the other man'! Really, this is too much, even for her."

"I am sensible of the unsuitability of such talk," he said, "but I exercise no control over your mother."

"You could if only you would take the trouble, Papa," I put in. "She would never go against your directive."

Papa and Jane looked at me, both with shocked expressions.

"What?" I asked, looking from one to the other.

Jane bit her bottom lip, looking as if she were suppressing a laugh. "You are very forthright, Mary."

I took it as a criticism and cringed inside. It was the kind of remark I used to offer so freely, but at present I was attempting to break the habit. Everybody said it was unbecoming.

"Thank you, Mary," Papa said, "for your sage advice. But it has been many years since my wife has listened to me. You will be gone to High Tor, removed from disgrace, and thus will be protected. Let us leave it at that."

I thought, for just a moment, I glimpsed tears in his eyes, so I said nothing further. As never before, I noticed the heavy pockets of flesh under his eyes and the deep furrows between his brows. He was growing old. Old and defeated by the antics of his youngest daughter.

"Very well, sir," Jane said. "But Mama should not allude to this with Lydia. It gives the appearance of sanctioning her behavior."

"Thank you both for your concern. Jane, I think you must remove to High Tor with Kitty and Mary as soon as possible."

Jane's eyes caught mine and she heaved a weighty sigh. "Yes, sir," she said. "I believe we have no other choice."

CHAPTER 4

Two days later we departed, planning to break our journey at the home of friends the first evening. Before we left, Lydia displayed all her ill temper by accusing Jane of being "high and mighty" and "butting in" when her "advice was not wanted." Mama took to her room and refused to come down to say good-bye. Papa emerged from his library long enough to wave us on our way, and I felt a rush of sympathy for him, being left alone to deal with both Mama and Lydia.

"Are there other guests at High Tor?" I asked after we'd set off.

"Mr. and Mrs. Ashton. I regret the timing of the visit, but there is nothing to be done."

"And they are?"

"Friends. Acquaintances, really. We don't know them well, but they seemed most eager to visit High Tor, so Charles thought we should invite them." She glanced out the

41

window for a moment, as if gathering her thoughts. "Regarding Lydia's situation, I think we must all guard our words when anyone outside of family is present, including the servants."

I nodded. When Kitty didn't acknowledge Jane's edict in any way, the latter said, "Kitty, do you understand?"

"Of course. Have I met Mr. and Mrs. Ashton before? Do they like to dance and play cards?"

"They have never stayed with us, so no, I do not believe you've made their acquaintance. I suppose they like dancing and cards as much as anybody else."

I groaned inside, picturing long evenings forced to make up a whist table. At least I could get out of dancing by situating myself at the pianoforte and providing the music.

"But who will be my dance partner, now that Mr. Walsh is no longer there?" Kitty asked.

"Perhaps you will have to content yourself with other pursuits," I said. "Like reading, sewing, or walking."

"One can't walk at night!" Kitty said. "Oh, why did Mr. Walsh have to leave?"

As indifferently as I was able, I asked where that gentleman had gone.

"He had business to see to at his estate,

but he promised to return sometime soon."

"He must be exceedingly fond of you and Mr. Bingley," I said, "to stay with you so often."

Kitty giggled. "There may be another he is fond of!"

Jane looked dismayed. "I beg you not to make any assumptions on that head, Kitty. Mr. Walsh has shown no particular preference for you."

"What? He always asks me to stand up with him, and sits beside me during evening entertainments."

"No more so than with other young ladies who have been present," Jane cautioned.

"More than with Mary when *she* was present," Kitty said.

"That is unkind and unworthy of you, Kitty." Jane gave her a severe look, and she had the decency to look ashamed.

"I am sorry, Mary," Kitty said.

I inclined my head to acknowledge the apology, even while my thoughts were drifting. Had no one else noticed Mr. Walsh watching me that evening? It was entirely possible I imagined his attentions. It had only been the one time, in any case.

"He and Charles are great friends," Jane said, looking at me. "They both love riding and shooting. And he is advising Charles regarding estate management. Now that he owns High Tor, Charles has a great deal more responsibility."

When Mr. Bingley first came into the country, he had let Netherfield Park, near Meryton, from its owners in London. As it turned out, they had possession of several properties — High Tor in Derbyshire being another one — and wished to divest themselves of some of them. Jane and Charles had hoped to live near Elizabeth and Mr. Darcy; it was thus to the satisfaction of all when they purchased High Tor. Charles had made many improvements to the land in the past few years.

"I thought only Mr. Darcy advised Charles," Kitty said, turning up her nose.

"Not at all. When he and Lizzy stay with us, though, the two men ride about the estate with the steward and single out areas that need improvement of one kind or another. And Kitty, please be more respectful when you speak of Mr. Darcy," Jane added.

It would be a tedious journey, trapped in the chaise with Kitty for two days. I pulled out a book from my reticule and began to read, thankful I was not one of those people who suffered from nausea in a carriage.

On the second evening, to Jane's surprise and delight, Charles met us at the inn where we were staying to escort us the remainder of the way. Papa had notified him by special messenger that we were en route. We dined early, in a private room.

"What news?" Jane asked. "How is my little David?"

"He's well, my dear. Teething and fussing, giving his nurse the fidgets, I'd wager. And I'm certain he misses his mother, although perhaps not as much as I have missed you."

Jane glowed.

"I have some news which might make your sisters happy," Charles said.

"Oh, do tell us!" Kitty demanded.

"Henry Walsh has returned. The matter he had to attend to was easily dealt with, as it turned out."

Kitty jumped to her feet and waltzed around the room. I said, "How nice for all of you, Charles, but there is no reason his presence should affect *me*." A look I couldn't interpret passed between him and Jane. Perhaps they pitied me, because I was not someone their friend could esteem.

After an early start and a long morning's

ride, we arrived at High Tor. Jane went directly to the nursery while Kitty and I took refreshment. Kitty fidgeted and, after what amounted to a significant amount of time for her, asked one of the servants where the other guests were.

"I believe I saw them walk out earlier, miss," came the answer.

When I'd finished eating, I took a plate to Jane in the nursery. David, my nephew, was now six months old. A little cherub, all rosy cheeks and rolls of fat, he'd become more lovable than a newborn, in my mind. He smiled, cooed, and fixed his eyes on my face. I played with him while Jane ate, and when he grew sleepy we made our way downstairs.

Since the day was fine, I suggested we walk. Kitty was opposed at first.

"We shall probably meet the other guests," Jane said.

Kitty reconsidered. "In that case, I shall come."

"Where has Charles gone?" I asked.

"He is with his steward, I believe. Charles and Mr. Cox are talking of going to the magistrate to complain of the poor condition of the local roads, and the difficulty of getting agricultural crops to market."

"The poor roads make travel difficult altogether," I said, "whether by post or private chaise or —"

"For the lord's sake, Mary, can't you think of something more interesting to talk about?" Kitty said.

I felt my cheeks flush, because she was right. I always had something boring and stupid to say.

Before I could form an answer, we heard voices in the lane. Approaching us from the other direction was a party of three. Mr. Walsh was one of them. I looked away at once, feeling my pulse quicken. I fancied the other two must be Mr. and Mrs. Ashton.

Jane made the introductions, and we performed all the necessary bows and curtsies. "I did not expect to see you today, Mr. Walsh," she said.

He looked a bit nonplussed but said smoothly, "Nor did I expect to have the pleasure of your company again so soon. My business was rapidly concluded. I was unaware you had other guests."

"Oh, say no more, please," Jane said, smiling. "You are most welcome at High Tor anytime, sir."

With that, we broke up into pairs so the lane could accommodate us. Mr. Walsh offered his arm to Jane, and Mr. Ashton did likewise to Kitty. That left me with Mrs.

Ashton, a petite blonde in a fashionable day dress, who eagerly linked her arm with mine.

"My dear Miss Bennet, I am in transports at meeting you at last," she said. I could think of many — well, a few — other things one might justifiably be in transports over, but meeting me was not one of them. I was on my guard instantly. "You have other sisters, I believe."

"Yes, ma'am, two." I remembered Jane's caution and offered no further information. "How did you become acquainted with Jane and Charles?"

"We met in Bath, of all places," she said. "We were there so my husband could drink the waters. He suffers from gout, you see." I nodded, inwardly drawing back. Mr. Ashton's condition was surely not meant to be shared with a virtual stranger. She smiled after divulging this, revealing pointy little teeth. They were quite bright and evenly spaced, though.

She went on. "We had the good fortune to meet your sister and Charles in the Pump Room one morning." I recalled, now that Mrs. Ashton reminded me, that Charles had taken Jane to Bath in the early stages of her pregnancy, when she was feeling ill most of the time, hoping the waters would ease her misery.

Mrs. Ashton continued her story. "Miss Porter, a mutual friend, introduced us. Quite in the middle of a sentence I interrupted her. 'Who *is* that charming couple over there?' I asked. 'Why, that's Mr. and Mrs. Charles Bingley,' said she. So we hurried right over. Jane was looking sadly hagged, you know."

"I believe she felt unwell at the beginning of her pregnancy."

We continued in silence for a few minutes, until Mrs. Ashton spoke again. "I simply adore Jane and Charles. They are both so exceedingly friendly and cheerful, one cannot help taking to them. And I do hope you and I will be great friends, Mary. May I call you Mary?"

"Ah, if you wish it." On such slight acquaintance, this was unusual. But I could not refuse without seeming impolite. Indeed, I could barely get a word in.

"And you must call me Amanda. I won't have you calling me 'Mrs.' or 'ma'am'! Reserve that for the old ladies!" Again, she smiled. This time I judged it to be more a stretching of the lips over her brilliant teeth than a genuine smile.

"One of your sisters is wed to Mr. Darcy of Pemberley. What an auspicious match that was for her." And for him, I wanted to say, but did not. "Upon my word, the Darcys are known to be one of the wealthiest families in England! And you have yet another sister married to an army officer, if my recollection is accurate."

I made no reply, but Mrs. Ashton kept up her barrage of questions anyway.

"Where is he quartered at present? Is your sister with him?"

This cursed woman did not give up easily, I realized. "He is in Newcastle, but Lydia is presently with my family at Longbourn, in Hertfordshire. She is expecting a child, and since her husband's duties could take him away at any time, it was deemed best that she come to us for the birth."

"And what is her married name, if I may inquire?"

"Mr. George Wickham is her husband." Before she could ask another impertinent question, I asked one of my own. "Of what duration is your stay at High Tor, ma'am?"

"*Amanda.* I insist!" She squeezed my arm to get her point across. "I would like it above all things to stay at least a fortnight, perhaps longer. But, however, we would not wish to be the type of guests who wear out their welcome!" In truth, I wondered at their receiving an invitation for a visit of any length. Had Charles taken leave of his senses?

We continued walking toward the house, Mrs. Ashton still clinging to my arm. Jane and Mr. Walsh were conversing cordially, his head bent toward hers. With alarm, I realized that Kitty was laughing, in a rather wild and uncontrolled manner, at something Mr. Ashton was saying. He, as Mr. Walsh had done with Jane, bent his head toward Kitty, but not in order to hear her. He rather seemed to be teasing her. "Flirting" would not be too strong a word. To my chagrin, Kitty showed neither command of herself nor good judgment. I saw Jane glance quickly her way and noticed the sudden increase in our pace, so that we were inside the house in only a few more minutes. I could not help wondering if Mrs. Ashton had noticed her husband's conduct. If so, it could only have caused her pain.

We all retired to our chambers to prepare for dinner. I lay down on my bed and stretched until most of the knots in my back and shoulders, put there by the lengthy carriage ride, had eased. Once I overcame my reluctance to be in society, I felt far more relaxed when I stayed at High Tor than I ever did at home. Although I enjoyed a degree of solitude at Longbourn, I carried a surfeit of anger and resentment in my chest — against my parents, against Kitty, and even against myself — and it sometimes burst out at inappropriate times. Mocking, and on occasion even cruel, thoughts spun inside my head, waiting for a chance to pounce on some unsuspecting victim. Most of the time they stayed trapped inside, but it demanded the utmost restraint to keep them there. Here, among people I admired and respected, I could often rid myself of such thoughts altogether.

Whenever I stayed with Jane, she shared Sara, her lady's maid, with me, and I saw she'd already been in my room and laid out a gown for me to wear that night. A pretty confection of sprigged muslin in a pale green, it was a cast-off from Jane. Her clothing fitted me well, as we were roughly of the same height and proportion, and I was glad to have something special to wear. I was seated at the dressing table pulling pins from my hair, so that Sara might arrange it for me, when I heard a soft knock at my door.

Jane came through, looking worried. *Oh, please, no more bad news.*

She sank down onto the edge of the bed and ran her hand lightly over the dress. "I always loved this gown. I'm glad you can wear it, Mary, now that I've quite grown out of it."

I laughed. "In a few more months, you may ask for it back. If you do, I shall have to hide it someplace." Jane fretted over the loss of her figure after giving birth, but she looked the same as always to me. Beautiful.

"I came to ask if you noticed the tête-à-tête between Kitty and Mr. Ashton."

I gave her a rueful smile. "I did, although Mrs. Ashton was demanding most of my attention with her questions. She talks incessantly."

"She's not so bad. He — her husband — pays her little notice, so I suppose she must seek it elsewhere."

"She had a great deal of interest in Lydia's situation. What could be the reason for that?"

"Hmm. She's never once alluded to it with me. That does seem unusual." A slight delay, then, "You gave nothing away, I trust?"

"I answered in only the most abbreviated terms. Mrs. Ashton said I am not to call her 'ma'am,' or 'Mrs. Ashton,' either, because both make her feel old. She insisted I call her Amanda."

"And will you do it, Mary? You, who are

so formal and serious?" Jane could not seem to repress a grin.

"I shall try, if forced. But I should tell you, avoiding her company seems the most sensible choice to me." I smiled at Jane's image in the mirror. Pulling the last of the pins from my hair, I turned to face her. "You are worried about Kitty."

She came to my side and began to slide the brush through my hair. "Your hair is lovely, Mary. Such a rich amber color. It matches your eyes. And yes, I am worried about our sister."

Jane thinks my hair is lovely. Nobody has ever told me that before.

"Thank you," I said, warming to the compliment.

"Given the circumstances of Lydia's marriage, and her current situation, one would think Kitty would be more prudent in her own behavior. Especially if she wishes to attract the suit of such a man as Henry Walsh."

"Have you spoken with her?"

"I just came from her room, and she was defiant. 'What would you have had me do?' she asked, when I told her she'd behaved in a most unseemly manner."

"What was the topic that sent her into such hysterical giggling?"

54

"Nothing fit for her ears, which John Ashton should have known. Something about a young couple eloping, who were staying in the same inn as the Ashtons. They dined together and heard the chief of the story."

I grimaced. "That sounds like just the sort of account Kitty would love."

"Lizzy and I rather thought her manners had improved because of her separation from Lydia. Do you not agree?"

"I have been aware — that is, it has not gone unnoticed — that her manner toward me has softened somewhat since Lydia's marriage and removal from home."

"I knew I was not mistaken!"

"But truth be told, Jane, we have few dealings with one another. She sits with Mama, takes up her needlework, or walks to Meryton. She sometimes expresses a longing to visit Lydia, which Papa forbids at once. And very often, she is away from home, with you or Elizabeth."

"It's quite disheartening to see her manners revert to their former state. Could this one brief exposure to Lydia have altered her to such an extent?"

"I have an idea that being in the company of Mr. Walsh affects her conduct. She desires his attention."

"And seeking it in an improper way will be of no benefit. Her silliness would never work on such a refined man as he. Do help me, Mary. Admonish her if her behavior calls for it."

I snorted. "You know she would never heed my advice."

"She is misguided, then. I have been watching you these last few months. You've changed, for the better."

I felt color creeping up from my neck. I *had* tried to change, and it was so like Jane to have noticed and acknowledged it. The change had come about gradually, after my exposure to both Jane's and Elizabeth's happy, contented lives. And after I'd begun to read and learn more of the world. I envied my sisters their happiness and knew I wanted it for myself. If not with a husband, then doing something on my own, independent of my family.

"I'm nobody to admire," I said.

Jane laid down the brush and took my hands. "There you are mistaken, dear Mary. Perhaps you have more work to do, but you are proving your worth, as both a sister and daughter. I was impressed with the manner in which you spoke to Papa."

"Were you? I thought you were appalled."

"Not at all. It was just what he needed to

hear, although I'm quite sure he will take no action as concerns my mother. But you tried." She stood and smoothed her dress. "I must make my preparations. I shall send Sara to you shortly."

I drew in a breath and took a chance. "Jane, before you go . . . how do you think Kitty fares in her bid for Mr. Walsh's affection?"

My sister was already in the doorway, with her back to me. Did her shoulders stiffen slightly, or was it my imagination? "It is as I described before. I see no partiality for her in his manner. He is in every way the gentleman, and so he takes pains to be courteous to her. I fear she may have misinterpreted his words or actions." With that, she spun back around and looked at me, perhaps to gauge my expression.

I nodded, and felt that repugnant color rising again. Since the light was fading, I didn't think Jane would notice.

Fool, I told myself. *Fool.*

CHAPTER 5

During dinner I was seated next to the wayward Mr. Ashton. Kitty, across the table, was flanked by Mr. Walsh on one side and Mrs. Ashton on the other. Although I doubted he would converse about anything untoward, I determined to speak with Mr. Ashton as little as I could without seeming rude. In truth, he seemed to have little interest in conversing with me.

"Bingley, did you work out your problems today?" he asked my brother.

Charles's eyes gleamed and he smiled. "We formed a plan."

"Meaning what?"

"We shall ask the magistrate to raise the road tax."

"But, Charles, won't that be difficult for poor families?" asked Jane.

"It would be, certainly, but we intend to specify that it be levied only on families above a certain income level."

"Well done, sir," I said, smiling at him. "But what is the chance of getting the magistrate to agree to your plan?"

"I think he must, before the roads become impassable."

"Good man, Bingley," Mr. Walsh said. "Something needs to be done."

"I found out a bit of news today that the ladies will like to hear," Charles said. He scooped up a bite of fish and chewed leisurely, waiting for Kitty to pounce. She didn't disappoint.

"Oh, do tell us, Charles!"

"We are to be invited to a ball given by the Penningtons."

Kitty squealed with delight. "When?"

"Within the month, I believe. Pennington said we would receive an invitation."

"Will we go?" asked Kitty.

Smiling, Jane said, "I see no reason why those in our party who wish to do so may not."

"We must walk to the village so I can purchase a bit of fancy lace for my gown," Kitty said. "And I need a bonnet. Or at the very least, new ribbons."

"No need to walk," Mr. Ashton said to Kitty. "I'll drive you in my curricle." Then he turned his attention to me. "And you, Miss Bennet, shall you go to the ball?" He spoke into a sudden silence, and I sensed everyone's eyes on me, waiting for my response.

"No, sir. I don't care for balls." When I was younger I used to be dragged to assemblies and private balls, and always felt the misfit. I would never forget the shame and humiliation of that horrible night at Netherfield when my father shouted at me halfway across the room to let someone else play and sing. Lizzy told me afterward she was sorry about the way Papa had treated me. She did not defend my playing and singing, however.

This produced a yelp of laughter from him. "Indeed, you must be the only young lady in the country who would say that."

"That is Mary for you," Kitty said. "Dull as a stick."

"Kitty," Jane hissed.

Smarting from the cruel taunt, I could barely swallow the bit of venison in my mouth. Oh, how I wished I could crawl under the table. Why couldn't I simply have said yes and been done with it? It wouldn't have meant I had to go.

"You must consider me dull as well, Miss Kitty, for I am not fond of balls, either," Mr. Walsh said. I glanced up. He was looking at me intently. Maybe he pitied me and felt obliged to come to my defense.

Kitty's mouth formed a moue. "But you like to dance, Mr. Walsh!"

"It isn't that. Only that it is so hard to converse in a ballroom."

"Balls are not for conversing," Mr. Ashton said. "They're for merrymaking."

"Perhaps you may both stay at home and play at cards or read," Mrs. Ashton said, snidely, I thought.

"Mary hates cards, too," Kitty said with an ill-tempered look.

"Mary is quite skilled at the pianoforte," said Jane, who no doubt believed she must now name all my accomplishments. That would take but little time.

"I hope we will have the pleasure of hearing her play tonight," Mr. Walsh said. "When last you were here, Miss Bennet, I recall your playing Mozart."

He remembers what I was playing that night. The night I noticed him watching me. I nodded. "My sister exaggerates my talents, I fear. But I have had the benefit of an accomplished master during the last few years."

My enjoyment of the excellent trifle Jane's cook had prepared was ruined. The candied fruit seemed dry as clumps of dirt and just as tasteless. At last we came to the end of the meal, with no further embarrassment for me, and Jane rose. "Ladies, shall we repair to the salon?"

I'd rather repair to a convent.

In the salon, Mrs. Ashton claimed a seat at the table, no doubt anticipating a game of whist. I watched Jane take Kitty aside and deliver what I was sure must have been a reproach. I wished she would not take the trouble. At the pianoforte, I perused the sheets of music, at last settling on a Mozart sonata. The first movement was calm and peaceful. I sank into it and let it soothe my spirits.

When the men joined us, John Ashton demanded a card table. "Who's for whist?"

Mr. Walsh walked quietly toward me and lowered himself onto one of the upholstered chairs. After a time he closed his eyes, and I hoped he was listening rather than dozing. Kitty's shrill voice suddenly intruded. "Mr. Walsh, won't you make a fourth at whist?"

His eyes opened, and he rose immediately. "Certainly, if you wish it." He glanced briefly in my direction and said, "Excuse me, Miss Bennet."

I finished the piece and found my book about Nelson, which I'd left lying on the table earlier. For a time, I read without distraction. Background noises hovered on the edges of my hearing: Kitty's laugh, Mr. Ashton's bark of triumph when he took a trick, Henry Walsh's chuckle, and Jane and Charles talking softly together on the chaise. They seemed to have such perfect harmony in their marriage. I realized my happiness for them was slightly tainted by regret for myself.

"Mary, come here for a moment, please," Jane said. When I was seated beside her she glanced at Charles.

"We received a message from Elizabeth earlier today," he said. "She and Darcy have been informed of all the recent developments in Lydia's situation, evidently by your father."

Charles paused, looking about the room to make sure nobody else was listening, I presumed. Jane took over. "Mr. Darcy is traveling to Newcastle to have it out with Wickham."

"He agreed to do it, then."

"It was his own integrity, and his vexation with Wickham, which decided him."

"What does he hope to accomplish?"

Charles kept his voice low. "To persuade Wickham it is in everyone's best interest for him to reunite with Lydia, even if the question of paternity is not settled. It is Wickham's duty to raise the child as his own, in any case."

"I wish he may be successful," I said. "I fear . . . do you think Wickham will demand money?"

"Given what we know of his character, it is hard to believe otherwise," Charles said.

While we were talking, a servant carried the tea tray in and placed it on a carved mahogany tea stand. Jane stepped over to pour. John Ashton brashly called for brandy. Soon thereafter, Mr. Walsh announced he no longer wished to play cards.

Mr. Ashton protested. "Walsh, you cannot beg off when you've been winning! Give us poor fools a chance to recoup our honor."

For a moment, Mr. Walsh seemed to be wavering. "Bingley will take my place," he said, sending a pleading glance to his friend.

"Oh, Mr. Walsh, please do not abandon me!" Kitty begged.

Charles willingly came to the rescue. Kitty screwed up her mouth in irritation. Suppressing a smile, I returned to my book.

Deeply absorbed, I scarcely noticed someone standing directly before me. When I looked up, Henry Walsh was holding out a cup of tea.

"Your sister fixed it the way you prefer."

"Milk, no sugar," I said, smiling. He sat

down next to me, jiggling his own cup a little.

"I've always admired those who are able to read while there is so much to distract them. How do you do it?"

Henry's voice was rich and pleasant to the ear, like something in nature. I laughed. "It is no great skill. I own it presents a challenge, but once I'm completely absorbed in the story, the distractions no longer . . . distract." Sipping my tea, I dared a quick glance at his face. Never before had I been this close to him. His good looks and masculine bearing were striking, although he wasn't perfect looking. He rather had the rugged appearance of one who spent a great deal of time out of doors. His eyes were extraordinary, the deep blue of the sea, or what I imagined the sea to look like.

"I'm sorry I missed your playing," Henry said. "I shall insist the men forgo their port if that's what is necessary for me to have that pleasure."

"I assure you, I am not so accomplished as that. I wouldn't want you to give up your port." *Am I flirting? Good heaven. Do I sound like Kitty?*

Amusement gleamed in his eyes. "It would be no sacrifice, Miss Bennet."

"Tell me about your home, sir," I said,

trying to turn the conversation. "I collect you live nearby."

I had hit on the right subject. His home was not so grand as High Tor, but it suited his needs. "My mother lives with me and deals with managing the household. There is yet more to be done inside, and the park is a work in progress."

"Has the estate been in your family a very long time?" I tried to ignore it but was sensible of the fact that Kitty had been glaring at me for the last several minutes.

"The property was entailed upon me."

"I see. How nice for *you,* but unfortunate for those who lost their home because of it." Then I blushed fiercely. Why was I cursed with candor? The poor man couldn't help being the beneficiary of an entailment.

He raised a brow. "I presume you speak from experience?"

This was the last topic I wished to discuss, but I had opened the door with my comments. "Our home, our land, everything, is entailed upon a distant cousin, who currently resides in Kent." I tried to keep my expression bland, but I felt one corner of my mouth tilt up and heard the disdain in my voice. "Mr. Collins. He is a vicar."

"I am sorry to hear it. In my case, and I am glad of it, no one was put out of their home. The previous entail had gone to a distant relative who died suddenly and had no living children, whereupon it came to me." He reached into a pocket and produced a white handkerchief. "You have a spot of something just here" — he pointed to the corner of his own mouth — "may I?" And before I could object, he leaned in and dabbed at my mouth. I felt my eyes closing, and my breath went shallow.

I was captivated by his hand and his exceptionally gentle touch, while at the same time cursing my slovenly habits. As soon as I recovered myself, my eyes flew open. Others in the room could have been watching, and this might have looked improper. "Oh! Please, sir, do not —" I flailed my hand pointlessly, since his had already removed itself.

The handkerchief disappeared. "Forgive me. I did not mean to give offense."

Since I'd been rendered senseless, I was actually grateful when Kitty joined us. "What are you talking about?" she asked. "Pray, don't keep secrets from me."

"Mr. Walsh was telling me about his home. It's not far from High Tor."

"It lies roughly five miles north of here," he said. "If the rest of the party has no objection, why don't we ride over and spend a day there? My mother would be pleased to make the acquaintance of all of you."

"Oh, yes!" Kitty said. "I am most keen to see your home, Mr. Walsh, and to meet your mother. Let's go tomorrow!"

"Kitty, I am sure Mr. Walsh did not mean —"

"Jane," Kitty shouted. "Mr. Walsh has invited all of us to visit his home tomorrow!"

I sneaked a glance at the gentleman, who seemed amused rather than irritated, and ducked my head when his eyes found mine. What must he think of us!

"It's all right, Miss Bennet," he said to me in a low voice. "Do not distress yourself."

I forced myself to look up. He seemed entertained, more than anything, and apparently didn't mind Kitty's exuberance. Everyone soon was apprised of the plan, and Mr. Walsh assured us of his mother's welcome. However, the day was fixed not for tomorrow, but the day after, as Jane had already planned a picnic for tomorrow afternoon.

After it was settled, I excused myself and retreated to a quiet corner of the room, where I eased back into my book. I could not resist a few glances now and then, though, to see what Mr. Walsh was up to.

Although I never caught him at it, I sensed he was watching me, too, and, had anyone asked, I could have said precisely what lines I was reading each time I felt his eyes upon me.

CHAPTER 6

I was late for breakfast, having been distracted by extra care with my toilette. Kitty was seated next to Mr. Walsh, while Jane sipped tea across the table from them. Charles, glancing idly at a newspaper, stood and smiled as I entered the breakfast parlor. "How well you look this morning, Mary."

"Thank you, Charles," I said.

"Good morning, Miss Bennet," Mr. Walsh said, also rising.

I dipped into a half curtsy. "Good morning, sir."

I was certain both men had addressed the same courtesies to Kitty when she entered, but nevertheless she glowered at me.

The Ashtons were not present.

I moved to the sideboard to fill my plate. The footman asked if I wanted tea or chocolate, and I chose the latter, probably because we seldom had it at home. After taking the chair next to Jane, I nibbled on toast and eggs.

"What would you say to a ride this morning, Walsh?" asked Charles.

"Splendid idea. The weather is perfect for it. Ladies, do you ride?" His gaze was directed at Kitty and me, but it was Jane who answered.

"I am afraid we are not horse riders," Jane said. "My father didn't keep mounts for the purpose. Just an old mare we rode now and then." Charles smiled fondly at her, probably recollecting the time she had ridden the mare to Netherfield in the rain. She caught a dreadful cold and had to remain there until she recovered. Jane believed wholeheartedly that that was when she and Charles fell in love.

"But I would love to learn!" Kitty said.

I sipped my chocolate. Mr. Walsh made no response to Kitty's none-too-subtle hint about riding lessons. His eyes were fixed on me when I noticed Jane making odd little motions toward her upper lip.

Oh! I'd done it again. What was wrong with me? I couldn't seem to eat or drink without something adhering to my lips or some other part of my body. I dabbed away the spot. That explained why Mr. Walsh was staring at me. Ladies should be fastidious. How many times had that been drummed into me?

"I do hope the weather stays fine for our picnic this afternoon," Kitty said. "Where shall it be, Jane?"

"At the lake," Charles and Jane said simultaneously.

Kitty immediately turned to Mr. Walsh. "Sir, would you be so good as to row me around the lake?"

"It would be my pleasure," he said, smiling.

For the Lord's sake, how much of her simpering was I to endure? *Have a care, Kitty. A good dunking would be just the thing for you.*

The Ashtons made an appearance, and Charles gently scolded his friend for being late. "Walsh and I have been awaiting your company for a ride."

"Kind of you," he said, "but I'm not in the mood for it. Go without me." Indeed, he looked as if he'd had a late night, gazing at us out of puffy and bloodshot eyes. His hair stuck up in odd places despite looking damp, as if he or his man had tried to tamp it down to no avail.

"Very well, then." Charles looked at Henry Walsh. "Are you ready?"

"I am. But first, I need to share some disappointing news. We must postpone our visit to Linden Hall."

Kitty groaned.

"Not for long," he said, glancing at her. "It occurred to me that repairs to the roof are under way." He smiled sheepishly. "I'd completely forgotten. We must delay our visit until next week at the earliest."

Jane inquired as to the day, and Mr. Walsh had barely replied before Kitty repeated her refrain about how keen she was to see his estate and meet his mother. *Ugh.* I had begun to wonder if I should accompany them at all, since I didn't know how much of Kitty's fawning I could tolerate without exploding.

God above, I was jealous. How lowering! Jealous of a sister whose behavior I abhorred much of the time.

The two riders excused themselves, and Mr. Ashton took up the newspaper.

"What shall we do this morning?" asked Kitty.

"I must see to organizing the picnic," Jane said. "The rest of you may do whatever you'd like."

"I'll practice at the pianoforte and walk afterward," I said.

Amanda Ashton glanced at me. "I declare, a walk sounds like just the thing! May I join you, Mary?"

My name on her lips grated. Courtesy demanded I assent, even though I didn't desire her company. A scheming look sparked in Kitty's eye. She turned to Mr. Ashton and said, "Sir, would you be so kind as to drive me to town in your curricle?"

"I would be honored," he answered.

I sneaked a glance at Jane, who appeared unsettled. "Your groom will accompany you, sir?"

Mr. Ashton looked entertained. "I am an old married man, Mrs. Bingley."

"Nevertheless . . . ," Jane said.

"If it will make you feel better, my groom, Thaddeus, shall escort us."

Jane nodded, and an awkward silence fell over the group. I gulped my remaining chocolate and took a few more bites of egg. Rising, I turned to Mrs. Ashton. "I'll play for an hour or so and then meet you in the front hall, if that suits you, ma'am."

"My dear Mary, I asked you to call me Amanda. I shall be most put out if you do not."

"Mary can barely bring herself to call our brother Charles instead of Mr. Bingley," Kitty said. "She is —"

Jane cut her off by loudly announcing, "I shall get to it, then. Kitty, may I have a word with you before you set out?"

I could finish Kitty's thought for her. *Mary is a prig. Ridiculous and boring, too.* That was the chief of it, I thought. *That was the whole of it.*

The morning passed much as we planned. Because of a letter she needed to write and post with all haste, Mrs. Ashton begged off walking with me. Relieved, I set off down the lane toward the shrubbery walk. Before long, I heard the sound of Mr. Ashton's curricle and matched pair, and soon they trotted into view. Beside him perched Kitty, bonnet strings flying. I was pleased to see the groom balanced behind them. Interesting that Mr. Ashton was not up to riding with Charles and Mr. Walsh but was quite keen to carry Kitty to the village.

It wasn't a comfortable feeling, to be jealous of one's sister. Henry Walsh was the cause of it, much as it gave me pain to admit it. He could not like me. He possessed a kind and generous nature, and most likely didn't approve of Kitty's — or Mr. Ashton's — rude remarks at my expense. I daresay that was the reason he'd pretended — and I was certain it *was* a pretense — he did not care for balls. Yes, he was a handsome man, and I enjoyed talking to him. But I vowed to avoid him from this moment on, since any true liking I developed for him would inevitably lead to heartbreak.

Kitty had already engaged him for rowing on the lake, which would occupy him for much of the afternoon. I would leave pursuit of him to her. Although her understanding was weak, and she sometimes showed a want of manners, she had never displayed a complete disregard for the good opinion of society, as Lydia had. With discreet encouragement on her part, Mr. Walsh might direct his attentions toward her.

Lydia. I wondered how she did, and whether Mr. Darcy had undertaken the journey to Newcastle. It was some distance from Derbyshire, probably a trip of several days. Could Wickham be persuaded to reunite with my sister and raise the child as his own? Since Mr. Darcy married Lizzy, his manners in company had become easier, but he remained a formidable man. Not a man to be denied.

The weather held, and we set out walking toward the lake around two o'clock.

"I never saw anything prettier than this! Do but look at how picturesque it is!" Mrs. Ashton said to her husband, waving her arm through the air.

"Hmph," was his only comment.

A footman had gone ahead of us, carrying heavy baskets of food. A second servant wheeled a cart with drinks, old coverlets to spread out on the grass, and toys for David. Clutching my book, I hung back, meandering and hoping to remain solitary. Kitty had her hand on Mr. Walsh's sleeve, and when I strayed closer, I heard her telling him about her shopping excursion, describing the lace she purchased for her gown and the style of her new bonnet. He laughed and said he would look forward to her wearing it. I slowed down so I would no longer be close enough to catch what they were saying. No reason to overhear what could only aggravate me.

Jane had given David's nursemaid the afternoon off, and we passed the child around so that Jane and Charles might have their turn at eating. When David squalled in Mr. Ashton's arms, Henry Walsh took him, handling him with all the ease one might see in a man who had spent time with infants. He walked about, settling David into the curve of his arm, pointing out trees, water, boat, birds, and anything else the child might find diverting. Not very comfortable with infants myself, I admired the skill in others. I had a great yearning to approach him and tell him so, but remembering my vow from that morning, I thought better of it.

"A man who possesses many talents. Do you not agree, Mary?"

"I beg your pardon?" I whirled around at the sound of Mrs. Ashton's voice. I had no idea how long she'd been watching me watch Mr. Walsh, and my face warmed.

"Henry Walsh. Never tell me you haven't noticed. A great man for sport, a prosperous landowner, and now we observe his benevolent way with children."

I laid down the chicken leg I'd been holding suspended halfway to my mouth. "Indeed," I said, trying to keep my composure.

"Your sister seems quite taken with him, but I sense his interests lie elsewhere. I told my dear John last night, 'Mr. Walsh has a vast deal of interest in Mary Bennet, do you not think so?' Of course, being a man, he had observed nothing extraordinary. But be assured, dear creature, I have!"

"I wouldn't know, ma'am. Amanda," I said hastily, before she could correct me again.

"Come now, my dear. Don't be sly with me. You cannot be blind to his preference for you."

"He is courteous and gentlemanly, that is all. I comprehend nothing more in his behavior toward me."

"Very well, then. I see I will not get you to own to it. You are too modest, or perhaps too shy to discuss the matter. We shall talk of something else in that case. How fares your sister in Longbourn?"

"You refer to Lydia? We have had no news."

"How she must long for her husband! A separation at this time would be hard to bear."

I murmured some meaningless response while casting about for another topic of conversation. "Do you have children, Amanda?" Generally, I would not dream of asking such an intimate question, but desperation trumped good breeding in this instance.

"We have not been so fortunate." She cast her eyes down, and I could not judge her sincerity. "Will your sister return to Newcastle after her lying-in?" she asked.

Now she raised her head, and I was looking straight into her eyes. They expressed more than a polite regard for my family's welfare. As she leaned toward me, her mouth opened enough to expose her sharp little teeth. I couldn't help thinking she had a rather vulpine countenance. She took an eager interest in Lydia and Wickham's affairs. Too eager. She wanted to gossip about them to her friends, I concluded. Some women took pleasure from talking about the misfortunes of others. It would not do.

"Pardon me, ma'am," I said, jumping to my feet. "I think I shall rescue Mr. Walsh."

My vow floated off into the breeze.

It was the first time I had approached him of my own accord. He watched me walking toward him and smiled. "Mr. Walsh, let me take David. Wouldn't you like to finish your meal?"

"Thank you, but I've eaten more than enough." He tucked David into my arms. "I believe he's growing sleepy. Perhaps he's ready for a nap?" We strolled in Jane's direction, David burying his head against my breast.

Jane saw us coming and rose. "Thank you, Mr. Walsh, for entertaining him. You seem to have a way with children."

His eyes gleamed with good humor. "I'm an experienced uncle. My three sisters have five — no, six — children among them."

Jane laughed. "I guess with so many, it is understandable you've lost track."

"And it's no wonder you are so accomplished," I said as I handed David over to Jane. "I hope to become more proficient with children one day." I winced. *What an embarrassing comment, as though I'm hinting at marriage and a child — with him.*

"You will, with practice," he said, not appearing to have misconstrued my words. "Miss Bennet, I was thinking of climbing to the top of that peak." He pointed in the general direction of High Tor. "Would you care to accompany me?"

I glanced at Jane for guidance. She laughed. "Go ahead, Mary. You'll be in full view of us, if you're worried about a chaperone."

I was more concerned about my resolve. What had happened to it? Only a few hours past, I'd vowed to keep my distance from the man, and now, as soon as I heard "climbing," "peak," and the most significant words of all, "accompany me," I was persuaded to do the opposite. So long did I pause, both he and Jane stared at me in puzzlement. "Thank you. I would like that," I said at last.

As we started off, I swiveled around to see what Kitty was doing. In conversation with the Ashtons, she didn't appear to notice me walking away with the man she wished to court her. I wondered if Amanda Ashton had been attempting to pry information out of her as well as me, and prayed if that were the case, she would be circumspect.

We walked at a leisurely pace. Hands clasped behind his back, Mr. Walsh seemed content with silence. I liked that about him, that he did not have to fill every empty space with the sound of his own voice. There was no bravado in him.

"What is your favorite season, Miss Bennet?"

I thought for a moment. "Autumn."

"And I prefer spring above every other. After the drudgery of a long winter, I am impatient to get out of doors again. Tell me what you like about autumn."

"I suppose I love the colors best of all, and the leaves underfoot. And there is something about the air on an autumn day. It shimmers."

"Does it?" His eyes held that little gleam of merriment I'd noticed the other night. "I shall have to take note of it this year."

We'd come to the base of the peak, where boulders and loose stone made the walking difficult. I slipped, nearly losing purchase, before Mr. Walsh took hold of my shoulders to steady me. When afterward he offered his hand, I hesitated. I felt his eyes watching me but could not look at him.

"Miss Bennet, if you will not take my hand, I fear we shall be forced to turn back.

The way is too rough for you to walk unaided. I promise to release your hand back to your keeping as soon as we arrive on the path."

I smiled, still not looking at him, and grasped his hand. In this way we progressed, and in a very short time, placing my hand in his seemed natural. Once we gained the path, the walk, though vigorous, was not difficult. At the top, we found a ledge to sit upon so that we might admire the view. We sat in silence for a few minutes, enjoying the vista.

"It's breathtaking, isn't it?" I said at last.

"Indeed it is. Now you may understand why I delight in spring. The trees are leafing out, gorse is blooming, and green spreads over hills and peaks like a coverlet. Will you not change your mind, Miss Bennet, and say you like spring best?"

I could not help laughing. "No, sir, I will not. I don't *dislike* it, though."

"Charles is a lucky man, to have such a grand estate."

"But you are content with your own estate, are you not?"

"Very much so. You shall see it next week, and I hope you will find it to your liking."

I dared to look up at him, and his eyes held mine for a moment. There was nothing

83

there of teasing or mocking, but still, I knew I must not read anything into his remark. He might have said the same to anyone who was soon to visit his home.

"Shall we go? I promised to row your sister around the lake." A reminder of the excellence of his manners and his desire to please. A climb up High Tor with me meant nothing more to him than a spin around the lake with Kitty.

On the way down, Mr. Walsh asked my opinion of Southey's biography of Nelson.

"On the whole, it seems balanced, if slightly biased in Lord Nelson's favor. Have you read it?"

"Yes. A great hero, although the Naples fiasco tarnishes him, as well as the conduct of his personal life."

"You speak of his . . . *flirtation* with Lady Hamilton?" My cheeks burned. I knew it had gone much further than a "flirtation," but I couldn't bring myself to say "affair."

"I do. Tell me, Miss Bennet, do you believe we should be judged by the totality of our lives, rather than each separate part?"

"You mean, should we consider the admiral's achievements over his whole lifetime rather than dissecting it piece by piece?"

"Precisely."

"I could more easily esteem his illustrious

deeds if he hadn't committed the imprudent ones."

"You cannot, then, set them aside? He was a great leader of men; his courage never faltered. He lost an arm, and ultimately his life, in service to his country."

"I do admire him for his accomplishments, and yet those imperfections in him . . ." My words tapered off. I wasn't sure what I wished to express.

"Is human perfection possible, Miss Bennet? I would hate to have my own faults examined too closely."

By now we were approaching the others. I wanted to tell him *I* could forgive his imperfections, but Kitty saved me from saying something so forward by accosting us with her demands. "Sir, I've been waiting a horrid long time for you to row me around the lake." She gave me a disapproving look. "You cannot keep Mr. Walsh all to yourself, Mary."

I was mortified.

Henry Walsh bowed slightly in my direccion. "Thank you for accompanying me, Miss Bennet."

I stood rooted to the spot while they walked away, staring after them. *Him.* As they pushed off from shore, a fierce desire to be the one in the boat with him took possession of me. We might have continued our conversation about his . . . faults. Whatever they were, they must be buried in the past, because at present, I could see none. It was just as well, then, that it was Kitty in the boat with him. I might have said something to regret later.

I spied a place to sit by myself with my book. Every so often, the sound of their laughter drifted toward me on the breeze. What Mr. Walsh and I had discussed was more serious in nature. I sighed. Men liked to be entertained by ladies, I thought. They liked to laugh.

I tried to put him out of my mind. But it was hopeless, because all I could think about was the feel of his warm flesh on mine. Our hands clasped together. I would have liked to etch the memory somewhere, so no one could take it away from me. I would have liked to hold it inside forever.

CHAPTER 7

The days boasted glorious spring weather, perfect for all those desirous of fresh air. The men spent hours riding, fishing, and shooting. Since most game was out of season, they had to content themselves with hunting gray squirrels and rabbits. "Not much sport in that," declared Mr. Ashton.

I walked alone much of the time, although occasionally Jane accompanied me. On one of my solitary rambles, as I passed near the riverbank, I heard a fine male voice singing "Annie Laurie." I knew it was not Charles, who couldn't sing at all, so that left one of the other two gentlemen. I sneaked toward the sound, hoping my half boots wouldn't land on a twig and give me away.

The singing ceased. "I hear you, so you'd best make yourself known." It was Mr. Walsh.

He must have uncannily good hearing, I thought, my cheeks already flushing. "It's

Mary Bennet," I said, walking toward him.

"Miss Bennet, you shock me. Sneaking up on a gentleman is a very risky business. What if I'd had my gun?" He set his rod and reel down and leaped to his feet. He'd shed his coat, and now looked around for it.

"I hardly believe you would have shot me," I said, chuckling.

He smiled. "Indeed. Your footstep is much lighter than a wild boar's." Having found his coat, he slipped it on. He wore no waistcoat or cravat.

"Do forgive me for the intrusion, but when I heard you singing, I had to see who it was. You have an impressive voice, sir."

"Thank you." He gave me a wry smile. "I don't usually sing with others about."

"Then we will not have the pleasure of hearing you after dinner one evening? I could accompany you, if you'd like."

"I would never live it down. Bingley and Ashton would make dreadful sport of me."

All I could do was smile at this. He was no doubt right.

"Perhaps if I could persuade you to sing a duet with me?" he said.

I flushed at the thought. "Oh, never. I have the worst voice imaginable. I have vowed never to sing in company again."

He laughed. "No! I cannot believe it." He took my elbow and began to steer me back toward the lane. "You walk every day, I think."

"When the weather allows, yes."

"May I join you?"

"Now?"

When he nodded, I said, "But your fishing gear — you don't want to leave it, do you?"

"I shall walk as far as the avenue, and then I'll return to my angling."

We talked only of mundane things. How long the excellent weather would last, the number of fish he'd caught that morning, and the length of his stay at High Tor. Probably a few more weeks, he said. Nothing noteworthy, like our conversation about Lord Nelson had been. When we reached the avenue, he bowed. "Enjoy the rest of your walk, Miss Bennet."

"I hope the fish continue to bite, and do please forgive me for sneaking up on you."

"Not at all. I'm glad you did."

His voice rang in my head during the rest of the way.

Her brow is like the snowdrift
Her throat is like the swan

Her face it is the fairest
That e'er the sun shone on.

I imagined he was singing about me. But Annie Laurie had blue eyes, not brown, like mine.

It was Kitty who had blue eyes.

Late one morning, Jane asked me to cut fresh flowers for the salon because the vicar was coming to dinner. I donned an apron and, knife in hand, carried my basket toward an area skirting the lane where daffodils grew in profusion. Cutting stems and humming a few bars from a Haydn piece I'd just been practicing, I started when Amanda Ashton came into view. I didn't bother looking up again until she spoke. " 'I saw some golden daffodils; / Beside the lake, beneath the trees, / Waving and dancing in the breeze.' "

I smiled, while inwardly cringing at her misquoting of Wordsworth.

"Mary, you look the very picture of the country wife," she said. Amanda looked the very picture of the kind of woman who never dirtied her hands with gardening. "Do you need any assistance?"

"No, thank you. I've only one knife. I'm nearly done, anyway."

"I do so love daffodils. They make one feel happy, with their bright color and merry aspect. How I would love to grow them! So charming."

"Why can you not grow them?"

She looked slightly perplexed, as if this were a weighty subject needing hours of thought. Ignoring my question, she asked one of her own. "Have you had any news from your dear family at Longbourn?"

Oh, not this again. I should have guessed she hadn't walked out here to tell me about her love of daffodils.

"No, we've heard nothing of any consequence." Papa had penned a few lines, informing us of matters we already knew or could have guessed at, such as: Mama had resumed visits to her sister but otherwise kept to her room; Lydia lay on the chaise most of the time complaining of boredom; he himself remained in his library as much as possible.

The only item of any interest was that they'd engaged a midwife for the birth of Lydia's child, which had given them, and us too, peace of mind regarding the upcoming event. And one final thing: Lydia had heard nothing from her husband. However, I was not inclined to share any of this with Amanda Ashton.

"Tell me, Miss Bennet, is George Wickham a relation of Mr. Darcy?"

The question was so unexpected, I swiveled to look at her, lost my balance, and fell backward, just managing to catch myself before tumbling completely over. I heard a snicker from Mrs. Ashton as I righted myself.

"A relation? Do you mean a blood relation?"

"I've been told they are half brothers."

"No, indeed, they are not. Mr. Wickham's father was the steward at Pemberley until his death. That's the only connection between them."

"I see."

If she could pry, I could do so in return. Keeping my voice even, I said, "Why do you ask? And who told you such a falsehood?"

Her mouth stretched into that odd representation of a smile. "I do not recall who told me; one of my acquaintances in Bath, I think. Although I didn't credit it, I wished to discover whether it was true or not. And I thought you and your family might want to know what was being said."

"If you didn't credit it, I rather wonder you took the trouble to ask me about it."

"I've offended you, Mary. I do beg your pardon."

"You have a remarkable curiosity regarding my sister and Mr. Wickham, and I cannot help wondering why."

"With no children of my own, and a husband who pays me scant attention — don't fret; I'm sure you've noticed — I have little else with which to entertain myself. Other people's predicaments are, therefore, of great interest to me."

What an extraordinary admission. I wasn't convinced she was telling the truth, however. For a moment, I challenged her with a skeptical look, but she said nothing further of any note. "I shall continue my walk, then, Mary, and hope you will forgive my impertinence."

To this I made no answer. I finished my flower gathering and rose, noticing as I did so that Mrs. Ashton was scurrying directly toward the house, seemingly with no intention of walking out any farther. A short while later, as I carried the daffodils to the house, I observed her and Mr. Ashton driving toward the village in his curricle.

It occurred to me then to wonder why she thought of Lydia's situation as a "predicament." An uneasy feeling settled at the back of my mind. Did she know something?

That evening, I met the vicar, Rev. Carstairs,

for the first time. A cousin of Mr. Walsh, he was quite young, surely no more than two-and-twenty, with a head of dark, unruly hair and a congenial manner. Kitty was seated between him and Mr. Ashton, while I was placed between Mr. Walsh and Mrs. Ashton. To my relief, Charles bore the burden of conversing with Amanda, leaving me free to talk to the other two gentlemen.

"When did you take orders, sir?" I asked between morsels of beef.

"Only last year. Henry was kind enough to offer me the living at Steadly."

"Andrew is the son of an earl's daughter," Mr. Walsh said. "He was in need of gainful employment."

Both men chuckled, and I saw that they had an easy camaraderie.

"So your father married the earl's daughter?" Kitty asked Andrew.

He nodded. "I'm sure the earl has long regretted it." This time the two men laughed out loud.

I found I liked Mr. Carstairs's sense of humor, but I wasn't sure if Kitty appreciated it. She smiled hesitantly and looked uncomfortable. Servants removed the platters of beef, replacing them with trays of raspberry and almond tarts, cakes, and custards in small cups. While everybody helped themselves to a sweet, I wondered why Mr. Walsh had never mentioned his own father. His mother was widowed, I knew. Would it be rude to ask?

I should have considered the matter more carefully before speaking. I turned to him and said, "What about your father, Mr. Walsh? Was it a recent loss?"

He studied me for a moment, his eyes darkening. "No. It's been five years since his death," he said coldly.

He added nothing further, and I wished I'd never asked. From his curt response, I could see this was not a subject he wished to converse about. He'd never spoken to me in that tone before, and I felt hurt burn in my chest. Was my question really so offensive?

After dinner, I played the pianoforte while Kitty seated herself next to Mr. Walsh, giggling and whispering. He seemed distracted. I noticed his eyes roving about the room, although his head was tilted toward her. Mr. Carstairs turned the pages for me, though it wasn't really necessary. I played poorly, making a hash of some difficult passages because my attention was not fully engaged. As soon as the piece was finished, I nearly leaped off the bench. Stealing from the room, I sought the privacy of my own chamber. It wasn't so difficult to escape from Henry Walsh if I applied myself to the task.

We had many such evenings. Mr. Carstairs was a frequent visitor and often made the fourth at the whist table. On a few occasions, Jane invited other guests, and I played so everybody else could dance. I grew irritated with seeing all the ladies save myself dancing with Mr. Walsh. My resentment was magnified because I did not feel we were on good terms. Although I'd felt his watchful eyes on more than one occasion, we had exchanged only a few perfunctory words ever since I had asked about his father. Perhaps the question had been impertinent, but it seemed a small thing to forgive.

If this was the way things were to be, I thought I may as well return to Longbourn. My feelings were in a tangle; I desperately wanted his attention but was afraid I wouldn't know how to behave if he bestowed it on me. For the present, his affection seemed directed at Kitty. He was solicitous of her comfort. He brought her tea, and once fetched her shawl when she said she was chilly. Frequently he was her dance partner, and he always played cards when she requested.

No. Allowing myself to feel anything for him would leave me far too vulnerable.

One evening while I was straightening the sheet music, he approached me.

"Miss Bennet, are we never to stand up together? Are you the only lady who plays?"

I felt warmth rising up from my neck. "I'm afraid I can't speak for Jane's acquaintances, but among my sisters, Elizabeth is the only other who plays."

"Perhaps Mrs. Bingley could extend her an invitation? She lives in Derbyshire, does she not?"

I laughed. "Some ten miles from here. She has twin daughters who keep her very busy, so I doubt she will visit for the sole purpose of our entertainment."

"A pity. Are you still set against attending the upcoming ball?"

Oh, why had I ever made that silly statement? Although I felt as if the words were stuck in my throat, I finally choked out an answer. "I-I've decided to go. To the ball."

If I were he, I would have laughed. But he was absolutely serious when said, "Will you promise, then, to stand up with me? The first set? And one other?"

"I will."

"I'm honored."

A smile — probably a very silly-looking

one — burst out. The world seemed not such a bad place after all.

CHAPTER 8

The day at last arrived for our visit to Linden Hall, Mr. Walsh's estate, and by now, I had developed a great curiosity about it. Jane, Mrs. Ashton, and I traveled in the chaise. The men rode, except for John Ashton, who insisted on driving Kitty in his curricle. His wife smiled tightly when he suggested it, and Jane made disapproving faces at Kitty, but to no avail. She didn't see, or pretended not to.

We turned off the road onto a lane, which soon broadened into an avenue lined with sycamores. The house came into view, set atop a gently rising slope, with a broad expanse of verdant lawn reaching toward a small lake. On one side of the house lay gardens crisscrossed with gravel paths, and on the other, a wood. The look of it surprised me. I had expected a more rustic setting.

The house itself featured evenly spaced,

linteled windows. A lady stood at the top of the stone steps, Henry's mother, no doubt. Flanked by a smiling Mr. Walsh and Charles, who had already arrived, she waited to greet us. John Ashton and Kitty had pulled up just ahead of the chaise, and we all ascended the steps together.

"Mama, allow me to present Mrs. Bingley," Mr. Walsh said.

"Welcome," she said warmly to Jane. "I'm glad to have the privilege of meeting you at last, since I have known your husband for quite some time now."

"I'm honored to make your acquaintance, ma'am," Jane said.

"And this is Mr. and Mrs. Ashton." Mrs. Ashton curtseyed prettily, while her husband gave a small bow. "And last, may I present Miss Mary Bennet and Miss Kitty Bennet?"

Edging closer to me while I acknowledged the introduction first, Kitty clamped her foot on the hem of my dress as I curtseyed, applying a firm pressure and making it impossible for me to rise fully. Not wishing to embarrass her, I spoke softly. "You're standing on my dress."

"How ridiculous, Mary. Of course I'm not standing on your dress." She moved her foot aside and I sprang upright. Jane's face wore an uneasy expression, and I exerted myself

100

to make up for the lapse in manners.

"How nice to meet you, ma'am," I said. "Your home is lovely."

Not content with stepping on my hem, now Kitty shouldered me aside to greet our hostess. "I've told Mr. Walsh over and over again how keen I was to meet you, ma'am," she said. "I declare, I thought I would never get the chance."

A warm smile lit Mrs. Walsh's eyes. She was a handsome woman, probably somewhere in her forties. "Shall we go in and have refreshments?" Her son offered her his arm, and they led the way.

The front door opened into a small rotunda. We passed through it into a sitting room warmed by an inviting fire. "What a delightful prospect you have from here!" said Amanda Ashton. "I never saw anything quite so charming. What do you say, John? Do you not agree?" With a bored look, her husband nodded.

When we had all arranged ourselves around a low table spread with platters of fruit, cheese, meats, and bread, Mrs. Walsh poured tea. Tall, arched windows lined one side of the room. "How nice to look out upon the woods from here," Jane said.

"We are very fond of walking there," said the older lady. "Henry has had paths constructed, winding all through the grove. It's quite enchanting." She looked at her son with motherly pride.

"I'll take you on a tour later," he said, "and most likely bore you senseless."

"Oh, no, never," Jane said, laughing. "Only think of all the tours of High Tor you have been forced to endure."

"Absolutely right, Walsh," Charles put in. "I for one am eager to see all the latest improvements."

"What a fine-looking instrument," I said, having spotted the pianoforte upon entering the room. "Do you play, ma'am?"

"Only tolerably," she said. "Henry has told me you are quite accomplished, however, Miss Bennet. I hope you may be persuaded to play for us later."

I was astonished to hear he had spoken to his mother about me but managed to stammer out my willingness to play. I looked up and caught Mr. Walsh's glance.

"Anyone for fishing?" he asked, turning to the men. "I know all the best spots, of course, and I do believe the trout are rising." This excited much interest, and finally it was arranged that they would spend the morning in that activity, leaving us ladies to talk, do needlework, or read.

The gentlemen went off to gather their

fishing rods and reels. After they left, I rose and walked to the windows, where I might look out on the imposing trees and ponder in private.

He has spoken of me to his mother; therefore he must, at times, think of me when we're apart. It means nothing, Mary, I scolded myself. *Only imagine what he has likely said of Kitty. It is she with whom he spends most of his time. Not you.*

By the time the men returned, I'd worn myself out with the flutters and began to count myself a simpleton. Kitty had been sending me evil looks all morning. When Mrs. Walsh asked me to play, I quickly agreed. Anything to take my mind off a certain gentleman. I chose *Moonlight Sonata,* then the adagio from a favorite Mozart piece. I should have chosen something bright and ebullient; instead, I chose lyrical.

"Who had the most fish in his creel?" Jane asked. The three men had washed and changed back into more formal attire.

"Much as it pains me to say it, your husband lays claim to that honor," Mr. Walsh said. "But I was a close second." We all waited expectantly for Mr. Ashton to chime in, but after a soft belch, he sprawled out on one of the chairs.

After the men had refreshed themselves, our host suggested a tour of the grounds. *Thank God.* I needed an activity besides playing the pianoforte and taking turns about the room. Mr. Ashton begged off, as did Mrs. Walsh, who she said must confer with the cook about dinner. As we exited through the front doors, Kitty pushed ahead and took Mr. Walsh's arm before he had the opportunity to offer it. Charles escorted Mrs. Ashton, and Jane and I walked arm in arm, trailing behind the others along the avenue toward the far end of the lake.

"I believe Mr. Ashton was in his cups," Jane said softly.

"Do you? How could you tell?"

"Charles says he always has a flask with him. His eyes looked bleary, and did you not take note of how quickly he seated himself? He could scarcely stand up! I'm certain he's sleeping it off right now."

I giggled, and then remembered I should tell Jane about Mrs. Ashton's peculiar behavior of late. "His wife has been pressing me about Lydia and Wickham. Again."

Jane frowned. "In what way?"

"At the picnic she expressed concern for Lydia's welfare and declared she must 'long' for her husband, even asking if Lydia was to return to Newcastle after the birth."

"That *is* strange. Poor creature. I believe she and her husband barely speak. I don't suspect her of malice, though."

"Of course not, Jane. You think too well of everybody!" I gave her arm a gentle tug. "Allow me to tell you the rest. When I was cutting flowers the other day, she came upon me and asked if Mr. Darcy and Wickham were half brothers."

"Wherever did she get such an idea? Mr. Darcy would be horrified if that notion got around!"

"She claimed an acquaintance in Bath told her, and although she didn't credit it, she wanted to know the truth."

"Well, perhaps that is all it was."

"Yet why are Lydia and Wickham such objects of interest to her? I had a strong sense she intended to learn what she could for a purpose."

"But what purpose could she possibly have?"

"I challenged her on that very thing, and she said since her husband paid her little attention, she was very much drawn to other people's predicaments."

"Just as I said. Only imagine the audacity of owning to it!"

"I don't trust her. I fancy she may be hiding something." I stopped in the middle of the path. "Jane, I think her outwardly foolish manners may be an act."

"That is pure speculation, dearest!" Jane said, raising her brows at me.

I shrugged. "Hear me out. I think she uses it to cover up her sharp questions. To make them seem innocent and inoffensive. Believe what you like, but surely we must be extra cautious around her."

"I think you are mistaken, Mary, but in any case, it wouldn't hurt to turn the conversation to other matters if Lydia comes up again."

"I only hope Kitty is using discretion. I saw her in animated discussion with both the Ashtons at the picnic."

Jane sighed, a wispy sound, expressing her doubts about Kitty's prudence. "I shall speak to her about it."

Up ahead, Charles called to us. "Ladies, make haste. Our host is in need of your opinion."

The group was situated on the lawn near the bank of the lake, looking back toward the house. "What do you think of this spot for a temple, or a folly, perhaps?" Mr. Walsh asked. He raised his brows at Jane and me.

"From here, the vista is lovely. One can see the house, wood, and gardens. But would the structure be visible from the house?" Jane asked.

"From the front door, the breakfast parlor, and the library, yes." He turned to me. "What do you think, Miss Bennet?"

Before I could answer, Kitty broke in. "I love follies and ruins and such! They make the wood seem inhabited by nymphs or . . . or spirits."

Mr. Walsh smiled at her. "Yes, Kitty. So you've said. But now I should like to hear your sister's opinion."

Usually, I did not scruple to tell the truth. But I had always given my opinion too freely, and often was sorry for it later. Although I found temples and follies artificial, it would have been horribly rude to say so. "It's as fine a spot as any, I believe. It would attract all the notice, since there are no trees nearby to draw the eye."

"Do I detect a note of disapproval, Miss Bennet?"

Caught out, I felt my color rising. "No, sir. That is, I —"

Kitty stepped between us. "La! Mary thinks such things are frippery. She likes everything plain and unadorned." It was true, but I rather wished she hadn't felt the need to point it out.

"I would be in raptures over it!" Mrs. Ashton said. Everybody ignored her.

Charles walked off with Jane and Amanda toward a wildflower garden vibrant with spring colors. From where we were standing, I could see cowslips, marsh marigold, rosemary, and flowering currant. A semicircle of lilac bushes bordered the rear of the garden. Jane called to Kitty, who gave a frustrated grunt before leaving Mr. Walsh and me alone.

I wished the earth would swallow me up, right after I pushed Kitty into the lake.

"Miss Bennet," Mr. Walsh said, "you may be honest with me. I promise not to take offense."

"Sir, it is your home and park. My opinion is of no consequence."

He watched me, hands clasped behind his back. "You are very wrong if you believe that," he said. "Come, tell me the truth."

What else was I to do, since he'd already guessed? "Very well. What Kitty said is true. I am not fond of temples, except for the original ones built by the Greeks and Romans. I think they are ostentatious."

He surprised me by laughing, a resonating sound that seemed to well up from his chest. I grinned ruefully in response. "Well said, Miss Bennet. You've taken me down a notch. I've often thought the same thing myself, but believed my mother would enjoy it. That is why I was considering it."

"If it would please your mother, then you should proceed with it, by all means. That is probably the best reason to build such a structure."

Humor flickered in his eyes. "Have you seen Greek and Roman temples then, Miss Bennet?"

"Of course not. Only my father has quite an extensive library, you see." My cheeks burned.

"I do see." He offered his arm. I accepted it, and we strolled toward the others. The heady scent of the lilacs filled the air. "Shall we go on? Let's take the gravel paths through the woods. I wish to show you the bridge I had constructed over the stream." He paused a moment, then said softly, "I hope you won't find it too ornate, Mary."

I couldn't stop a tiny chuckle sounding at the back of my throat. When I looked up at him, I realized he was laughing softly. I looked away, and it was a long while before I realized he'd called me Mary.

When we came to the bridge, everybody remarked on its simplicity of style. Ha! Jane winked at me. The stream rippled beneath the stone structure, seemingly in no hurry on its route to the lake. By now, clouds obscured the sun, and the wood had taken on a mysterious aura. I moved away from Mr. Walsh to gain a better view.

"Your wood reminds me of a scene from Shakespeare," I said, spinning around.

"That's what I was thinking, too," Kitty said. I held back a smile, since I was quite certain my sister had never read a single line of the Bard.

Our host glanced at her. "Enlighten us, Miss Kitty. Which play does it put you in mind of?"

An awkward pause ensued, and I heard a barely muffled giggle from Mrs. Ashton. "I- I'm not sure —"

A moment ago I would have she said deserved her comeuppance, but now that it was upon her, I was sorry for her. "She was thinking of *As You Like It,* were you not, Kitty?"

"Or *A Midsummer Night's Dream,*" said Jane, who must have been feeling the same as I.

"Yes," Kitty said, looking relieved. "Both of those. I think." To my surprise, she caught my eye, and I recognized in her odd half smile an expression of gratitude.

"Ah," Mr. Walsh said, letting the matter drop. He was not a man who lacked sensibility, yet his comment to Kitty seemed a deliberate attempt to shame her. Why would he have wished to do so? I considered this as we wound our way toward the house but could arrive at no definitive answer. Could he have wished to embarrass her, as she had embarrassed me? That was an idiotic notion if ever there was one, yet it pleased me to think it might be so.

CHAPTER 9

Mr. Carstairs joined our party for dinner. "Andrew is the youngest vicar in all of England," Mrs. Walsh said, looking fondly upon her nephew. I wondered if she knew this to be true or if it was merely speculation on her part.

He blushed. "One of the youngest," he said, correcting her.

"Our vicar is the opposite," Kitty said. "He is so exceedingly ancient, sometimes I fear he will totter right out of the pulpit onto the floor!"

I winced, but Mr. Carstairs took no offense, smiling along with my sister.

"I'm rather fond of the old man," Charles said, "since he performed our wedding ceremony." He and Jane smiled at one another. Sometimes it was hard to bear such wedded bliss.

The meal was simple fare, turbot followed by beef and spring vegetables. I ate a little of everything, saving room for a small piece of pound cake. Afterward, the ladies retired to the sitting room while the men partook of their port.

As soon as we entered, Kitty approached me. "Mary, will you play some dance tunes? I do long to dance!"

"Mr. Ashton will want to play cards," said his wife.

Jane looked sympathetic. "Perhaps he will agree to a few dances first. Mary?"

"Yes, of course." I supposed I would not be dancing, then. Apparently I would have to wait for the Pennington ball to stand up with Mr. Walsh.

I wandered over to the instrument and began to look through the sheets of music. Mrs. Walsh entered the room and, when she heard what we were about, insisted on playing.

"Miss Bennet, you must take part in the dancing. I have no desire to do so and am perfectly happy to remain at the pianoforte." She smiled warmly. To refuse would have been rude.

"Thank you, ma'am." While waiting for the men, I picked up a book lying on the table, a novel as it turned out, called *The History of Sir Charles Grandison.* I had never heard of it.

The men wandered in, and Kitty informed them of the plan.

"Good God! Must we?" asked Mr. Ashton. "We only have four couples. Where's the fun in that?"

"Sit out, if you wish," Charles said.

"Excellent advice," John Ashton replied. His wife looked put out but joined him at the card table.

"Grimstock, then?" Mrs. Walsh asked. "It's best for three couples."

Everybody nodded, and I sighed with relief. It was an easy dance that even I could perform with grace.

Kitty was gazing expectantly toward our host, who, without hesitation, went to her and said, "May I have the honor?" I had no justification to feel hurt by this, but the fact that they simply seemed to know they would dance together stung.

Charles said, "Well, then, I shall have the pleasure of dancing with my wife."

That left me with Mr. Carstairs. "Miss Bennet? You'll have to put the book down, I think." I smiled sheepishly, not even realizing I was still clutching it.

The music started, and we doubled forward and back, then performed the set and turn. Kitty and Henry were in front of us. She had always been a fine dancer, and he danced well, too, though he seemed rather to be going through the motions than truly enjoying himself. Mr. Carstairs, to my surprise, was exceptionally light on his feet. I actually caught Kitty watching him once or twice.

As soon as one dance finished, we barely had time to catch our breath before Mrs. Walsh struck up another tune. Varying the steps, or the order, made it seem like we weren't doing the same dance over and over. I wished we would vary the partners. The nearest I came to Henry was when we went through the arches, but that happened so quickly it didn't count.

And then we were done, quite worn out and ready for refreshment. I thanked Mr. Carstairs and wandered over to where Mrs. Walsh, assisted by Jane, was pouring tea. I accepted a cup, picked up my book, and retreated to a chair set a little away from the others.

Suddenly, the air stirred, and Mr. Walsh was making his way toward me, his eyes never drifting from my face.

"Whist, anyone?" Mr. Ashton called out. "And some brandy, Walsh?"

Henry, ever the polite host, veered abruptly back toward the others. He poured a brandy for his guest and chatted amiably

115

with his cousin while his mother served them tea. Kitty and Charles had joined the Ashtons at the whist table. I waited, my foot tapping the floor. I wanted Henry to hurry back to me. And I wanted him to keep his distance from me. Why was it that every time I was convinced it was Kitty in whom he was interested, he began to take notice of me? It was most vexing.

To distract myself, I opened the copy of *Sir Charles Grandison* and read the beginning paragraphs twice through without absorbing a single word. And then Henry was there, lowering himself onto the chair next to me.

He glanced at the book in my hands. "Do you read novels, Miss Bennet?"

"No, I don't. That is to say, I never have, but I might." *Keep to simple answers, Mary. "No, I don't" would have sufficed.*

"Are you one of those people who think them frivolous and lacking in moral value?" He sipped his tea, not taking his eyes off me.

"Not at all. I read mainly what is in my father's library, and there are no novels among his personal collection."

"I shall lend you one of Richardson's earlier volumes, *Clarissa*. I am still reading this one, which is quite different. My mother

116

is a great novel reader, and I read chiefly what she recommends." He set his cup on a table and leaned forward, hands resting on his thighs. "You may borrow from my collection anytime."

"Thank you. I may take you up on your offer whenever I'm visiting Jane and Charles. Novels will be a welcome change for me."

"How much longer do you plan to remain in Derbyshire?"

"A few more weeks, I should think. Our youngest sister is currently at Longbourn awaiting the birth of a child. Her husband's regiment —"

"Yes, Charles told me of her circumstances."

This was awkward. How much had Charles told him? Most likely the same story we were telling everybody. "Jane and I will be expected at home when the child is born."

"Why you rather than Kitty?"

Shocked at his rather impertinent question and not at all certain what answer to give, I stammered out a completely nonsensical response. "It is only that Jane knows about babies and I . . ." *Oh, Lord, what am I meant to say?* "My mother believes you will offer for Kitty any day now, whereas I am the *designated nursemaid"*?

Aware of my distress, he quickly said, "It is of no consequence, Miss Bennet. But I shall be sorry when you go."

All at once my cheeks flamed, and at the same time, a jolt of pleasure so great I could scarcely contain it stabbed through me. I looked down, afraid to meet his eyes for fear they would show mockery, or even worse, sarcasm.

"Mary," he said softly. "Will you look at me?"

Shyly, I glanced up at his face.

"It is neither a good time nor place to express what is in my heart, but if I may, for now, I should like to say . . . I admire you very much."

I felt an irrepressible smile steal across my face and for once was bold enough to fix my eyes on his. What else was in his heart that he could not express?

A footman entered the room, breaking the spell cast between us. He hurried over to Mr. Walsh and handed him a folded paper.

"Sir, an express for Mr. and Mrs. Bingley has come."

"Ah. Thank you, Harris. Pardon me, Miss Bennet."

He rose and carried the note to Charles, who said, "It's from Elizabeth, my dear."

118

Jane blanched but remained outwardly calm.

"I'm afraid we must take our leave," she said, rising. "I hate to curtail the pleasures of our evening, but family matters summon us home."

"Oh, my dear," Mrs. Walsh said, "I do hope your child is well."

"Perfectly so, ma'am. It is nothing to do with David. Thank you most heartily for a pleasant day and evening."

The others had seen the message delivered and heard that we must depart. "Oh, mightn't we stay for more dancing?" Kitty said to Jane.

Mr. Carstairs stepped in. "Another time, Miss Kitty. We will have many other op- portunities." Kitty clamped her mouth shut, thank goodness, and simply bade him good night.

We gathered wraps and reticules and waited outside for the chaise. "Would you like to ride with the ladies, Bingley?" Mr. Walsh asked. "I can ride your mount over tomorrow if you prefer."

Not until then did I understand he wouldn't be returning to High Tor with us. I had assumed he would be riding alongside Charles, as he had done that morning. I recalled now that there had been a bag strapped to the top of the chaise. My tranquility was shattered. When would I see him again?

Charles declined his offer, no doubt preferring to be anywhere other than in the carriage with the ladies. Due to Mrs. Ashton's presence, there would be no opportunity to speculate as to the contents of Lizzy's message.

"Kitty," Jane said, "you will ride in the chaise with us." Her tone brooked no argument, and for once, Kitty complied without a fuss.

Mr. Walsh had disappeared, and so I shook hands with his mother. "It was most kind of you to invite us, ma'am. Thank you."

She enfolded my hand in both of hers. "Everything my son told me of you is true, Miss Bennet. I am hopeful of our seeing a great deal more of each other."

Everything? More astonishment. "I hope so, too." *Should I have said that? For what, precisely, am I hoping?*

We were waiting now only to say good night to our host, who at last dashed toward us carrying a book. The one he promised to lend me, I thought.

"Will you wait a moment, Miss Bennet?" he said after bidding everyone else adieu. His mother, I noticed, had unobtrusively withdrawn into the house, taking Mr. Carstairs with her. I could see Kitty ogling us from the carriage, and perhaps Mr. Walsh saw too. He touched my arm, drawing me into the shadows, where we couldn't be observed by anybody. "Here is my copy of *Clarissa*. After you've had time to read it, will you share your views with me?"

"Thank you, sir. I'm not shy when it comes to offering my opinion."

He laughed quietly, handing me the volume. I cradled it with one arm, and we both walked toward the chaise. When he held out his hand to help me up the steps, I clung to it.

I was lost.

"I do hope your letter does not carry bad news," Mrs. Ashton said. Her tone invited the sharing of secrets. Jane quelled her curiosity, at least for the present, by simply saying, "Indeed."

We were quiet during the ride, and my mind was left to roam free over all that had transpired today. Mrs. Walsh's kindness, and the implication that her son had told her more about me than the simple fact of my proficiency at the pianoforte. I could not help wondering what else he might have said. He had singled me out during the walk about the grounds, and even though he danced with Kitty and not me, he had sat beside me afterward and made that thrilling revelation.

He called me Mary. Twice. I heard his voice in my head, and I wished he'd said my name a dozen times. I should have protested by saying I hadn't given him leave to call me by my Christian name. But he did it in such a tender way — and not within the others' hearing — that I could not be affronted.

I knew I was in a fair way to risking my heart and should flee back to Longbourn. I should beg Jane to allow me to leave immediately before anything else happened. From my knowledge of these matters, after years of hearing my sisters speak of such things, it was possible that Mr. Walsh's declaration was leading up to a proposal of marriage. I'd always believed I would remain a spinster. I would disappoint as a wife. I had not the easy compliance, the ability to defer to a husband, and worst of all, I lacked beauty, conduct, and, at times, even common sense. But Jane said I had changed. Truly, I valued her opinion above that of anyone else.

From Kitty's manner and countenance, her anger with me was obvious. She viewed

Mr. Walsh as her suitor, and perhaps my whole family felt the same. Was I willing to risk their censure by stealing Kitty's beau? I knew my parents — my mother at least — had every expectation of my remaining at home and caring for her and my father as they grew old. Mama neither hoped for nor anticipated a marriage for me. Nothing about a union between Henry Walsh and me would sit well with her.

Still in a quandary about what to do when we arrived at High Tor, thoughts of the letter nevertheless distracted me from my own dilemma. Jane and Charles and Kitty and I congregated in the library. Charles poured himself a brandy and offered sherry to the ladies, but we all declined. He handed Jane the letter and said, "My dear, you should be the one to read it."

My sister broke the wax seal and studied the missive for a moment before reading it out loud:

21 March
Pemberley

Dear Jane,
    Do not be alarmed. We are all well.
    This letter is to inform you that my husband arrived in Newcastle yesterday.

After making inquiries, he was able to ascertain that Wickham had sold his commission and left town. Nobody seems to know where he might have gone.

After further investigation, Fitzwilliam discovered that Miss Susan Bradford, the lady to whom, according to Lydia, Wickham had become attached, is also missing. A gossiping regiment wife confirmed Lydia's tale of an affair between the two, and also revealed the name of the officer with whom Lydia was seen to have spent her time. Fitzwilliam will attempt to interview the man tomorrow.

He will stay one more day in the hope that he may be able to find someone who knows where Wickham is, or at least one who is willing to tell him. It seems an exercise in futility to me, but I leave it to my husband's judgment.

I shall write again when there is more news. I have also written to Papa.

Yours,
Elizabeth

Collectively, we drew a shaky breath. Charles spoke first. "Reprobate!" I knew he wished to say more, but the presence of ladies prevented him. Instead, he got to his feet and strode about the room.

"I rue the day Lydia became involved with that man!" Jane said, upon which words Kitty began to wail.

"What will happen to our poor sister?"

"We must remember Lydia shares a good portion of the blame for this muddle," I said, eyeing all of them. "Had she behaved differently . . ." I stopped myself from further recrimination. It would not be helpful. "This is bad news, but let us not forget Mr. Darcy's inquiries are not concluded. He may yet find some useful information to lead him to Wickham, and his powers of persuasion are great with that man."

"To have sold his commission!" Jane said. "His only means of supporting his family. Is the care of Lydia and her child to fall upon our parents?"

Charles intervened. "Mary is right. We are too hasty in our assumptions. Let us yet hope for a good outcome. If anyone can achieve it, it's Darcy."

"Of course," Jane said, distractedly fingering the cameo she wore round her neck. "All is not lost. It's not too late to discover his whereabouts."

Mr. Darcy could achieve a "good outcome," I thought, but it would be at great personal expense. My parents could barely afford to support those of us still unmarried, let alone all the Wickhams. Mr. Darcy would be the one, yet again, who would be forced not only to bear the cost of their living expenses, but also to discharge any debts Wickham had incurred while in Newcastle. Knowing Wickham, these could have been considerable.

"I am going to bed," Kitty said through her tears. "Wicked man! It is unbearable."

"Good night, dear. Perhaps we shall have better news tomorrow," Jane said.

I had turned to follow Kitty when I felt Jane's hand on my sleeve. "Mary, may I speak to you privately, after I check on David? I'll join you in my sitting room, if that is all right?"

"Of course," I said, feeling an apprehension I couldn't quite explain.

Chapter 10

"All is well," Jane said as she whisked through the door of her private sitting room. "Apparently David fussed a bit when his nurse put him to bed, but he's sleeping now."

"So you'll sleep well tonight, too," I said, smiling at my sister.

"Yes. But I *am* at his beck and call. You'll understand, someday."

"Not according to Lydia. Or my own mother." My smile faltered at that thought.

"Do not set store by their opinions, Mary. They are the last two who should be giving you advice." An embarrassed looked washed over her face. "I do love them, of course —"

"Naturally. Nobody would ever think otherwise." I held a hand up to stay further guilty declarations. "You wished to speak to me?"

"Yes, about Mr. Walsh."

My heart plunged. Had I said or done something improper?

"Let's sit by the fire." Jane insisted I take the chair. She lowered herself to the small footstool directly in front of me. "It's just that, well, Charles and I have noticed Henry Walsh seems to be enjoying your company."

I stared at the guttering flames while I decided how to respond. "Perhaps," I said noncommittally. "But I'm sure you have also noticed he enjoys Kitty's company as well."

"Because she invites his attentions! Did you not see the way she looked at him before the dancing tonight? To choose you instead of her would have humiliated her. He was trapped."

"I don't know, Jane. He's very kind to me and we have had some interesting conversations, but that's the extent of it."

"My dear Mary, any fool can see he is smitten with you. Surely you're aware of the way he singles you out. And I've seen him watching you."

"Yes, all right, at times I believe he shows a preference for me, but I think it is only kindness on his part. I'm not the sort of girl men love."

"Don't be ridiculous! Do you return his feelings, Mary?"

I looked down and ran my hand along the rich silk fabric of the chair. "Yes. No! I don't know. If I don't believe his to be genuine, how can I return them?"

"Why do you think he would play you false?"

"Because he was meant to be Kitty's beau! She wants to marry him. And our parents — Mama, to be sure — expect it."

"That does not mean he wishes it! And Mama would welcome the news of another daughter wed — it doesn't matter which one." She drew in an exasperated breath. "Kitty misinterpreted his courteous and gentlemanly behavior toward her as something more, and then foolishly told Mama he was paying his addresses to her. Remember my warning to her on the trip to High Tor?"

"But she will be exceedingly disappointed, not to mention angry with me. She's been glowering at me for days."

"All because she misjudged the situation. If she's angry with you, it is because she perceives the truth and is hurt by it."

"So I am to be the cause of my sister's unhappiness?" I stood so rapidly, spots danced before my eyes. I was suddenly intolerably warm and moved toward the windows.

"Has Mr. Walsh indicated with words, as well as actions, his fondness for you?"

"Yes," I said softly, "he asked me to stand up with him at the Pennington ball. The first set and one other. And he said . . ." But I could not tell Jane. His words still whispered to me. I wished to keep them for myself.

"Never mind. You don't need to tell me." From the faraway look in Jane's eyes, I sensed she was remembering something, perhaps sentiments expressed between her and Charles when they were courting. "I urge you, Mary, to encourage his suit," Jane said, "if indeed you do feel affection for him. He's a fine man, all that a gentleman should be."

"But Kitty will hate me forever."

"Hang Kitty!"

"Jane! She's our sister."

"And she'll find another beau, one more suited to her. In many ways, she is still a silly girl. You must do what's best for you — and Mr. Walsh. I'm convinced he and Kitty would not get on well together; they're too dissimilar. In fact, a union between them could well be a disaster."

I sighed. "Enough on this subject for tonight. I'm taking my poor, befuddled brain to bed." I kissed Jane's cheek and walked down the hall to my chamber. Once in my bed, I lay awake for hours, my mind alive with opposing thoughts. When I finally drifted off to sleep, Henry Walsh haunted my dreams, with his piercing blue eyes and sweetly tender voice.

I slept so poorly, Jane asked me at breakfast if I was feeling well. "You have dark shadows beneath your eyes."

"I'm fine, thank you. My only complaint is a poor night's sleep."

She gave me a kindhearted smile, acknowledging her understanding of the reason for my wakefulness. Kitty seemed distracted and made no comment, but when we rose from the table, she asked if she might accompany me on my morning walk. Surprised, I agreed, and after fetching bonnets and pelisses, we set off. The air had turned cooler and carried the promise of a rain shower. I hoped it would wait until after our walk.

Kitty didn't speak at first, although I noticed her gaze fixed on me when she thought I wasn't paying attention. Then, in a hurried outburst, she said, "I know I have been less than kind to you on occasion, Mary. I am sincerely sorry if I have caused you pain."

I didn't believe for a minute she had asked to walk with me to apologize for all the years she'd treated me so ill. When she resumed her speech, the nature of the apology soon became clear.

"Mr. Walsh is courting me, not you. It's me he admires."

I looked down, exhaling an impatient breath. "If that is the case, you can have nothing to worry about."

"If you left High Tor, it would show him you have no regard for him."

I'd spent half the night agonizing over whether to flee from Henry or to encourage his suit. To embrace the chance for personal happiness or simply leave it to Kitty to find hers. I'd been leaning toward the latter course of action, because vying with my sister for the same man left a bad taste in my mouth. Not to mention my own worries about my suitability as a wife and the wishes of my parents. But now that Kitty was demanding it, resistance rose in my chest until I felt it would burn a hole through my dress.

"But I do have regard for him, and, in any case, I cannot make him like you if he does not."

Her face flooded with color. "But he does!" Indignantly, she said, "Speaking plainly, Mary, gentlemen do not care for girls who read and study and are as serious as you. He may admire you now, but it won't last. Those qualities are not what men want in a wife."

How dare she? "What you say may be true of many, perhaps even most men, but it is not a fair description of Henry Walsh."

"Only think, Mary. Where are your looks? Your fashion?"

My temper yearned to break free, but I managed to keep it in check. "In one breath you apologize to me for treating me unkindly, and in the next you deliberately insult me. I'm not inclined to agree to your demands in the circumstances."

I increased my pace so Kitty would have to hurry to keep up, but suddenly she stopped, so abruptly I had to turn back to hear what she was saying. "I have tried to be a better girl, so as not to end up like Lydia." Tears welled up in her eyes and trickled down her face. "I have changed. I'm not so silly as I used to be. I've learned something about how to be in company from Jane and Lizzy."

"You seem unwilling to show off your newly acquired manners here. You flirt with John Ashton, spend your time in foolish pursuits, and brazenly treat Mr. Walsh as though he were already your betrothed."

Her crying increased to full-scale sobs, interspersed with little hiccups. My mind roiled. *What should I do?* We walked on for some moments in silence, me a little ahead of Kitty, who continued her weeping. "Please, Mary," she said as we reached the turning onto the avenue. "It may be my last chance to get a husband." Her voice was a pitiful rasp.

While I didn't believe that, I could not be so coldhearted as to ignore her pain. Did she truly care for Henry Walsh? I decided to ask her what I'd been wondering about all along. Something Papa had questioned in that conversation I'd overheard between him and my mother. "Can you describe to me, Kitty, the nature of your feelings for Mr. Walsh? What do you admire in him?" I stood watching her, my arms folded in front of my chest.

She was still whimpering when she said, "Whatever do you mean?"

"It is not so difficult a question, is it? What makes you want to marry him?"

"You're being mean, Mary!"

"Indulge me. I'm trying to understand your feelings so I can decide what to do about my own."

She glared at me with reddened eyes. "He

is quite handsome." A little smile curved her mouth. "While not as wealthy as Charles or Mr. Darcy, he's comfortably well-off, and his home is lovely. He would make any girl a good husband."

"What can you tell me of his character?"

She stamped her foot. "You're tormenting me! What do you care?"

"I think if you are to marry him, you must know something of his interests, his likes and dislikes, his tastes, morals, and judgment."

Petulantly, she said, "He likes to shoot and ride." *Jane told us that.* "He has excellent taste, as anyone could see who has been to his home. It's fitted up beautifully." *His mother's design.* "And those other things I guess I'll learn about in time. They're not that important, anyway."

Everything superficial and nothing to do with the Henry Walsh I'd come to know. The one who loved music, read books, and thought deeply about character. Nothing she had learned from the man himself. But I knew this was the best I would have from Kitty. Perhaps she *could* learn more in time.

"Does it not . . . have you not questioned why he singles me out for conversation?"

"Yes! I wish he would not." She swiped at her tears and gave me a venomous look.

"But it's me he dances with, and flirts with, and —"

"Yes, point taken," I said.

"And I'm a good talker. It's not my fault he doesn't want to talk to me. It's yours, because you always try to keep him for yourself."

It was hard not to laugh at that pronouncement.

"Show him," I said. "Prove to him that you would make him a wife to admire and love."

"How? What should I do?" She was blinking rapidly and appeared completely baffled.

"To start, spend time each day reading. You might begin with Shakespeare."

A look of horror passed over my sister's face, but her crying ceased.

"Write letters to our parents, and Lydia and Elizabeth. Walk out every day. Pay no more heed to Mr. Ashton, and good heaven, tone down your advances to Mr. Walsh. Allow *him* to ask *you* to row on the lake, climb a peak, or dance."

"But he's not even here."

"He will call on us soon enough. If you can do all those things, I believe you'll stand a better chance of gaining his admiration. Do remember what I said, though. You are the only one who can earn his affection."

She narrowed her eyes at me. "Why are you helping me?"

"Out of a misguided sense of sisterly duty, I suppose." If Kitty caught the sarcasm, she didn't show it.

"And what about you, Mary? Will you leave High Tor, so —"

"So I will not stand in your way?"

"Precisely!"

"Don't forget, only a few moments ago you said I had no looks or fashion and wasn't someone Henry could care for. If you take that view, I rather wonder why my presence here should be of the least concern to you."

"But —"

An obstinacy I didn't even know I possessed sprang up. "I will not leave. It's in Henry Walsh's hands now. He must choose."

"He might choose you," she wailed.

"Perhaps. But he might choose you. And there's a third possibility we haven't even considered."

"What?" she said impatiently.

I moved very close to her and lowered my voice. "He may not decide in favor of either of us. For all we know, there are other ladies in the running."

She took a step back. "You're being horrid, Mary."

"I'm simply being realistic." I motioned toward the house. "Why don't you turn back? I think I'd like to walk on by myself." I strode off down the avenue alone, my heart thudding bleakly in my chest.

"How many letters must I write each day?" Kitty called.

I kept walking.

"How many hours must I read?" she shouted. "Oh, this isn't fair. I do so dislike reading!"

I called over my shoulder. "You want to marry him, don't you? You must show Mr. Walsh you are capable of being the wife he deserves." I squeezed my eyes shut, not caring where I stepped. The gravel crunched; in the wood, chaffinches sang. The pungent smell of newly turned earth drifted toward me. I sped up and, eyes still shut tight, stepped into a small crater and pitched forward onto my hands and knees.

For a long time I stayed that way, my breath coming in harsh, ragged gasps. Only after my palms began to sting and my knee grew damp did I sit back on my heels. I had just offered Kitty a way to get Henry Walsh for herself, so it seemed quite at odds for me to hope, indeed pray, she would fail. Because I wanted him to choose me. *God help me, I wanted him to choose me.*

On my way back to the house, the skies opened and a drenching rain soaked me. It seemed fitting, somehow.

The next several days passed at a wretchedly slow pace. Charles was visiting tenants, checking on spring plantings, needed repairs to cottages and outbuildings, and other such business. Since my nephew had caught a cold, we saw little of Jane, who spent most of her time in the nursery.

Because Mrs. Ashton preferred to keep to her chamber in the morning, Kitty and I sat alone in the salon, reading or writing letters. My sister was making an effort, reading *As You Like It* and penning missives daily, though I noticed they were about the same length as my father's letters. Which is to say, very short indeed. Often, I caught her staring aimlessly, but I neither reproached nor chided her. Once she said, "Mr. Shakespeare used a prodigious amount of words to say the simplest things! Why could he not be more direct?"

I couldn't help smiling. "He wouldn't be Shakespeare if he wrote like everybody else. It takes time to accustom yourself to his style. Once you've done that, the reading will go faster."

She sighed. "I suppose so."

I was having a decidedly difficult time concentrating on anything, be it music, reading, or needlework. Always on my mind was the expectation of a visit from Henry and what I would do when that occurred. *Just be yourself.* There was no reason to try to change, except that Kitty's comments rankled. Did I indeed have no looks? No fashion? Was I as unattractive as she had implied?

One morning Jane entered the room carrying a letter. "I received another message from Lizzy," she said. "Still no trace of Wickham or Miss Bradford. Mr. Darcy did interview the officer with whom Lydia had an affair."

"Oh, do tell us about that!" Kitty begged.

"There is nothing much to tell," Jane said. "He admitted to it and apologized. He even told Mr. Darcy that he and Wickham still counted themselves as friends. Can you imagine? Any other husband but Wickham would have called him out!"

"Probably not, under the circumstances," I said.

"Mr. Darcy did uncover one lead. Wickham told more than one person he was traveling to London."

"To what end, I wonder."

"Perhaps the lady . . . his lady friend is

there."

After that conversation, I couldn't settle to anything. "I'm in need of some fresh air," I informed my sisters, hoping neither of them felt the same. On an impulse, I hurried to my chamber and found my reticule. I had an idea to walk to the village to see if the dressmaker had any recent copies of *La Belle Assemblée* or *Ackermann's Repository* she would allow me to peruse. Perhaps I could bone up on my fashion sense and find out how to improve upon my looks. Not that I could ever resemble the ladies pictured in the fashion plates, but Kitty's comments made me think maybe I ought to try. I borrowed Jane's cashmere shawl, draped across a bench in the hall, and slipped out the front door.

What a great disappointment to find, when I'd reached the dressmaker's shop, that they were closed. I lingered a few moments before their window, where a selection of fabrics was on display. A sage-green silk was especially lovely but far beyond my price range. I stood there a bit longer, gazing at my reflection in the glass and thinking about what I might do to enhance my appearance. My hand strayed to my hair, tugging loose some strands around my face. I cocked my head back and forth, studying the effect. After a while, I sighed in frustration and made my way home.

By the time I reached High Tor, I'd been gone nearly two hours. When I returned, things were in a bit of an uproar. I'd barely gotten through the entrance hall before Kitty, hurrying out of the sitting room, nearly knocked into me.

"Mary! Your stupid advice did not work."

"I beg your pardon?"

"After asking after my health, Mr. Walsh paid me no attention whatsoever. Indeed, he spent the chief of his time talking to Jane, while I sat on the chaise with my embroidery."

"Mr. Walsh was here? While I was walking?" Blast! I had managed to disappear at the very time he called. Now I most likely wouldn't see him until the ball.

"Of course. Aren't you listening?"

I struggled to recall what Kitty had said when I walked through the door. "Did you try to join in the conversation? Did you ask if his mother was well? Or what he'd been doing since we saw him last?"

"Jane did all that, so I had nothing more to add. I'm done reading boring Shakespeare and writing those tedious letters! How you persuaded me such a scheme would work in my favor, I shall never know."

And with that, she dashed toward the stairs, flushed and angry. "It wasn't a scheme," I shouted after her. "And you cannot expect immediate results!"

Jane appeared in the doorway, a suspicious look on her face. "May I speak to you, Mary?" She spun on her heel; I had no choice but to follow. Having faced down the enemy on one side, it seemed I now had to outmaneuver on the other.

Jane didn't even wait until we were seated. "Would you care to tell me what you're up to? What is this scheme you cooked up with Kitty?"

"There is no scheme, Jane. I simply gave her some sisterly advice, which, on the whole, I thought would improve her chance to gain Mr. Walsh's regard."

"I've been wondering why she suddenly took up reading and letter writing. And her new, more decorous manner has been quite impressive. Now I discover this has come about at your urging."

I settled myself on the chaise and smiled sardonically. "I hope you haven't become accustomed to her new ways. She just told me she was giving them up."

Jane rolled her eyes. "You should have heard her railing after Henry left. She was in high temper and sounded very much like

Mama. I don't care what advice you gave her, such behavior will never attract a man like him." She caught her breath, then said, "Tell me, Mary, have your feelings toward Mr. Walsh changed since we spoke a few nights ago?"

"Not in the least, but —"

"I will tell you then that he could barely contain his feelings the whole time he was here, which was above an hour, far longer than is customary. He asked after you and dearly wanted, I could see, to walk out and find you. Only his good breeding forbade him to do so. He looked at Kitty not at all."

A deep well of joy settled around my heart. "Honestly?"

"I wouldn't lie about such a thing!"

"I started to say . . . to tell you that Kitty and I had a talk. Or to be more precise, she had a talk with me. This was the morning after we visited Linden Hall."

Jane looked at me steadily. "Go on."

"She asked me to leave High Tor so she might have a clear path toward winning Mr. Walsh. I refused."

"The nerve of her! Good for you for refusing." Jane's look rapidly changed from excited to puzzled. "Then why are you giving her advice?"

I rubbed at a nonexistent spot on my

dress. "I merely suggested some changes in her behavior that might make Henry wish to converse with her. A test, perhaps, to see if she were capable of engaging him in other ways besides dancing and flirting. But as she just announced, she's abandoned them already. I ended up telling Kitty that he may not want either one of us. He gets to choose." I glanced up at Jane. "It seems rather unfair, doesn't it? That men always get to choose?"

She gave me an arch look. "But what we women do goes a long way in persuading them to make the correct choice."

CHAPTER 11

The day of the ball allowed no tranquility, no peace of mind. What I had hoped would be a time of sweet anticipation turned rapidly into a nightmare, beginning with Kitty's swoons over likely dance partners and Amanda Ashton's incessant chatter about gowns, jewelry, wraps, slippers, and everything else one associates with such an occasion.

When I could no longer bear it, I took to my room, pleading a headache. Jane was concerned. "Mary, you must lie down until it is time to prepare. We can't have your evening spoiled by a megrim."

"No, of course not. I shall rest until dinner." Instead, I paced in my room as though it were a prison cell. I wanted to be out of doors and walking. But that would never do for one who'd just complained of a headache. After a long while, I heard a light tapping on my door and dived onto the bed before Jane stepped in.

"How are you feeling, dear?" she asked. Her arms were overflowing with gowns.

I slowly raised my head, as though by great effort. "Better, I think."

"Good, because we must determine which one of these will best suit you. We should have done this long before now. Let's hope no extensive alterations prove necessary."

I groaned inside. Even though I wanted to attend the ball, I hated bothering about gowns and slippers and fans. "I was planning to wear one of my white gowns."

"No, you must wear something with a little color. You're not eighteen anymore, and you can dress in something other than white. Come, now, up you go."

I dragged myself off the bed while Jane began laying the gowns — of silk, crape, and sarcenet — out across its width. "Your white muslins are looking a little faded, in any case. They're not very becoming. If you wish to make an impression on a certain gentleman . . ."

I conceded the point, smiling. "I suppose you're right."

"Which do you like? The green silk is striking and would complement your hair nicely."

"No. It's too revealing. Look how low the

neckline is."

Jane rolled her eyes. "The apricot crape, then. That's also a good match for your hair, and I love the pearl embroidery at the neckline. It is a little more modest than the green."

"Very well, the apricot crape it is. I do like the pearls." Never before had I worn anything so grand as this. It had a flounce at the hem, too. I could hardly imagine myself in it.

"Please do try it on, so that we can see if Sara needs to take it in or let it out anywhere." Jane examined the gown closely for any spots, tears, or loose pearls. Once satisfied, she gathered up the remaining gowns. "I'm off to see if Kitty may wish to wear one of these. I'll come back to help you after I've spoken to her. I cannot wait to see how beautiful you will look tonight, Mary!"

Me, beautiful? *Never.*

Kitty, I knew, had planned her ball attire weeks ago and would have no need of Jane's help. I dropped down onto the stool at the dressing table, chin in my hands, and pictured myself in the apricot dress, moving gracefully onto the dance floor to stand up with Henry Walsh. He would send me frankly admiring looks; I would smile mysteriously. As always, we would converse easily on any number of subjects, but there would be an aura of something new between us. A physical attraction. I shivered, but not because I was cold.

I could barely contain my excitement.

The Penningtons lived in an imposing stone house in Clifton, the town nearest High Tor. We arrived in style, in Mr. Ashton's barouche, which could accommodate all six of us. Since it was a private ball, we did not have long to wait our turn to be let out. The driver set the steps down, and Charles and Mr. Ashton alighted first, afterward assisting all the ladies.

Flambeaux lit the outside of the house. Reflected off the glass-fronted façade, the flames nearly made one believe it was on fire. Two footmen stood at the front doors, flung open to admit the guests. Music, voices, and laughter beckoned to us, and a surge of anticipation raced through me. After giving our wraps to a servant, we moved to the receiving line. I glanced around the room, taking in the grandeur of the great rotunda, the extravagant gowns of the other ladies, and the fashionable black and white evening clothes worn by the gentlemen. The only man I had an interest in seeing was not in view, however.

When we were getting dressed, Jane had stopped by my chamber and pronounced me "astonishing" in the newly altered apricot gown. As soon as she'd left, I summoned Sara and asked her to arrange my hair.

"Can you do something special with it? Perhaps a few ringlets loose at the neck and on my forehead."

"Oh, yes, miss. And Mrs. Bingley gave me these pearls to weave into your hair. Said they was just the thing to match your dress."

When Sara was finished, I stood before the glass, transfixed. With both hair and gown, I did look, if not astonishing, rather prettier than usual. My face shone with a mix of elation and anxiety, which lent my cheeks a soft pink blush.

"You're quite smart, miss, if I may say," Sara had remarked.

And now, still waiting in the receiving line, I noticed how lovely Kitty looked. To my surprise, she was wearing the green silk, and showing plenty of décolletage. Her coffee-colored hair looked well with the gown. My sister had barely spoken to me since yesterday, and I thought maybe I should make peace with her. "That dress becomes you, Kitty," I said.

"You look nice too, I suppose," she answered, her gaze settling somewhere over my left shoulder.

I smiled to myself, refusing to allow her to spoil my exuberant mood. At last we reached our host and hostess and, after greeting them, made our way upstairs to the ballroom. In all the bustle, we'd become separated from the Ashtons. Almost immediately, we spied Mr. Darcy and Elizabeth. She had written to say they planned to spend the night with us at High Tor and travel to Pemberley in the morning.

"Lizzy!" Jane said.

Elizabeth's eyes danced. She had a new, cropped hairstyle, which suited her very well. The curls bounced around her face, making her look like a young girl again. "How elegant you all are," she said.

Charles and Mr. Darcy had moved off to one side and were now in close conversation. One could only assume they were discussing the quest for Wickham. Elizabeth looked at us and said, "I shall give you the news later. Let's go to the ballroom. We should enjoy ourselves tonight."

No sooner had I entered the room than I glimpsed Mr. Walsh. He was standing with a group of men, only one of whom I recognized — his cousin, Mr. Carstairs. Upon seeing us, both men approached.

After we greeted them, Elizabeth asked if she might be introduced to our friends. Mr. Walsh, looking uncommonly handsome in black and white evening clothes, bowed to Lizzy. "Mrs. Darcy, at last I make your acquaintance. This is an unexpected pleasure."

"The pleasure is mine, sir. I have heard a great deal about you from my sisters."

"Nothing too damaging to my reputation, I hope, ma'am."

Lizzy laughed. "No, indeed. I think they can find no fault in you at all."

The music for the first set was striking up, and I expected Henry to claim me for the dance. But before he could act, Kitty stepped forward and said, "I've saved the first dance for you, sir."

Although he appeared a bit flummoxed, he smiled down at her and said, "I'm honored, Miss Kitty." And then, to rub salt in the raw wound, I heard him tell her how pretty she looked. She planted her hand on his sleeve, and off they went to the dance floor. Henry hadn't even glanced my way, nor given any indication that he was sorry about having to dance with Kitty rather than me.

Suddenly the room seemed to draw closer; the voices became more strident, the crush of people nearly unbearable. I took a step back, closer to the wall, desperate for somewhere to hide. I had been accustomed to doing this at balls in the past, but fancied tonight would be different. Both Jane and Lizzy were casting sympathetic looks my way, but even they couldn't summon any comforting words. As if it wasn't enough that the man I was trying so hard to impress with my borrowed gown and more fashionable hairstyle had completely ignored me, I also had to bear the pity of my kind and well-meaning family.

It was only the first set, I reminded myself. Perhaps he would find me for the second one. After all, it wasn't his fault Kitty had tricked him into dancing with her. The set ended, and they began walking toward us, Kitty chattering away. Abruptly their progress was halted by an onslaught of matrons wearing plumed headdresses. It was obvious that they sought introductions to Mr. Walsh for their daughters, all gowned in white, who were hovering at the sides of their mothers and appeared barely old enough to be out in society. Charles, who saw what was happening, rescued Kitty and escorted her back to us, where she stood fuming and fussing over her ill luck.

"The nerve of those women, thrusting

their daughters upon Mr. Walsh when he was still with me."

She was right; it was rude of them. *But you, dear sister, thought nothing of thrusting yourself upon him.*

Meanwhile, I watched while Henry danced the next set with a lively young lady, possibly as old as eighteen. When that set had finished, his next partner awaited him. The mothers eyed each other triumphantly, if somewhat warily.

I felt tears glazing my eyes and drew in a long breath to steady myself. This would never do. Somehow I had to survive what was sure to be a very long evening. Charles, no doubt at Jane's prodding, asked me to dance. I partnered with Mr. Darcy as well, and Mr. Carstairs. Not once did I allow my stilted smile to droop or my mock-carefree manner to slip. I spotted Henry Walsh several times dancing with various ladies. Did he not even remember asking me to stand up with him? What had I done to deserve such ill treatment? Maybe he was not the gentleman I thought him to be.

Jane and Elizabeth came over to stand beside me during a break for the musicians. When Lizzy started to speak, I cut her off. "Don't say anything, please, Lizzy. I warn you, I'm dangerously close to either weeping or screaming."

Jane's lips were tightly compressed, and she looked as if she were about to cry. Elizabeth linked arms with me. "No, dear. Of course not."

I realized I hadn't asked about Mr. Darcy's trip to Newcastle. That seemed a safe subject. "Can you give me any news? Did Mr. Darcy learn anything more?"

The man in question appeared, bearing glasses of lemonade for us. Charles was right behind him with a glass for Jane. "I shall let him tell you," Elizabeth said.

"What did you discover about our errant brother, Mr. Darcy?" I asked, accepting the lemonade from him.

A look passed between him and Elizabeth, from which I gathered the news was not good. "When I found out all I could in Newcastle, I traveled to London and located Wickham not far from the area he'd frequented before. He swears he will never go back to Lydia."

"Oh no," I said, momentarily forgetting my own troubles. "Did you offer an . . . inducement?"

"I did, and when he turned it down, I concluded his lady friend must be wealthy. He has no money of his own and no connections except for myself."

"Is there anything else to be done?" I asked.

"Not by me, I'm afraid." Mr. Darcy smiled ruefully at Elizabeth. "It was a fool's errand, I think."

Elizabeth grasped his arm. "You did all you could, Fitzwilliam. More than we had any right to ask of you."

"Yes, I agree," I said. "We are again in your debt, Mr. Darcy." What was to become of poor Lydia? And what damage would her husband's desertion inflict upon our family's reputation?

Mr. Darcy was shrugging off our thanks when the supper dance was called. I felt pathetically grateful that Andrew Carstairs asked me to stand up with him. The dance was a quadrille, and I noticed Kitty partnered with Henry Walsh. How had she contrived that? They were not in our group of eight, thank heaven. Had he asked her this time, or had she trapped him into it again?

At Linden Hall, he'd said he admired me very much, and even before that, he'd requested the dances. I began to believe he was trifling with me. Kitty was right. I had no looks or fashion. Despite my efforts to look well tonight, even pretty, I'd failed to gain Henry's attention. I could never be an

Elizabeth or a Jane. I might as well revert to the old Mary. I may have been loathsome to others, but, naïve and unaware, at least I wasn't miserable. The hurt I'd been feeling now turned into anger. At Henry Walsh, at the world, at myself. Chiefly at myself. I was a fool to have thought I could compete with Kitty, or, indeed, the flock of young beauties trailing after Henry.

Still simmering inside, I dragged my attention back to the intricate steps of the quadrille. Afterward, Mr. Carstairs escorted me into the adjacent hall, where tables had been readied for supper. "May I fill a plate for you, Miss Bennet?" he asked.

I nodded my acceptance of his offer, although I didn't think I'd be able to swallow a single bite. While I waited, a footman filled my wineglass, and Kitty and Mr. Walsh claimed the chairs across from me. Although I sensed him watching me, I didn't meet his gaze. I couldn't bear for him to see the misery in my eyes. He went off directly to find refreshment for himself and my sister. The Bingleys, Darcys, and Ashtons joined us.

The minute Jane and Lizzy were seated, Kitty leaned across the table and said, "I think it must mean something, that he asked me for the supper dance, don't you?" Her face was flushed with pleasure. She must have known I would hear too, but obviously didn't care.

"Perhaps it means the same as Mr. Carstairs asking Mary," Lizzy said, eyebrows raised. Kitty huffed with irritation. I ducked my head. I couldn't help smiling at that.

The gentlemen returned with plates of delectable-looking crab puffs, miniature cakes, and dried fruits. Having no appetite, I pushed the food around my plate. While I sipped my wine, I listened intently for openings in the conversation. Opportunities to do my worst. If Mr. Walsh didn't like the new Mary, let him have a taste of the old.

"Did you see Lucinda Bright, Jane?" Lizzy asked. The Brights were close friends of Mr. Darcy and his sister, Georgiana; I had met them on occasion at Pemberley. Lucinda had always struck me as somewhat vain of her appearance.

"We spoke briefly. She looks beautiful in her rose gown," Jane said.

"Vanity corrupts her, I fear. She does not choose to attain true excellence nor the favor of our Lord," I said. *Oh God. Loathsome Mary rises from the ashes, reborn like the phoenix.*

"Mary, please," Elizabeth said softly, managing to look simultaneously alarmed and astonished. Kitty and Mrs. Ashton both giggled. I held myself stiffly, waiting for another opportunity.

"Is your mother in good health, Mr. Walsh?" asked Mrs. Ashton.

"Yes, indeed. She's kept busy visiting tenants, many of whom have been ill with colds and fevers of one kind or another. These things spread like fire among hayricks."

"She is an unselfish sort of lady, who will always take pains to help others," Amanda Ashton said. Was she vying with me for stupidest remark?

Again I broke in. "One is naturally benevolent when no selfish interest interferes. It speaks well of one's own superiority."

At last I had Henry's attention. I glanced his way briefly and saw the confusion in his eyes.

Jane shoved her chair back so forcefully, Charles had to grab hold of it to prevent its falling over. "Mary, do play for us, dear. I think we would all enjoy a bit of soothing music," she bit out.

"Of course." I rose and, on wobbling legs, made my way to the pianoforte. I felt feverish, my face hot but my body chilled. I perused the music, trying to find just the right piece. One I could play *and* sing. I glanced up for a moment and caught Mr.

Walsh staring at me.

His intense gaze rattled me, so I chose a couple of sonatinas I knew well to begin. I needed a brief respite from my self-imposed humiliation. I played softly and noticed the group at our table had resumed talking, and even found something to laugh at. It would not have surprised me if I were the object of their laughter.

Now for the coup de grâce. I chose an old tune called "Oh, Nancy." Perfect for my purposes, it had numerous high notes I had not the smallest hope of reaching. I cleared my throat, set the music on the rack, and began. As soon as Jane and Lizzy heard the opening notes, their heads swiveled toward me. Conversation ceased.

When I missed the first high note, a few titters broke out among the guests. I plowed on, breathing deeply and pushing to reach the top of my vocal range, but missing every time. During one particularly difficult passage, I lost my voice altogether and emitted a few squeaks. Risking a glance toward my table, I studied the reactions. Some people, like Kitty and the Ashtons, obviously were trying not to laugh. Charles and Mr. Darcy had twisted their faces into pained expressions. Lizzy and Jane sat quietly, Jane with her eyes cast down and Lizzy staring fiercely at everyone, as though daring them to make sport of her sister. Oddly, I didn't see Mr. Walsh, and in a moment, I understood why.

"Miss Bennet." A calm voice, a kind one, spoke at my side.

I stopped singing abruptly. "Mr. Walsh." My heart raced, and I looked not at him, but at the floor.

"Do you recall the day by the river, when you heard me singing 'Annie Laurie'? I shall sing it now, if you'll accompany me."

"I-I don't . . . you vowed you would never sing in company."

"No," he said gently. "That was you."

I gulped, feeling my mouth form an ironic grin.

"I'll help you look for the music."

As he reached for the stack of sheet music, I put my hand on his wrist. "I know it. I don't need the music."

"Very well, then. Shall we begin?"

I played the opening notes, and his baritone voice joined in. I was glad I knew the music so well, because his singing lifted me, took me to a place where I could forget everything except him.

Like dew on th' gowan lying
Is th' fa' o' her fairy feet
And like the winds in summer sighing

Her voice is low and sweet.
And she's a' the world to me
And for bonnie Annie Laurie
I'd lay me doon and dee.

The guests begged for another song, and then a third, after which they demanded a bow from the singer. I seized on the opportunity to quietly disappear. Tears had begun to trickle down my cheeks, and it would never do to lose my composure in public. I could make myself look foolish in every other way, but I would not be caught crying.

My feet carried me back to the ballroom. I found a chair against the wall and sank down on it, thinking over what had just transpired. Henry Walsh had rescued me from complete humiliation. Since he had avoided me all evening, I could not account for it. Especially after I'd insulted his mother and, on the whole, made myself look ridiculous in his eyes — as well as those of everybody else. Not only had he possessed the presence of mind to come to my aid, he had chosen the most inconspicuous and natural way of doing so, providing a partial redemption for me. It was too good of him and made my decision to behave in such a way seem shameful.

Before long, the orchestra was tuning their instruments and guests were drifting back in from supper. I was considering whether or not to find a more secluded spot when the gentleman occupying my thoughts appeared before me.

"Will you dance with me, Miss Bennet? You promised to stand up with me twice, you know."

Had I heard correctly? After taking no notice of me all evening, he was finally claiming his dances? I could find no explanation for it, except that he felt sorry for me. "Sir, I have a headache. I am sorry to disappoint you," I said, rushing the words.

Immediately, he sat down beside me. Taking my hand, he said, "Forgive me. I didn't know you were feeling ill. Shall I find Jane?"

"No! No, I need only to rest here a while."

"Are you certain? It would be no trouble to carry you back to High Tor."

"Quite certain, thank you. I don't wish to leave." I couldn't let the moment pass without acknowledging what he'd done for me. "I am in your debt, sir. You came to my rescue in a most gentlemanly way, and I thank you for it."

He studied me so intently I had to look away. "Miss Bennet —"

Kitty, who had been hovering nearby, now

163

sat down on my other side. Dancers were gathering for the next set. "Mr. Walsh, I'm sure my sister would enjoy another dance with you."

"Oh, yes!" Kitty said.

"Of course." Before rising, he leaned in and whispered to me. "I hope you will forgive me for . . . for my —"

"Please, sir," I said, my cheeks warming. "No apologies are necessary."

After a quick nod, he walked away with my sister, and I was glad I hadn't let him say what he wished to be forgiven for.

CHAPTER 12

When at last the long, torturous evening had ended, and the Ashton barouche had delivered us to High Tor, I tried to slip away without talking to anybody. Jane stopped me as I began to ascend the stairs. "Mary, don't rush off. Lizzy and I would like a little chat."

"But —" My elder sisters both wore determined looks, and I knew they were not to be denied. Kitty flounced past me, apparently floating on a cloud of bliss, and Charles and Mr. Darcy headed off to the library for a brandy, no doubt. The Ashtons had retired to their chambers. I was cornered and knew what the poor fox must feel like.

We went into the salon, where Jane lit a branch of candles from the one already burning. Elizabeth said, "I'm having some sherry. Would either of you care to join me?"

Although I usually didn't drink spirits, I

accepted a glass, and so did Jane. Perhaps we all needed fortification. We sat, the two of them on the chaise and me in one of the silk-upholstered chairs. I waited, sipping slowly, feeling the liquid heat slide down my throat into my stomach.

"That was quite an impressive performance, Mary," Lizzy said after a moment. "Why did you do it?"

"I don't know what you mean."

"You were hurt because Henry Walsh didn't dance with you. Jane told me he had requested two dances, so I understand the pain you must have been suffering. But why make matters worse by acting so outrageously?"

My temper, usually kept in check, flared. "I did nothing wrong."

Lizzy fixed me with a scathing look.

I backed down a bit. "Even if I may have erred a little, what does it matter to you and Jane? In a few weeks, nobody will remember I was your relation."

"We're not concerned for ourselves," Jane said.

I felt my resistance to their questions shrinking. What did it matter if I told them the truth? But how to explain? I gathered my thoughts while they stared at me impatiently. "Before tonight, Mr. Walsh had shown an interest in me — indeed, had singled me out several times. Ask Jane, Lizzy, if you do not believe me."

"I don't need to ask Jane," she said. "Of course I believe you."

"After Kitty said what she did about my looks, I decided that for the ball I would take more care with my appearance." A puzzled glance passed from one sister to the other, and I realized I hadn't told either of them about Kitty's insulting remarks. But I didn't want to explain now. "Especially since Mr. Walsh had already made it clear that he liked me. So I thought." A humorless laugh burst out. "And look what happened. He couldn't have been less interested if I'd turned into a hideous old crone since the last time we met. Most of the evening, he ignored me."

"Because he was lured by Kitty and then accosted by matrons attempting to snatch him up for their daughters! What could he have done that wouldn't have been exceedingly rude?"

"He might have looked at me, shown me with a glance that he was sorry! He danced with Kitty for the supper dance — why didn't he ask me?"

"I don't know," Jane said. "Perhaps she waylaid him again."

"Doesn't he possess the strength to refuse her? Couldn't he have said he'd asked *me* for that dance?"

Elizabeth began pacing the perimeter of the room. "All this doesn't explain your actions. Why you chose to talk such nonsense. And *sing*!"

Wincing, I said, "I was angry. With Henry, but mostly with myself, for thinking I could ever be any different from what I've always been. I desired his attention, even if it had to be gained by acting like the old Mary." I looked down. It was easier than looking at my accusers. "And I wanted to hurt him, I suppose."

"And you succeeded only in hurting yourself!" Lizzy barked.

"He cares for you," Jane said. "I'm certain he does. You shouldn't give up on him."

"He has an odd way of showing it." I choked down the rest of my sherry and flew up so fast I nearly lost my balance. "I know you mean well. Both of you." I stretched out my arms toward them. "You're not to blame, nor am I, for misinterpreting his behavior. He simply enjoys good conversation, and I've been providing that. After tonight, I'm quite certain whatever interest he may have had in me has been soundly quashed."

When I paused to catch my breath, Jane started to protest. I spoke over her. "It's all right. His regard was more than I had any right to expect." It was the truth, and the first time I'd admitted it to myself. "Now, if you don't mind, I'd like to go to bed." The feigned headache I'd been complaining of all day now seemed to have clamped down on my head. Maybe it was the sherry. Or retribution.

Elizabeth had circled back and planted herself in front of me. "I wonder, Mary, why you are so unwilling to forgive him. Many of tonight's events were beyond his control." Her voice softened. "I think you are afraid. It is easier to pretend you don't care."

This was too much. "Don't be ridiculous!" I snapped.

"Of what?" Jane asked. "Of what are you afraid, Mary?"

"Ask Lizzy. I have never heard of anything so nonsensical." I spun around before they drove me to say something I would regret and had made it halfway to the door when Elizabeth resumed speaking. Although she was talking to Jane, there was no doubt I was meant to hear.

"She's afraid of risking her heart. Of accepting love, I think. Because she has always felt unloved." Her voice was gentle, pitying.

"We, and all our family, must take responsibility for that."

Closing the door quietly, I hurried to my chamber. I had told Sara I would not need her after the ball. After undressing and plaiting my hair, I eased under the covers. A candle still burned on my night table, and in the faint light I saw the apricot gown draped over a chair. I rose to put it away, wanting it out of my sight. It smelled faintly of the light lavender scent Jane wore. Just for a moment, I held it against my face and reveled in the soft, gauzy feel of it. The truth of Lizzy's remarks buckled my knees, and I dropped to the floor, still clutching the gown. Burying my face in its folds, I cried. Sobbed, to own the truth. Using the dress to muffle the sound, I kept on crying until I had exhausted myself.

After a while, I crawled back into bed, blew out the candle, and finally fell asleep.

Elizabeth and Mr. Darcy, after eating breakfast with us, departed for Pemberley. Lizzy said no more about last evening, only hugged me tightly before her husband helped her into the chaise.

I had awakened feeling hollow and empty. At breakfast, I forced down a roll and drank some chocolate. As we waved farewell to

Lizzy, I contemplated a walk, especially since the weather was fine. I had just turned to fetch my bonnet when Amanda Ashton approached me.

"What a handsome couple your sister and Mr. Darcy make," she said.

"Yes, indeed."

"I suppose they spend a great deal of time with the Wickhams, since, as you told me, Mr. Darcy and Wickham were boyhood friends."

In actuality, I had told her no such thing, but merely had said Wickham's father had been the Pemberley steward. Not knowing what answer to make, I settled with "Not often, since Newcastle is some distance away. My sister and Mr. Darcy visit Jane and Charles more frequently."

"I see."

What does she see?

"It appeared Mr. Bingley and Mr. Darcy had secret business to discuss last night. Their heads were together at the ball, and afterward, I imagine."

Ever since the day she had questioned me about Mr. Darcy's relationship with Wickham, and I had challenged her, she'd left me alone. I'd not had another word from her on the subject. Until now. "They've been the closest of friends for many years

171

and always have much to discuss. Some of it is private, not even shared with their wives." I spoke through clenched teeth.

Apparently, she realized her inquiries were ill judged. She dropped the subject and went on to another. "I was shocked at Mr. Walsh's neglect of you last night. One could hardly help noticing."

I drew in a deep breath and released it audibly, wishing I could unleash my temper on her. Turning on my heel, I walked toward the house to collect my bonnet and pelisse. A walk now seemed a necessity. Mrs. Ashton hurried after me. "Well?" she said.

I noticed she'd completely dropped her silly female pose. I had to think to form an appropriate response. "What he chooses to do as regards me is his own affair, Amanda. It should be of no concern to you." With that, I strode briskly ahead of her so there would be no further opportunity for questions. The woman was a scourge.

On my way out, I stopped by the kitchen and asked the cook for a basket. I thought to walk along the river and gather watercress.

"I do like a salad with watercress," she said. "Spices things up a bit."

I smiled and took the basket, which she'd lined with a clean, white cloth.

"Here, dear, you'll be needing a knife, too."

I tossed the knife into the basket and set out. Walking through the shrubbery lane, I soon gained the avenue and made my way toward the part of the river where I knew watercress grew abundantly. It was a bit early in the season, but perhaps I'd find tender, new shoots. They had the best flavor.

Something I had scarcely allowed myself to think of came to mind. It was Elizabeth's extraordinary assertion from last night, that I was afraid of accepting love. For my whole life, I had felt unloved by most of my family. Not mistreated, but left out. Jane and Lizzy were the only ones who showed me affection — and more recently, my father, in his own peculiar way. In the past, when I was at my most pompous and overbearing, even they'd sometimes become irritated with me. If my own family didn't love me, how could such a man as Henry Walsh do so? I knew, even if my sisters refused to admit it, that the reason he'd avoided me last night was because his regard for me extended only as far as a few stimulating discussions. When it came to dancing, or anything remotely romantic, he avoided me.

I turned off the avenue onto a path leading to the river. It was lined with ferns, moss, and other low-growing foliage I couldn't identify, and soon gave way to a grassy riverbank. I set my basket down and lowered myself onto a rock, wrapping my arms around my knees. The sound of the water was soothing.

Was Lizzy right? Was I afraid? When I was with Henry, and we were deeply involved in a conversation, I felt no doubt of his regard for me, and mine for him. I was completely relaxed and comfortable in his presence. Even last night, when he'd saved me from myself, he was tender and gentle with me. But his behavior for most of the evening made me realize I no longer trusted him. Lizzy was right about this much: I was scared to risk my heart when I couldn't be sure of his feelings. Kitty and the other girls at the ball were prettier and more vivacious, and he'd made his preference for them painfully obvious.

The morning had warmed, and I shed my pelisse. Walking close by the river, I looked for watercress along the edge. To my dismay, most of it seemed to be pushing up too far out for me to reach. There was nothing for it but to remove my shoes, stockings, and garters. I laid them in a pile with my pelisse, rucked my skirts up with one hand, and clung to my knife with the other.

I'd had to do this before and knew the river bottom could be slippery. I stepped forward with caution and, when I reached the bed of watercress, awkwardly pressed my skirts against my waist with my elbow, while I bent over and cut the shoots using both hands. It was in this less-than-elegant posture, my bare legs exposed, that Mr. Walsh found me.

Chapter 13

He spoke in a very low voice. "It's Henry Walsh, Miss Bennet."

I reared up, embarrassment flooding me, and dropped my skirts in the process. "Oh, dear. What have I done?" I said stupidly.

"Forgive me. You must allow me to help you."

I simply stood there, watching the lower part of my dress sink into the river.

"Hand me the knife," he said, splashing right into the water. I did so, and he tossed it onto the bank.

"Your boots will be ruined!" I said, as if it mattered at this point.

Before I could guess what he intended, he bent over and picked me up, one arm beneath my legs, the other protectively around my back. I had no choice but to throw my arm around his neck. It was either that or try to hold myself upright, which would have been ridiculous. My face brushed the fine wool cloth of his coat, and the desire to sink against him was strong. I clung to him while we made our way to the bank. After setting me down, he took out his handkerchief and spread it on the ground for me to stand on.

"There's a cloth in the basket," I said, and he handed it to me. I was mortified. In clear view were my stockings and garters! And there I stood, in my bare feet, my ankles showing as I bent over to squeeze some of the water from my dress and blot it with the cloth.

I rose. "Mr. Walsh —"

"I'll walk back to the avenue while you . . . attend to your toilette," he said. "Call me when you've finished."

I had a strong suspicion he'd been trying not to smile. Good heaven! Did I have to choose *this* morning to wade into the river? I wondered why he had come to High Tor, and most especially why he had sought me out. I dried off as best I could and tugged my stockings on over damp legs, securing them with the garters. The dress was hopeless. I could squeeze and blot for hours, but time was the only real remedy. I put my pelisse on, to hide my sodden hem, and called to him.

Henry strolled down the path, smiling at

me. Why did he have to be so handsome, with his irresistible smile and those deep blue eyes? "I'm glad you find this amusing, sir," I said in my most affronted voice.

"Forgive me. If you could have seen the look on your face . . ."

Imagining myself in his place, coming down the path and watching me drop my skirts into the river, I couldn't help grinning.

"Why don't we walk?" he asked. "The avenue is sunny and your dress will dry faster." He retrieved the knife and threw it into the basket. When I tried to take it, he insisted on carrying it for me.

For a brief moment, a sense of profound happiness flooded my chest. Best not to let it linger too long. "How did you know where to find me? Have you been to the house?"

"One of the servants told Mrs. Bingley you were gathering watercress. She directed me this way." He stopped abruptly, grasped my arm, and stepped a bit closer. "I wish to apologize for what happened last night at the ball."

I felt my cheeks turn pink. Or perhaps rose red would be more accurate, so acute was my embarrassment. I didn't want his apologies.

"Miss Bennet, Mary, I-I had every intention of dancing the first set with you, but your sister —"

"Oh, please, don't apologize." I glanced down at his hand, still holding my arm. He removed it. "You were under no obligation to me," I said.

"Obligation?" He huffed a laugh. "I did not consider it as such. I'd been looking forward to dancing with you at last, but events contrived to keep me from you. I was disappointed."

Not having the smallest idea of how to respond, I looked away.

"Were you perhaps upset too, Mary? Even a little?"

Don't admit it. But when I glanced at his face, at the pleading look in his eyes, I nodded.

He smiled, and the warmth of it melted whatever resentment I had left. "Let's sit down," he said, taking my elbow and guiding me toward a bench, one of several along the lane. "Are you too warm? Would you like to remove your wrap?"

He helped me take off the garment, and I spread out the hem of my dress so it would catch the sun. The merino wool would dry quickly in the warm air.

"Miss Bennet, there is something I wish

to say to you before you hear it from a third party. Something which may be distressing to you."

I must have been gawping at him, because he let out a bark of laughter. In truth, I had no idea what he was talking about. "What is it? Is something wrong?" Wildly irrational thoughts made my head spin. Mr. Walsh was dying, or perhaps his mother was. He was a gambler and had to sell his estate to pay debts of honor. He had a wife and kept her hidden in a cottage in the wood —

"I have a daughter, Mary."

I must have misunderstood. Wouldn't Jane and Charles have told me such a thing by now? "You have a daughter?"

His face colored slightly. "Yes. Her name is Amelia, and she is eight years old. At present, she lives with my eldest sister, but I very much wish for her to live with me."

"Amelia is . . . your daughter. You want her to live with you?" *Blast! Must I repeat everything he said?* But my mind was reeling, and I couldn't think of a sensible response.

He smiled, at my ineptitude, I supposed. "Do you remember when we talked about Lord Nelson, and I said I would not care to have my own faults examined too closely?"

I nodded, and he went on. "When I was

twenty years old, I fell in love with a girl from the local village. I wanted to wed her, but my father wouldn't permit it. I was too young, he believed, and she too much older than I. This was an infatuation I would grow out of. She was not my equal, in his opinion. He was a retired army officer, a very imposing man, and I was too young and naïve to go against his wishes."

"But you married anyway? Without his approval?"

"No. I told Beth I couldn't marry her. I ended our relationship, even though it broke her heart, and mine, too." I stole a glance at him. He stared into the distance, his eyes unfocused, his thoughts riveted on the past.

"A year passed, and I didn't see her, heard nothing of her. That was best, my father said. One day, out of the blue, I received a letter from her family. A virulent fever had swept through the village. Beth caught it and died."

"Oh no!" Now I understood his extreme reaction when I'd asked about his father.

He wrapped my hand inside both of his, as if to draw strength from me. "It was many years ago now, and I do not often think of her anymore. The letter said she'd left something for me, and I must come to them to claim it. I was bereft. Guilt-ridden and furious with myself for giving in to my father. I went to see her family within days of receiving the news.

"Imagine my surprise when I discovered what it was she had left me. A child. Our child. An infant girl who had her mother's fair coloring and sweet nature. I brought her home, over my father's objections, and my mother and I spoiled her terribly.

"Eventually my sister Beatrice insisted it would serve Amelia best to be in the company of other children. She must learn manners and decorum. This she could do at my sister's home, as well as share in the benefits of the governess and masters employed for her own children."

Still reeling from this revelation, I hardly knew what to say. "D-do you see her often?" I finally stammered out.

"Yes, Beatrice lives only some five miles away. Amelia is a delight, and I want you to meet her. That is, if I haven't shocked you too greatly."

It *was* a shocking confession, but it seemed to me he had done all he might to make amends. He described Beth as being several years older than himself, so it was no seduction of an innocent girl. From his telling of the tale, it sounded as if he had truly loved her. Still . . . he'd had a child out of wedlock. And he'd kept it a secret from all of us.

He rose and gazed down at me. "Please believe me, Mary, if I had known Beth was with child, I would have wed her, my father be damned." He flushed. "Pardon my language."

When I made no response, he went on. "I was young. I made a mistake, and I will always regret the hurt I caused. But I will never regret Amelia." He said this as though daring me to suggest he should have sent her to a home for orphans and foundlings.

"I'm persuaded you are the best of fathers, Mr. Walsh. Amelia is a lucky child, to be so loved by you and all your family. What I don't understand is why you've made me privy to your secret."

He lowered himself to the bench and reached for my hands, which I gave willingly. "Can you not guess, Mary? Have you no idea?"

I stared, openmouthed. He could not mean what I thought he meant.

Apparently he found my bewilderment amusing, because he laughed. And then he said, "I wish to marry you."

I jerked my hands away and nearly leaped off the bench. To say I was astonished would be understating my feelings. I needed to gather my thoughts before making a coherent response.

"Mary, please —"

I interrupted before he could go further, speaking with my back to him. "How could I possibly have guessed? Your behavior of last night was hardly that of a man who was serious about gaining my affection."

"I apologized. I thought you had forgiven me."

"Yes. *No.*" I whirled around to face him. "That was before . . . this." I flung my hand out, as if "this" was an actual thing I could point to. "Before you told me about Amelia, and before your proposal."

"So my proposal makes you *less* inclined to forgive me?"

"Forgiveness aside, Mr. Walsh, other than enjoying our conversations, I've noticed that you never choose me as a dance partner, rarely offer me your arm, and never compliment my appearance. You have done all those things for Kitty, many times. Isn't it perhaps she you wish to make your wife?" I was vaguely aware of sounding petulant and whining as I reeled off these faults. And the last part about making Kitty his wife may have gone rather too far.

Now he stood, agitated. "Your sister would be no substitute for you, dear Mary.

We have nothing in common. She has an annoying knack for coming between us. Surely you've noticed that."

"I would have to be blind not to have noticed. But why can you never refuse her? You danced with her twice last night, while never seeking me out or even looking at me. And this was after you had made a point of asking me for the first dance and one other!"

He studied me, a pained expression on his face. "I'm sorry if I hurt you. It was the opposite of what I intended." He gave his head a shake and went on. "I've tried to avoid being rude to Kitty, though perhaps I should have been more forthright with her. And I did seek you out after supper."

"A bit late, wasn't it?"

"Perhaps so." His voice trembled a little as he continued. "All the times you and I have been together, walking and talking — and I did offer you my arm on those occasions," he said wryly. "I felt drawn to you. I admire your intellect and your directness. There's an essential part of your character I'm attracted to. I believed you felt the same."

Such a lack of tenderness, of warmth, in those words. *My character.* It always came back to that. His feelings for me had nothing to do with love or true affection. I'd seen enough of loveless marriages. I didn't want one for myself, especially after observing the joyful unions of my elder sisters.

And then I was struck by a thought more unbearable than any other I'd considered. I now understood the reason he had chosen me over Kitty. Why he couldn't consider marriage to any of the younger ladies. He believed I would be the better mother! Hadn't his tale of Beth and Amelia led directly to the proposal?

He didn't love me. This had nothing to do with love. It was my good sense (how my family would laugh at that!), my devotion to reading and learning, and perhaps most of all, an open declaration of my desire to "become more proficient with children one day." And what had been his answer? "You will, with practice." Oh, yes, practice with a conveniently available child.

I could no longer wonder at his rescuing me last night at the ball — he would hardly sit by and laugh while the future mother to Amelia made a great fool of herself. I only wondered why it took him so long.

He cared chiefly about those qualities he deemed necessary for motherhood. Well, Kitty could change. If she truly cared for him, as she claimed, she would accept his daughter and learn to mother her. Or if she were incapable of doing so, perhaps one of the other girls Henry had so assiduously danced attendance on last night would do. I drew in a sharp breath and spoke before I could change my mind.

"Thank you for honoring me with your proposal, Mr. Walsh, but I cannot accept."

Restively, he paced in front of me. "Have I so badly misinterpreted your feelings toward me? You never appeared anything but glad of my notice and my company. Did you lead me on, then, with every intention of rejecting me?"

"No! I had not the least idea you would offer for me." *But I wanted him to, didn't I?* "Please forgive me if I misled you, but can you now deny you have misled *me*? All of us? You kept your daughter's existence a secret, because the fact that you even have a daughter is no small thing."

"Ah. So you now believe me unfit to be your husband."

"You need a mother for Amelia; you believed I would do for the job."

His color heightened. "This is what you think? That you have my regard only as a mother to Amelia? You misjudge me!" He stopped abruptly, not two feet from me, and I could see his eyes had darkened with anger.

"To own the truth, I don't know what to think."

"While we're on the subject of truth, how do you explain your odd behavior of last night? Were you attempting to discourage my suit, even before you knew about Amelia?"

Oh, I wished he would not have raised the issue of *my* conduct. "No, sir. I was angry with you for taking no notice of me. And even angrier with myself for believing you would."

Jaw clenched, he took another step closer to me. "You're a mystery to me, Miss Bennet. You were furious with me because I neglected you at the ball, and yet today, when I pay you the greatest compliment a man can pay, you reject me."

"Your proposal was hardly the kind girls dream of, sir."

"My pardon if I didn't live up to your girlish ideals!"

Every time we lashed out at each other, it seemed we'd drawn a step or two closer, until we were now standing eye to eye, both of us breathing hard. Henry's eyes sparked with anger; I was certain mine did too.

"It would seem we've reached an impasse," he said, moving away from me. "You've given me your answer. I won't trouble you further." Anger still clouded his expression, but his temper had subsided. He reached for his hat and turned to leave. "Good day, then. Be assured of my continued good wishes." Fixing his hat in place, he strode off down the avenue. Suddenly, he stopped in his tracks and spun to look at me. "Oh, one other thing, Miss Bennet. You looked elegant in your apricot gown. And your hair, with the pearls. Beautiful. It was remiss of me not to have told you." He nodded curtly and went on his way.

I dropped onto the bench, moaning out loud. He *had* noticed my appearance, even recalled it in some detail. Blast the man! Why couldn't he have told me last night? Was I wrong to think love so important? Many, if not most, marriages were made between two people who barely knew each other.

Perhaps, as Elizabeth had implied, I should forgive his faults. The lack of affection, the coldness of the proposal, and the fact that he had a child. Henry possessed many qualities to esteem. I began to believe Lizzy was right. I was afraid of endangering my heart, of taking a chance on a man whose feelings for me would never go beyond respect and appreciation for my intellect. I stood and began walking. After a few paces, I saw I was headed in the wrong direction. My mind was in a muddle.

Henry had chosen me, not Kitty. And I had rebuffed him.

CHAPTER 14

When I returned to the house, any hopes I'd entertained of being left alone were immediately disappointed. Kitty was pacing around the front entrance, waiting for me with some impatience. Servants were running to and fro, carrying trunks and bags toward the door. "What's all the hustle and bustle?" I asked. I set the basket down, empty of watercress, and removed my hat and pelisse.

Her glance briefly took in the activity, then settled on me. "The Ashtons are leaving. Where have you been, Mary? We received a letter from Papa. Lydia's child has been born. Jane wishes to depart for Longbourn immediately."

At that moment, Jane came rushing down the stairs. "Mary, did Kitty tell you the news? Lydia has been brought to bed of a girl! We must be on our way within the hour. Can you be ready?"

I wasn't sure what the rush was, since the babe had already made her appearance, apparently without any mishaps, but I nodded my agreement. "Of course, if that is what you wish."

"If there is a reason for you to stay, Kitty can accompany me," she said in a low voice. "Nothing has happened to keep you here?"

From her quizzical look, I knew she'd been hoping Mr. Walsh and I had pledged our undying love to each other while gathering watercress. I put an end to her hopes. "No. Nothing. I'll pack my things."

"Sara has already begun, but you had best check on her."

I started up the stairs, then turned and asked, "What did Papa's letter say?"

"The midwife attended Lydia, with Mama and Aunt Gardiner's help. Fortunately it was an easy birth. Off you go! I'll tell you the rest in the chaise."

We departed right on schedule, leaving poor Kitty to her dreams of Mr. Walsh. Although everything he'd said persuaded me he would not pursue her, she would need to discover it for herself. Apparently, she was ignorant of his visit. I felt sure she would have lashed out at me if she'd known he had been at High Tor and sought me out rather than her.

"Good-bye!" Kitty called, waving as Jane and I drove away. She looked rather pitiful, and I hoped her heart, soon to be broken, would mend quickly.

I wished I could curl up in a corner of the chaise and weep. If turning down Mr. Walsh's offer was the right decision, why did I feel so bleak? I could tell all to Jane, but I didn't want her to endure listening to the trials of one sister while on her way to aid another. She must have sensed my sadness, because she left me to my disordered thoughts. Only think, Henry Walsh had a child, one he had kept secret all this time! I wondered if Jane and Charles knew. I recalled at the picnic noticing his skill when handling David and his stumbling over the number of nieces and nephews he had.

If only he'd told me at the start that he had a daughter! Although I wasn't sure if revealing the truth about his situation would have mattered. I didn't wish to wed a man who simply needed a mother for his child. A man who kept secrets. A man who proposed as though he were arranging a business transaction. Marriage and security in exchange for raising his child. In the end, we would barely tolerate each other, like my parents. It was too appalling to contemplate.

■ ■ ■ ■

Jane and I spent two unpleasant nights at coaching inns. At the first, the inn yard was noisy with comings and goings until the wee hours. And the second — suffice it to say the condition of the bed linens didn't bear thinking about. Worried about vermin, we slept in our clothes with our pelisses on. When we arrived at home, only Papa stood out front to greet us, shading the sun from his eyes with one hand.

"Welcome, my dear girls. We are sadly in need of your help."

"Is something wrong, sir?" Jane asked.

"Your aunt Gardiner left a few days ago, and without a nursemaid, things are in a sorry state. Your mother has taken to her bed, and Lydia has done nothing but complain since the child's birth."

"Should we go to Mama or Lydia first?" Jane asked when we'd put off our wraps.

"You'd best greet your mother, or she'll be vexed."

As Jane and I hurried upstairs, I thought I heard the baby crying. We looked at each other in dismay. Mama lay on her bed surrounded by pillows, her smelling salts close to hand. "Oh!" she said as we entered the room. "I thought you would never get here."

"We came as soon as we received Papa's letter," Jane assured her. The baby's cries grew louder and more insistent, and I glanced nervously at my sister.

Clutching a handkerchief, Mama swept a hand through the air. "Your father! I am most sorely displeased with him! He refused to write to you until my sister Gardiner was to take her leave." Her arm sank down onto her pillows, as if exhausted by so much effort. "He said we must learn to get along on our own. Have you ever heard such nonsense?" She paused for a breath, then continued in a more reasonable voice. "We are all in an uproar since your aunt decamped. I do not know why she could not have stayed longer. She was not with us even a month, and had no great need to return home, I'm sure! In my state, I can hardly bear a baby in the house."

I frowned. "Mama, Aunt Gardiner's own children probably missed her keenly. Not to mention Mr. Gardiner."

"Oh, what does that signify next to a new baby?" She twisted her face into a grimace, dismissing any claims the Gardiners had over their beloved wife and mother.

"How is Lydia?" Jane asked.

"How do you think? Since we received

Lizzy's letter about Wickham's refusal to take her back, she's in very low spirits. Cruel, heartless man!" I refrained from pointing out that Lydia bore some responsibility for her predicament.

The baby's screams rose to an earsplitting pitch. "We'd better go to our sister," Jane said.

"Yes, do, or that child will never stop her caterwauling."

Lydia's bedchamber was just down the hall. It looked as if someone had taken a pile of things and simply thrown them in the air, leaving them to land where they might. Ladies' magazines, discarded clothing, bonnets, reticules, baby clothes, all lay strewn about. It was hard to see how matters could have gotten this much out of hand in the short time since my aunt's departure. Jane went directly to the baby, while I, stepping around the mess on the floor, made my way to Lydia. She was propped up by a multitude of pillows, so like Mama. I eased myself onto the edge of the bed. "You have a baby daughter, Lydia. Congratulations!"

She scowled at me. "You've never given birth, Mary, and can't know what a nightmare it is. It took a monstrous long time! And the baby cries constantly. What am

I to do?"

Jane approached the bedside with the little bundle, a doting smile on her face. "She's beautiful, Lydia. And Papa's letter said your labor was not too difficult."

"He would say that, wouldn't he? It was no hardship on him."

Except for taking you in and having his life completely disrupted.

With Jane's swaying movements and clucking noises, the child was already quieting. "What have you named her?" she asked.

"Felicity."

"Ah . . . lovely name," Jane said.

Lydia must have found it in a magazine. Nobody we knew had ever named her child Felicity. I stood up and peeked at her. She had an abundance of almost black, curly hair and dark eyes, and stared up at me in a bewildered way. With her brows drawn together, she resembled a scholar trying to work out a philosophical problem, and I giggled. Jane held the little bundle out to me, and I accepted it, feeling awkward and ignorant of what to do. So I kept on with what Jane had been doing, walking about and cooing.

"Is she hungry? Perhaps that's why she's fussing," I said. If I were to be of any help, I'd need to learn about feedings and changing nappies and bathing. And many other baby matters. For a moment, I remembered Mr. Walsh holding little David and how comfortable he seemed. I'd told him I envied his skill, and I did all the more now. A sharp pinprick of regret took me by surprise, for the way things might have been, but I could not indulge those feelings now.

"How should I know? How I long for a nursemaid, but Papa won't pay for one. I need my rest, you know. I declare, it's exceedingly mean of him. He says Wickham should pay, only I don't even know how to contact him. Horrid Mr. Darcy won't give me his direction."

"Wickham told him he was leaving within hours, so his current direction would not have been helpful. Mr. Darcy went to a great deal of trouble to track down your husband. You should be grateful to him for his efforts on your behalf," Jane said.

"Well, why should that signify since nothing good came about as a result? I didn't ask for Darcy's help. You and Lizzy did that."

Jane cast Lydia a reproachful glance but held her tongue. I was certain Lydia would be oblivious to a rebuke, in any case.

"How long has it been since her last feeding?" Jane asked.

"A few hours."

"It's time then. With infants, it's best to put them to the breast when they fuss."

"She doesn't suck properly," Lydia complained.

"Why don't I help you?" asked Jane. "Let me see how you're going about this, and maybe I can offer some advice."

"Mary must leave," Lydia commanded. "I don't want her watching me, and she doesn't know anything about it."

"I want to talk to Papa anyway," I said, grateful for the chance to make my escape.

"Mrs. Hill, do you know where my father is?" His library door was standing open, but he wasn't there. The familiar odors of ink, leather-bound volumes, and aging parchment made me glad to be home, despite Lydia's complaints and Mama's nerves.

"Off to visit a tenant. Wouldn't be gone too long, he said."

I nodded my thanks and decided to walk out. Perhaps I'd meet him on his way back. I strolled in the direction of the tenants' cottages, breathing in the scents of spring — loam, manure, fresh-cut grass — and thought over the talk I'd had with Jane earlier.

On the first few days of our journey, she had waited with all consideration for my feelings, but doubtless hoping I would raise the subject of Mr. Walsh. I did not. After we'd jounced along an hour or so this morning, and I still hadn't said a word, she'd raised it herself. Very circumspect in her questions, Jane had shown a great deal of patience and kindness.

"Mary, may I know what happened between you and Henry Walsh?" she hesitantly asked. Weary with keeping my feelings in check, I told her the chief of it, leaving out only the story of Amelia. If they didn't know about her, I felt strongly it was not my place to tell them.

I hadn't even realized I was crying until Jane reached for my hand and held it tightly. Only then did I feel the wetness on my cheeks and the burning behind my eyes. *Not again.* I never used to weep. Crying was for silly girls like Lydia and Kitty. For someone opposed to it on principle, I'd lately been doing more than my share. Once I realized my eyes were dripping tears, I couldn't stop the tremors that overtook me. Jane bore with me, all the while patting my hand and murmuring comforting little noises.

"Why did you refuse him? Is it as Lizzy guessed? Are you afraid?"

I avoided a direct answer. "He doesn't love me, Jane. He thinks I have an admirable character," I said between little gasps. I couldn't say he only wanted me because he thought I possessed commendable mothering attributes. *Oh, blast!* Even though he'd deceived me, I couldn't shake off the feeling I'd made a horrible mistake. Henry was a good man, even if he was not violently in love with me.

"There are worse reasons to marry. And I'm sure he would grow to love you. Look how you've changed for the better in the past few years!" She handed me a handkerchief from her reticule.

"Forgive me if I tell you I don't agree with the idea that couples grow to love each other," I said, my voice thick and rasping. "It seems to me more common that they grow apart."

Jane grimaced. "Do you think he'll offer for Kitty?"

"He said they have nothing in common, so I think not."

"Well, that shows good sense, although Kitty will be hurt. But she'll recover and, if I know her, will be on the hunt for another man soon enough."

"I've made such a tangle of things," I said, eventually raising my head. "Now when I see Mr. Walsh at High Tor, it will be very awkward and unpleasant. If he doesn't offer for Kitty, though, he probably won't be there very often."

"I think he'll continue to be a frequent visitor because he and Charles are so close. But don't fret over it now, Mary. You will not be there for some time, and you'll have plenty of other matters to occupy you at Longbourn."

Like learning to care for a baby, I thought now, ambling along the avenue and keeping an eye out for Papa. Clearly, Lydia was no fit mother. I hoped Jane could give her — give us both — some instruction before she returned to High Tor.

"Mary!" Papa's voice, hailing me. He walked toward me swinging a walking stick.

"I was hoping to find you," I said. "Do you have more visits to make?"

"No, only the one. Mr. Calvert's pasture is sorely in need of drainage. I had the unpleasant duty of informing him I couldn't help him achieve it."

I had a vague memory of Charles and Mr. Walsh discussing drainage systems the day we visited Linden Hall. "I think Charles knows something about this," I said. "Perhaps he would be willing to help."

Papa held up a restraining hand. "I cannot ask Charles or Mr. Darcy for any more help. Out of the question."

"So it is true, then, that a nursemaid for Lydia is also out of the question?"

"You disapprove, I see. I have done a poor job of managing our income over the years, Mary. I'm determined to hold on to the money set aside for marriage settlements for you and Kitty. Apart from that, there's simply not enough for a nurse."

"But Papa, by all means, use my portion. I am quite sure I will never wed."

"*You* may be sure of that, but I am not. Lydia is strong and healthy, and there is no reason why she cannot tend to the babe herself."

I arched my eyebrows at him. "Except that she has absolutely no inclination to do so."

"Even so, she'll manage. According to Jane's letter, you've come home in order to offer assistance?"

"I'll do what I can, but I'm afraid I'm ill prepared for the job. Has Lydia heard nothing from Wickham, then? No word at all?"

"None." He was silent a moment. "Although she has received a few letters from someone else. She refuses to say from whom, but I have a strong suspicion they are from the man she —"

"No need to explain, Papa. I take your

meaning. That seems rather . . . *scandalous,* does it not?"

"Just so. I told her in no uncertain terms that I would confiscate any further communication from him. She laughed and said it was none of my affair. You know her too well to doubt me on that head."

"Oh, I am sorry, sir." *Ungrateful wretch of a girl, to speak so to Papa.*

"It is your mother and I who are to blame. If I hadn't been so remiss as a parent, if I had been more severe on Lydia, we might not have come to this pass. I foolishly assumed she would turn out to be a good girl, like the rest of you. Kitty excepted, although she has improved of late."

"We must make the best of a bad situation," I said, and we strolled toward home, both lost in our thoughts of missed opportunities and irresponsible acts.

CHAPTER 15

The days flew by, and the dread of Jane's leaving us burrowed into the pit of my stomach. What would I do, left alone with Mama, Lydia, and a newborn babe?

Jane made good use of her time with us to instruct Lydia and me on swaddling, bathing, feedings, changing nappies, and various ways to comfort the baby when all else failed. With Jane's patient coaching, Lydia became more proficient at nursing the child, who had at last learned to latch on to the nipple.

I closely observed Lydia performing these tasks, and it was disturbing to see her impassivity. She took no joy in any of it, nd handed Felicity to me or Jane directly after a bath or feeding. And she always left us to deal with the soiled nappies, wrinkling up her nose and saying, "Eww," as she 'anded Felicity over.

One day Jane said, in a voice that brooked

no argument, "Lydia, today you are going to get out of that bed, bathe, and dress. Then, since it's a very fine day, we will all take your daughter outside for a walk."

"You and Mary may walk, but I'm not recovered from the birth yet. I still feel rather weak, you know."

"Nonsense. Felicity will be a month old tomorrow! You will never regain your figure or your strength if you keep coddling yourself in this way," Jane said. "What do you intend to do? Wither away up here? It's time to rejoin the world, dear." From then on, Lydia bathed and dressed every day, although she continued to keep to her chamber or the upstairs sitting room most of the time and displayed little if any motherly tenderness.

The morning Jane was to leave, I took her aside. "I must speak with you before you depart."

"What is it, Mary?" The footman was strapping her bags onto the chaise, and if she sounded impatient with me, I didn't blame her. She'd been here almost a month, and I was certain she missed Charles and David exceedingly.

"I won't keep you but a moment. I'm concerned about Lydia . . ." My voice tapered off, since I didn't know precisely how to describe the reason for my unease.

Jane grabbed my hand and pulled me into the dining room. The servants had finished clearing it of breakfast things, so it stood empty and quiet. "She shows no affection for Felicity. Is that what you're trying to say?"

I nodded. "Do you think it's because" — I felt my face color — "she doesn't know if Wickham or the other man is the father?"

"Hmm. Possibly, but I think it more likely that she's simply taking longer than usual to form an attachment with her child. I've heard of that happening to some women, along with other strange behaviors, especially with a first child."

"She's so listless and lethargic. Is that part of it?"

"It very well could be."

"Can anything be done?"

"I think not. It simply takes time, and I'm afraid the burden of caring for the baby is going to fall on your shoulders until Lydia has come through this. I am certain Charles and Mr. Darcy would pay for a nursemaid, but Papa will not hear of it."

I thought back to the day I'd overheard my mother saying I'd have to help Lydia when her child was born. I'd been so consumed with anger. Lydia had arrived in the middle of that conversation. All things considered, I supposed I should be glad I hadn't had to travel to Newcastle to attend her.

"Now, if there's nothing else, I must go. If the circumstances become too taxing for you, you can always visit High Tor. I'm sure it would do you good."

Shortly afterward, she climbed into the chaise and left me to my new occupation of nursemaid.

My adoration of Felicity began the first time she smiled her gummy little smile at me. I'd taken her from Lydia after a feeding, intending to tuck her back into bed. It was early, not past six o'clock, and most days she fell back to sleep. As I walked down the hall, her tiny hand shot out and brushed my face. The soft touch of her flesh felt sweet beyond measure. I entered the nursery and lowered myself into the rocking chair, propping her in my arms and gazing down at her. She'd changed so much in the weeks since Jane had left us. Her eyes had taken on a deep brown hue and were focusing well, now that she was nearly two months old. Having lost a great deal of her dark hair — perfectly normal, according to Mama — at present only soft fuzz covered her scalp. And then the smile flashed.

It was such a lovely thing. So honest and trusting. I wasn't sure if she had smiled before, or if I was seeing the first one. I wanted to dash in to tell Lydia, but I knew she'd be angry if I woke her up. Instead, I tickled Felicity's chin and cheeks, made faces, recited a few nursery rhymes — whatever I could do to elicit another one of the wondrous smiles. I was rewarded for my trouble with two more toothless grins before she fell asleep in my arms.

The thought of parting with her pained me, so I carried her to my own chamber and tucked her beside me in my bed. I fell asleep listening to the cooing noises she made in her sleep, and when I awoke later, she was still sleeping. After I'd washed and dressed, I laid Felicity in her cradle and walked down to the breakfast room.

Lydia, already seated, clutched what appeared to be a letter in one hand while eating bites of toast with the other. She started when she saw me and jerked the hand with the letter down to the folds of her dress.

I couldn't resist goading her a little. "What is so secret that you must hide your letter from me, Lydia?"

"Nothing concerning you. Just a letter from a friend."

"Which friend?" I asked, pressing her.

"One of the regiment wives, if you must know. She asked a lot of nosy questions, to say the truth. I suppose they find my situation vastly diverting." She looked crestfallen, and I felt sorry about baiting her.

Mama came in just then. I poured myself some coffee and buttered a cold roll, all the while surreptitiously studying Lydia. I noticed she slid the letter into her lap and kept it there throughout breakfast. If it was truly from one of the regiment wives, why was she so bent on hiding it? Perhaps Papa was correct in believing these missives to be from her . . . friend.

"Lydia, dear," Mama said, "I think this would be a fine day to make some morning calls. Lady Lucas and your aunt Philips both wish to see the baby. What do you say?"

Say yes. It will help you become acquainted with your daughter.

"I don't know," Lydia said. "Sir William and Lady Lucas will go on about Charlotte Collins's babies until I shall wish to scream. And I'll have to pack up the baby's things and get her ready to go, which means bathing her and feeding her —"

"That doesn't signify," Mama said with a nod in my direction. "Mary will do all that for you, won't you, Mary?"

210

I pretended to think about it. "I believe I can manage except for the feeding. You shall have to do that yourself," I said.

Felicity cried at that moment, as though letting us know she desired to be out in society. "Why don't you feed her now, Lydia, and I'll prepare a bath and set out her clothing."

"Very well then," she said, rolling her eyes heavenward. "You and Mama will hound me until I agree." She scraped her chair back and, keeping the mysterious letter concealed at her side, left the room.

I bathed the baby in Lydia's chamber, which served the purpose better because it was warmer and more spacious. While Lydia performed her toilette, I dressed Felicity in a long pink frock with lace trim. "Has she smiled at you yet?" I asked.

"What? Has who smiled at me?"

"Felicity, of course."

"No. She seems a disagreeable child, always fussing and crying."

"Lydia! She smiled at me this morning after you fed her. If you would only take the time to play with her yourself, she would smile at you. After her feeding she is most content and happy."

"I suppose you think you know everything there is to know about babies," Lydia said, turning away from her vanity table and glaring at me, "now that you've looked after Felicity for a few weeks."

"Not at all," I said. "I happen to believe you're wrong in calling her a disagreeable baby. To me she seems most amiable."

"Well, and you would know. You've raised so many babies yourself."

I expelled a frustrated breath and realized I'd made a terrible mistake. She'd taken offense at my words; I had spoken too impulsively, as I used to do. Lydia said not another word, but none-too-gently scooped Felicity up, grabbed the child's bonnet, and marched downstairs in a huff.

The footman carried a bag of Felicity's things to the carriage, and grandmother, mother, and baby soon departed, Lydia with a scowl on her face. I didn't mind her being angry, as long as Felicity did not suffer for it. Perhaps spending the day with her child would enable her to reap some of the rewards of motherhood, and she would begin to care for Felicity. How could she be content to be nothing more than a wet nurse to her own baby?

In less than ten minutes they were back. Upstairs straightening Lydia's room, I heard first the carriage and then the baby's cries. I hurried down to see what was wrong.

Felicity had soiled her diaper and was screaming, and neither my mother nor Lydia seemed to have the least idea what was to be done.

The carriage door was summarily opened. Lydia held out a wiggling, wailing Felicity toward me. Astonished, I said, "You came back just so that I should change her nappie?"

"No," Lydia said after I had safely taken the baby into my arms. "I've decided not to take her. It's my first outing, and I don't want it to be ruined by a crying, bad-tempered baby!"

"I rather thought showing off the baby was the point. I can't feed her, you know. How long will you be gone?"

The carriage already in motion, Mama stuck her head out the window and yelled, "Mix a little honey with water and drip it into her mouth with your finger!"

"Ta!" Lydia called, heaving the bag of baby things onto the ground.

I knew Fee would be hungry before they returned, but she'd be content for a time, would probably even nap. I carried her in, changed her, and went downstairs to find Mrs. Hill. "Felicity and I are going on a picnic," I said. "We may be gone a while. Would you ask Cook to fix me a few bites of something to take along?"

"Certainly, miss."

"Mama said a little honey mixed with water might stave off the baby's hunger. Could you see to that, too?"

Mrs. Hill looked as though she wanted to say something, but she kept it to herself. "Of course, miss." Muttering under her breath, she walked toward the kitchen, and I wondered if she thought me foolish to take the baby on such an expedition. Spring was giving way to summer, and I did not wish to waste a sunny day inside. I might catch a glimpse of bluebells or wild garlic blooming in the woods.

While I waited for the food, I searched the sewing room until I found a piece of sturdy fabric from which to fashion a carrying sling for the baby. I laid her on the floor on a blanket, and, after taking a few measurements, cut and hemmed and arrived at something I thought would serve the purpose. Mrs. Hill helped me drape it across my chest and tie the ends in a knot at one side of my waist. I tucked Felicity inside, making sure she was comfortable and able to breathe.

"There now, miss, that's very clever of you. I wondered how you would carry everything. If you don't mind my saying, you've been more of a mother to that child than Miss Lydia. Mrs. Wickham, I mean."

I probably should not have allowed myself to smile, but these were the first words of praise I'd received regarding my care of Felicity, and I was ridiculously pleased. "Thank you, Mrs. Hill." I gathered she had been grumbling about Lydia earlier, not me.

On my way out, I saw the post had come. Sorting through it quickly, I found a letter addressed to me from Jane. I tucked it into the basket holding the food, and off we went.

Even with the sling, it was difficult to handle everything. I carried Mr. Walsh's copy of *Clarissa* in my free hand, and its size was such that my hand and arm were aching by the time I found a spot near the stream to rest and eat. Felicity had fallen asleep, and I laid her on a blanket Mrs. Hill had thoughtfully tucked in beside the food. No sooner had I extracted cold mutton, cheese, and fruit tarts from the basket than I remembered Jane's letter. After setting aside the food, I wiped my fingers with a napkin and broke the seal.

Sat. 2 June
High Tor

My dear Mary,

I fear I have neglected you by not writing sooner. It has taken me the better part of three weeks to set things to rights here. Cook and Mrs. Nicholls locked horns over menus, among other things, while I was at Longbourn, and it took a good bit of diplomacy to sort things out between them. Charles of course keeps out of such matters, and Kitty was unable to deal with the situation. Also, David's nurse came down with a bilious stomach and had to be sent home for a week. Fortunately she is strong and generally healthy, and returned to us a few days ago.

You will be interested, and I daresay surprised, to learn that Kitty and Mr. Carstairs have developed a fondness for each other! I wish I could see your expression right now, as you read those words. According to Charles, Mr. Walsh did not call the entire time I was at Longbourn, but his cousin did. In fact, HW has only been here once since I've been back, which I believe could be described as a courtesy call to welcome me home. Charles rides over to Linden Hall once a week at least, where the two discourse on their favorite topics — horse riding and estate management — and catch up on news. They do not discuss the reason why Mr. Walsh no longer calls upon us.

When it became obvious to Kitty that your removal to Longbourn was not going to advance her suit with him, she gave up and transferred her affections to Mr. Walsh's cousin. Forgive me if I sound cavalier about it; they do seem to have a great liking for each other. He calls nearly every day, and I expect he will offer for her soon. Are you shocked? Kitty is keeping her own counsel, but she seems very much happier and more content than formerly. I think when next you see her, you will notice a great change in her character.

Henry Walsh asks after you whenever Charles sees him. I think he still cares for you, Mary. It is my belief that should you return to High Tor in the near future, he, with some encouragement from you, would still be interested. I have heard from a few of the local gossips that he was seen dancing with the daughter of the local magistrate at a recent assembly, and he called on her the next day. I met Miss Bellcourt once at a private ball; she is a person of delicacy and fashion and plays the harp most beautifully. It is said she will inherit a fortune of £20,000. Enough on that subject!

Please write and tell me how things fare with you. I would particularly like to know if the matter we discussed the morning I left has been improved upon. Do not mention Kitty's situation to our parents or Lydia. I know I may depend upon your discretion.

Yours,
Jane

Kitty and Mr. Carstairs? How odd! Although I did recall his treating her in quite the gallant manner, she never seemed the least affected. Because she had her sights set on Mr. Walsh, she'd ignored his cousin. Even though he was a member of the clergy, Mr. Carstairs had an easy affability, which would suit Kitty. He wasn't at all a groveling or overly formal sort of man, like Mr. Collins. I hoped she would accept him, if he indeed made his offer.

I wouldn't allow myself to think about Mr. Walsh. Naturally he would be attending assemblies and balls, and I was sure he may have danced with a dozen girls. He was pursuing other young ladies with far more to recommend them than I could ever lay claim to. Fashion, beauty, and fortune — what man could resist all three? And in his case, one more quality would be required. The woman he wedded would also need to prove herself an acceptable mother to Amelia. One day he would find someone to love as he had once loved Beth. I hoped he would have the good judgment to tell her — whoever she would be — about his daughter at the outset.

Felicity had awakened and was crying. Having lost all appetite, I laid back, propping myself on my elbow, and leaned over her. "What is it, little Fee?" I said. "I hope you're not too hungry yet." I rubbed her stomach and continued to speak nonsense to her. I didn't know when I'd taken to calling her "little Fee." It seemed to suit her.

I sat up and lifted her into my arms. Swinging her back and forth in wide arcs, I heard a joyful little chuckle, followed by a sharp intake of breath. She was laughing! Delighted, I carried her out to the avenue, talking to her as though she could understand every word I said, most of which was nonsensical.

I had Felicity, and she would make anything bearable. She would make me happy.

After a while, I repacked the basket, leaving some of the food for the birds to devour. I drank a few sips of very warm ale and decided against feeding Felicity any of the honey water, since she seemed content at present. After arranging the carrying sling across my body, I settled her against my chest and glanced around to make certain I had everything. I spied the volume of *Clarissa,* with Jane's letter tucked inside, lying on the ground. Both reminders of Henry Walsh. A spike of pain demolished the sense of well-being I'd felt only moments ago while I played with Felicity. And I had to carry the heavy book home, having read not one sentence of it.

CHAPTER 16

For a long while, I did everything in my power to encourage Lydia to form an attachment to Felicity. Every few days, I either pleaded a headache, lied about Mama needing my help, or sneaked out of the house for a walk, forcing her to tend the baby by herself. Each time I returned, the poor thing would be lying in the middle of Lydia's bed sleeping, but more often, wailing pitifully, while her mother leafed through old issues of *The Lady's Magazine* or arranged her hair in a new style. When I entered the room, Lydia would glower at me and say, "Where were you, Mary? She's been crying for hours." I knew she wouldn't tolerate my lecturing her about her treatment of Felicity; she had already made that clear.

Even Mama noticed not all was well. One evening after her last feeding, I brought Felicity downstairs to the drawing room after I'd readied her for bed. Papa had retreated to his library by then, so it was only Mama, Lydia, and me in attendance. "Oh, let me see my darling granddaughter!" my mother exclaimed, and so I placed the babe in her arms.

My mother did seem genuinely to enjoy her granddaughter — when she was not crying or fussing, of course. Now she held the child out in front of her, raising her brows, puffing out her cheeks, and making all manner of funny faces, which delighted Felicity. "Oh, will you look at that smile? She looks like you when you were a baby, Lydia."

For the first time ever, at least in my presence, Lydia took notice of her daughter, smiling and asking, "Did I really look like that?" For the briefest moment, I saw a spark of curiosity flash in her eyes. Mama, to my surprise, set the baby into Lydia's accepting arms. "There's a pretty girl," Lydia said. "There's my sweet girl."

A sharp jolt of jealousy nearly overwhelmed me. It caught me by surprise, and I had to make an effort to keep command of my expression. Wasn't this what I wanted? For Lydia to love Felicity? Yes. Decidedly. *Then what was wrong with me?*

"I declare, she is a cute little thing, is she not?" After a moment or two, Felicity began fussing, and Lydia said, "Take her, Mary.

She's sleepy."

"You put her to bed, Lydia," I said irritably. "You're her mother, and you must accustom yourself to doing more for her," I added.

"Don't you take that tone with me, Mary! It is your responsibility to take her upstairs."

"Oh? I beg your pardon. You are Felicity's mother; therefore, you are responsible for her care. I thought I was merely helping you through a difficult time."

"Mary is right, Lydia. You have been very lax in your attentions to Felicity. She will soon think Mary, not you, is her mama."

My sister leaped up, jostling the baby. I reacted without thinking, reaching out to steady Lydia. She recoiled from me, turned, and made it as far as the door before she said, "What should I do if she cries?"

"Rock her for a while. That usually soothes her."

When enough time had elapsed for Lydia to be out of earshot, Mama said, "I have been very much worried about Lydia and her child. She does not seem to have the natural feelings of a mother."

Still trying to gain the upper hand over my confused emotions, I didn't answer for a time. I leaned against the back of the chair, forcing a calm I did not feel. "Jane told me

223

this happens sometimes. That some mothers take longer than others to form an attachment with their child, and there's nothing to be done but wait."

"I think you should insist, Mary, that Lydia take more responsibility for Felicity. Someday, when she and Wickham get their marital problems sorted out, and she returns to Newcastle, caring for her baby will be on her shoulders. Then what will she do?"

My mother had the fantastic notion that any day now, Wickham would arrive and carry his wife and child off with him and all would be well. Even though we had explained the situation to her on more than one occasion, she simply couldn't take it in. But this was not the time to attempt to set her straight. "I've tried everything, but so far, nothing has worked. Just now, when she held Felicity and smiled at her . . . it was the first time she's ever done so."

"She's an indolent girl, I know, and even if she someday loves Felicity, she'll still not want to be bothered with her. From now on, I shall try to encourage her, Mary."

"Thank you, Mama."

"Whom are you encouraging?" Papa had emerged from his cocoon in the library into the middle of our discussion.

"Oh, it's nothing, Mr. Bennet," Mama

said, winking at me. Both of us knew too well, even though he asked, his interest would wane as soon as we tried to explain.

"I have some news," he said, surprising us both.

"Well, don't keep us in suspense! What is it?"

"We are to have guests."

"Guests? Who?" Mama asked. "Why did you not tell me sooner?"

"Because I just learned of it myself, in today's post."

"But that was hours ago!" Mama said.

My father's face folded into his characteristic look of impatience. "Mary, I took your advice and wrote to Charles about the drainage problems some of the tenants are having. Mr. Calvert's barley crop will be ruined if something is not done soon, you see."

"Charles is coming, then? And Jane and the baby?" Mama asked.

"No, no. Charles and two friends are coming, men who know of these things and can advise the farmers on how to drain their fields."

I felt the blood seep from my face. "Which friends?"

"Henry Walsh for one, and the other is a Mr. Carstairs, whom I've not met. You must

be acquainted with him, Mary. He's the local vicar."

With some difficulty, I kept a measured
tone. "Yes, I met him during my recent stay
at High Tor. He's Mr. Walsh's cousin, and a
most amiable man." I knew, however, he
was extremely unlikely to be knowledgeable
about draining fields. So his purpose in
coming must be to speak to Papa about
Kitty.

"Mr. Bennet, they cannot stay here. Not
with the baby and our most unusual situation. They shall have to stay at the inn in
Meryton."

My parents continued to talk about ac-
commodations for the guests, and my mind
drifted away. Henry Walsh coming here! I
would have to see him; there would be no
avoiding it. How terribly uncomfortable it
would be. I heard my father saying something about Netherfield Hall, but the words
sounded distant and incomprehensible. A
little glimmer of excitement was forming
inside me, demanding all my attention.

Stupid girl. Nothing has changed. He no
longer liked me; in fact, he believed I had
purposely misled him as to my feelings. Add
to that my unwillingness to overlook his
faults, and I wondered if he could ever
forgive me for rejecting me.

"When do they come?" I asked, interrupting my parents' discussion.

"In a fortnight. Possibly longer," Papa said. "I wish it didn't have to wait, but the time had to suit all three."

"Mr. Walsh," Mama said, making a face. "I wish we did not have to accept help from a man who did not want our Kitty."

I wondered if my younger sister had written to my parents, or if Jane had delivered the news. It suddenly occurred to me that after I'd left High Tor, Henry had done nothing to engage Kitty's affections. He'd said she was no substitute for me, and it seemed he'd been sincere about that. Nor was he paying his addresses to any of the other young ladies from the ball. There was Miss Bellcourt, whom Jane had mentioned in her letter, but thus far what we knew of his dealings with her consisted of gossip and speculation. As far as I was aware, Henry had not actively sought a wife after I'd left. The realization left me shaken and forced me to question all that had passed between us, and all I had believed about him.

"I would remind you, Mrs. Bennet, we do not know the true nature of their association — only what Kitty believed it to be — and we must welcome him as we would any other guest."

"Oh, I know, I know. But still, I do not like it," she said, lifting her brows.

"Try as I might, my dear, I find it difficult to put us in the way of your liking anything." With that, he rose and said he was returning to his library.

The fortnight passed in a blur. I tried to think reasonably, telling myself Mr. Walsh could no longer be interested in me after my behavior at High Tor. Even if he were, would I be able to accept his regard, and be persuaded of its depth and strength? And that his interest went beyond viewing me as a mother for Amelia? These questions lingered in the back of my mind, but I could no longer deny my overwhelming desire to see him again, and to wonder what might transpire during his time with us.

What saved me from running mad was the rhythm of daily life with Felicity. After the evening when Lydia first paid attention to her daughter and I'd reacted so strongly, I closely examined my feelings, which I now realized were a mix of resentment and jealousy. How dare she call Felicity her "sweet girl"? What right did she have, when it was I who bathed Felicity, changed her, comforted her when she fussed, played with her, did everything but feed her? How I longed for that indelible bond.

Felicity slept the night through most of the time, but there were still occasions of her waking and fussing. I always tried to quiet her myself before rousing Lydia. I would tie on a fresh nappie, walk about the room with her, even let her suck the honey-and-water mixture from my finger. One night, when nothing seemed to help, I sank down on the rocking chair and held her close against me. Her little mouth puckered, making sucking sounds, and she turned her head toward my breast. Through my thin night rail, she found my nipple and began to suck. Her tiny hand shot up and pressed against me as she latched on.

A feeling of complete contentment stole over me, so tangible I ached with it. It was visceral, unlike anything I'd ever imagined. At last I was able to experience that most primal connection to the child whom I'd come to love and who meant everything to me. Any moment, I expected her to grow frustrated and cry because no milk was forthcoming, but she continued to suck until she finally drifted off to sleep. It seemed the sucking was what she needed, not the milk.

I crawled back in bed and lay there thinking about what I'd done. My nipples were tingling with the oddest sensation. I knew I shouldn't have done it, yet it seemed so natural. What if Lydia or Mama had come in and discovered me? They would have been outraged if they found out, possibly have thought me deranged.

But I knew I would do it again, because suckling Felicity was the only way in which I could become her mother. Lydia didn't want the job, so why not me? That was how I justified my actions, that night and in the days to come.

Unlike my mother, I held no improbable hopes regarding a reconciliation between Lydia and Wickham. But I suspected she might be communicating with him. Since the morning I'd seen her concealing the mysterious letter, I'd caught her reading other missives a few times, once in her chamber, when I entered unexpectedly. She quickly pressed the parchment into the pages of one of her magazines. I pretended not to have noticed. Another time, she expressed a desire to walk. When I offered to accompany her, she said I must stay to see to Felicity, although she was asleep and Mama was perfectly capable of looking after her for a short time even if she did wake up. I watched Lydia out the window as she strode away from the house. She hadn't gone ten feet before I saw her extract a letter from her reticule and slow her pace while she read it. That answered the question of why she needed her reticule on a walk.

If she wasn't writing to Wickham, who then? The man who may be Felicity's true father? Lydia never spoke of him. Of course, she could not in front of our parents, but since she was generally indiscreet, why wouldn't she have mentioned him to me? I began to fear that she was planning to run off with the man, taking Felicity with her. And then I would have nothing.

I fervently wished I could draw, so I might sketch Felicity. My sisters and I were woefully untutored in art. Since they had married, Jane and Lizzy both had begun instruction in drawing, but now they were occupied with their children. Not for the first time, I wished our parents had been more diligent about our education.

I had attended a few private parties at which a profile artist had done portraits of the guests. Some had simply studied their subject's profile and cut. Other artists had used candlelight to cast a shadow and worked from that. In either case, it didn't seem especially difficult.

I walked to Meryton and purchased some sheets of a delicate black paper, and that evening, persuaded Lydia to hold Felicity while I cut, using my sewing scissors. I had arranged two branches of candles so that Fee's shadow would be cast upon the wall. Lydia complained of being inconvenienced, but Mama, to my surprise, stood off to the side, clucking and making faces so Felicity would stare at her and thus keep her profile to me.

The scissors felt awkward, and my fingers heavy and unwilling to move properly. When I finished, Lydia proclaimed, "La, Mary, that one looks like Sir William Lucas!"

Sadly, she was right. The face was much too long, the features too large. Blast! This was going to take some practice. "Let me try one more."

"Well, hurry up, then," Lydia said. "I'm tired of keeping Felicity from fidgeting."

My second attempt was slightly improved, but not by much, and by the time I had finished, Fee was fussy and miserable. The profile no longer looked like Sir William, but rather resembled one of his grand-children. I sighed. "Perhaps in daylight I shall simply try cutting the profile without using the shadow."

I knew my humble efforts would never

match the skills of a true profilist, but I was determined. Whenever I could convince Lydia and Mama to assist me, I cut profiles of Felicity, and at last created a few that did not look completely ludicrous. I asked Mr. Hill to frame one for me. If Lydia took her daughter away from me, I would have these likenesses of her to look upon every day, and remember the blessings she had brought to my life. The pure, undiluted love.

CHAPTER 17

I lay on the bed with Felicity asleep beside me, listening to her whispery breaths and the sucking sounds she made with her mouth. In the distance, I heard the clatter of carriage wheels, and a thrill of anticipation raced through me. Today was the day our guests were to arrive. The day I would see Henry Walsh again.

During the two weeks of waiting, I'd succeeded in banishing him from my thoughts much of the time. Felicity's waking hours had increased, and I threw myself into her care and amusement. I'd given up my attempts to force Lydia to take more interest in her, having reached the point of feeling like her mother myself. I had put her to my breast several times when she awoke during the night. Miraculously, after a few minutes of sucking, she would fall back to sleep.

Felicity loved me. I could feel it in the way her hands reached out to explore my face, in her joyful smiles when she saw me first thing every morning, and in her nuzzling against me, so close I was sure she could feel the beat of my heart. When Lydia fed her, held her, showed her any affection, I fought against anger and jealousy, and an uneasy feeling that might have been fear of what was to come.

I bolted upright, my heartbeat speeding up at the sound of male voices out front. I moved quietly from the bed to the windows and pushed the curtain aside. A carriage had indeed pulled up, and from it emerged . . . Kitty! Mama would be surprised and delighted. Mr. Carstairs followed her. Charles and Mr. Walsh, on horseback, were dismounting and turning their horses over to a groom.

Mama was shouting, "They are here, Mr. Bennet, they are here! And Kitty, too!"

Footsteps sounded in the hall. That would be Lydia heading downstairs. She had likely spent the last hour preening while I lay stretched out with the baby. A sharp knock n the door and she burst in. "Mary, they've arrived! You must come down. Lord, you look a fright! Fix your hair and put on a different dress — that one is exceedingly rinkled."

"Shh! Felicity is still asleep." She didn't so

much as glance at her daughter. "I'll come in a minute." I walked down the hall to my own chamber and hastily washed, repinned my hair, and hesitated over what dress to wear. I settled on a pale yellow sprigged muslin. It was cut a bit low across the bust, so I threw a netted fichu around my neck and shoulders. Before going down, I peeked in at Felicity, wondering if I should put her in her cradle. Although she was now able to push herself up and turn over on her own, there was little risk in leaving her in the middle of the bed. She couldn't move very far. And when she awakened she would cry, and I'd hear her. I glanced once more out the window, where introductions were in progress. Lydia was shaking Mr. Walsh's hand. I turned and dashed downstairs and out the front door.

Charles noticed me first. "Mary!" he said, planting a kiss on my cheek. He turned and looked toward his friends. "You need no introduction to these gentlemen, I believe."

"No, indeed." My heart was thudding against my ribs, so marked I was sure everybody would notice. Mr. Walsh stepped forward and I held out my hand. His hand, warm and so familiar, claimed mine, and I said, "How do you do, sir?"

"Miss Bennet. You are well, I hope?"

"Quite well, thank you. How is Mrs. Walsh?"

"Just over a cold, but otherwise fine. She sends her best." His eyes were veiled, and I thought I detected a slight clenching of his jaw.

I turned to his cousin. "Mr. Carstairs, how nice to see you again."

"Miss Bennet. The pleasure is mine." His eyes were dancing, and I assumed he knew Jane had revealed the secret.

Kitty approached and embraced me warmly. "Hello, Mary." Her face wore an odd look, a bit wistful and perhaps somewhat . . . repentant. I kissed her cheek and remarked upon how well she looked. Her eyes, too, held a gleam that spoke volumes.

Once inside, we entered the downstairs drawing room, and Mama rang for tea. "Please, be seated," she said. "You must be tired after your long journey. I do apologize that at present we have no spare chambers to accommodate you. Except for Kitty, of course."

Charles shrugged it off. "It is of no consequence, ma'am. My friend at Netherfield was more than happy to let us invade the premises. You have a full house here at present, I believe."

The youngest occupant of the house made

herself known at that moment with an earsplitting scream. What on earth? Terrified, I leaped from my chair and dashed from the room. Felicity never screamed upon awakening; she merely cried, and never in a vociferous manner. I heard Mama say, "Lydia, you had better go with Mary."

I groaned, much preferring to see what had happened on my own. But I soon heard footsteps behind me and realized not only Lydia but Kitty, too, was on my heels. I burst through the nursery door, stunned when I glimpsed the poor babe lying on the floor screaming, her legs and arms jerking reflexively. "Good God!" I knelt down beside her and gently lifted her into my arms. "Are you all right, little Fee?"

"Did you lay her on the bed again, Mary?" Lydia asked. "If she'd been in her cradle where she belonged, this never would have happened."

Ignoring Lydia, I ran my fingers over the tender skin at the back of Felicity's head, then over her neck, torso, and limbs. Her cries had tapered off into little gulps by this time. Fortunately, she'd fallen onto a rug. Perhaps she'd only had the wind knocked out of her and been badly frightened, with no real harm done.

Lydia said in a cold voice, "Let me have her."

Astonished, I gently laid the child in her arms. Felicity scrutinized her mother and resumed her wailing. It took all of ten seconds for her to be handed back to me. Lydia turned to go, but I called to her. "I'll dress her, but she'll be hungry. She always is after her nap."

Lydia heaved an impatient sigh. "Botheration, can't she wait for a while?"

Kitty sent me a look behind our sister's back. "Lydia —"

"Oh, don't you start, Kitty. You know even less than Mary about babies!"

"I believe Mary knows more than either of us," Kitty said. "I was simply going to suggest you return to the drawing room, and Mary will bring the baby to you when she's ready for her feeding. Will that suit, Mary?"

"Perfectly," I said, and Lydia beat a hasty path to the door.

"She doesn't seem to . . . Jane said she hasn't yet developed motherly feelings for Felicity," Kitty said hesitantly. Her hands flew up to straighten her coiffure.

"No." My conscience wouldn't allow me to lay all the blame on Lydia. "Perhaps it is partly my fault. I've been too eager to

239

step in."

"I don't think so, Mary. Look how hastily she left the room, hardly before you had determined Felicity wasn't hurt." She had dropped down on the bed, and her foot swung back and forth. Clearly, she was nervous about something, and I thought I knew what.

"Yes. But do consider how long she has been deprived of company other than her family. I think she's desperate to be in society again." Why was I defending her? *Guilt,* came the answer, insistent and unmistakable. I set about tying a fresh nappie on the baby, who did not appear to have sustained any injury from her unfortunate encounter with the floor.

"Will you watch her while I find her a fresh dress?"

"Of course." Kitty jumped up and fastened her eyes on Felicity. "Oh, she smiled at me! She really is adorable."

I had walked over to the little trunk where I kept Felicity's clothes, and when I returned, Kitty was looking at me in an odd way. From the glow in her eyes, and her inability to sit still, I could tell she was bursting to tell me of her betrothal.

She grabbed hold of my hand. "Mary, I have some exciting news."

240

I smiled. "What is it? Don't keep me in suspense."

"Mr. Carstairs and I are engaged!"

I did not have the wherewithal to pretend total ignorance of the situation. "I confess Jane told me she thought you two might make a match." She looked a little dejected, so I quickly embraced her and kissed her cheek. "I'm so happy for you, Kitty. I think he is a fine man."

"Do you, Mary? I-I hardly allowed myself to become acquainted with him until after you left High Tor." Her face flushed, but she went on. "I had so foolishly fixed my affections on Henry — he says I must call him by his Christian name now that I'm to be in the family — I had overlooked his cousin altogether. But I believe we are much better suited than Henry and I ever would have been."

She hadn't said she loved Mr. Carstairs, but her obvious delight at her betrothal signaled deep feelings for him. I tugged the vhite dress over Fee's head and asked, "When did you first begin to feel an attraction to him?"

"After you left, Henry quit calling, but Andrew visited us every few days. He always had a funny story to tell me about one of his parishioners, or the things he and Henry got up to when they were boys. And he was so solicitous of my comfort. I felt more and more at ease with him, and after that, my esteem for him grew." She smiled playfully. "It didn't hurt that he was such a fine dancer!"

"I remember that," I said, "from the evening at Linden Hall when we all danced. But I don't believe you liked him then."

I began pushing Felicity's arms into the sleeves. We were quiet for a moment, and then Kitty said, "I'm sorry, Mary. My foolishness has caused pain for both you and Henry. I only hope it is not too late to repair things between you."

I glanced up. Kitty's head was tilted slightly and her brows were drawn together in a frown. Her expression was quite sincere, a quality not in evidence on the morning she apologized to me and then demanded I leave High Tor. I was astonished at her new-found confidence and maturity, proven by her willingness to shoulder some of the blame for the way things stood between Henry and me. Andrew Carstairs must be having a salutary effect on my sister. And it would have surprised me if Jane had not also had a hand in Kitty's transformation.

I wasn't certain, but I strongly suspected Jane had told Kitty of Henry's proposal.

"I've been foolish too, Kitty. I wasn't sure what I wanted, and I am still not. Mr. Walsh and I parted on very ill terms. He expressed a good deal of anger and bitterness toward me. I'm not sure 'repairing things' is possible, or even desirable," I said, picking up the baby and starting for the door. "Will Andrew speak to Papa today?" I asked, hoping to discourage any further questions.

"I believe he is doing so right now."

We heard Lydia's giggles on the way downstairs, and when we entered the drawing room, Mr. Carstairs and my father were indeed absent. Mr. Walsh and Charles were stranded with Mama and Lydia. Both men rose, and Charles immediately said, "At last, I have the pleasure of meeting my newest niece! May I hold her?" I passed Felicity into his arms.

"It's surprising she is still alive, after Mary let her fall off the bed," Lydia said in a scornful tone.

The room went quiet. I bit my lip, furious with myself because I could feel the cursed flush spreading upward from my neck. Now that I'd handed Fee over to Charles, I had nothing to do with my hands, nothing to occupy myself, so I simply stood there. Nobody leaped to my defense, and Lydia nattered on. "But she is the next best thing to a nursemaid. I declare, sometimes I believe Mary considers herself Felicity's mama."

That was too close to the truth to deny. I found a vacant seat and snapped out of my daze to see Henry Walsh studying me with kind eyes. He handed me a cup of tea, as he'd done on another occasion, at High Tor.

"Thank you," I said, watching him. His look had swiftly reverted to one of indifference. He nodded briefly before walking over to Charles and taking Felicity from him. I gulped my tea, hoping its restorative powers would prop me up.

The drawing room door was thrown open, and Papa and Mr. Carstairs came through. "Well, Mrs. Bennet," said my father. "It seems we are to have another wedding."

CHAPTER 18

"What?" asked Mama, genuinely astonished. "I believe I misunderstood you."

"No, no, you did not. Mr. Carstairs has asked for Kitty's hand, and after he assured me she had already accepted him, I gave my consent."

"Kitty! I am most put out that you did not tell your mama. But I forgive you, since this is such good news!" She wrapped her arms around Kitty and kissed her.

Setting my cup on the table, I rose and went to Mr. Carstairs. "May I wish you happy, sir?" I said, holding out my hand. He took it, and then kissed my cheek.

"You must call me Andrew from now on, Miss Bennet."

"Then you must call me Mary, since we're to be brother and sister." I stepped aside so Mama could speak to him, and only then did I notice Lydia. Her eyes had gone cold. The laughing, carefree demeanor she'd shown when I first entered the drawing room had vanished. She was the only person still seated. Whether she was out of countenance because all the attention was now on Kitty and her intended or because she was thinking of the sad state of her own marriage, I could not say.

Charles and Papa were talking and smiling, and Mr. Walsh was still circling the room with Felicity in his arms. I knew she must be hungry, because she'd begun to fuss a little. After a moment, he stopped and said something to Lydia. "La!" I heard her say. "Not me. Give her to Mary."

We walked toward each other, and he handed Felicity over to me.

"I'm afraid there's not much I can do in this instance. She's hungry, you see," I said.

"Ah. I thought as much. But your sister —"

"No need to explain. I'll speak to her."

He half-smiled and nodded, and I went over to Lydia. "You must take her upstairs now."

She scowled at me. "Don't tell me what to do, Mary." Then, when I hesitated before placing Felicity in her arms, "Oh, very well. Nobody here is paying me any notice."

Just then Kitty approached. "Are you not going to wish me happy, Lydia?"

Lydia bristled. "I'm exceedingly vexed at you for keeping this a secret. You could have written. And I thought you were in love with that . . . other one." She cocked her head toward Henry.

Kitty's cheeks turned scarlet. "Keep your voice down! That was a . . . mistake. And you must see, I could not tell anyone before my parents knew," Kitty said.

"Well, of course I wish you happy," Lydia said, just before she marched out of the room with her child. Since this terse expression of good wishes had been forced out of her, I didn't think it went too far in soothing Kitty's hurt feelings. Andrew stood nearby and had witnessed the conversation. He and Kitty exchanged a look, and she actually smiled. In the past, Lydia's displeasure would have upset her, and she might have remained out of spirits the rest of the evening. I thought Mr. Carstairs may have been the best thing that ever happened to Kitty.

"The problem is, the new methods of drainage are expensive," Charles said. "At least, that's what Walsh tells me."

Over our dinner of lamb and vegetables, the general air of cheerfulness that comes with happy news prevailed. Everyone except

Lydia, who hunched over her meal in stony silence, was in good humor. I thought I'd perceived a slight thaw in Mr. Walsh's smile earlier. Enough to allow me to hope he didn't hate me. I couldn't have borne it if he did. Had I forgiven him, then? He had neither apologized nor asked for forgiveness, so it was rather a moot point.

"One must use hollowed-out bricks or roofing tiles, so, yes, it is costly," Mr. Walsh said. "What system are they using now?"

"Chiefly stones or faggots," Papa said.

"That sort of deep trenching doesn't last," Mr. Walsh said. "In the end it is more expensive, because it must be repaired so often."

"I fear it may be all we can afford," said my father.

"Oh, may we not talk of something else?" asked Mama. "You men can talk of trenches and tiles over your port. For myself, I would like to know when this wedding will take place."

Kitty darted a glance at her betrothed. "We should like it to be right away, Mama," she said. "As soon as we can settle things."

"The banns must be read, of course, and we must arrange for your bride clothes, my dear," Mama said. "Meryton may not do . . . we may have to journey to Ware, or even

London."

I held back a laugh. Even Jane and Lizzy, who had both been betrothed to wealthy men, had had their bride clothes made by local seamstresses.

"That won't be necessary, Mrs. Bennet," Papa said. "It's not one of the princesses marrying, but our Kitty." Everyone laughed, including Kitty and her fiancé.

Mama harrumphed. "You will be married from Longbourn, will you not?" she asked.

Kitty and her intended agreed this was their intention. Looking up, I noticed Mrs. Hill in the doorway.

"Is it Felicity?" I asked.

"Yes, miss."

"I'll go to her." I excused myself and rose.

Little Fee had the habit of falling asleep for half an hour or so around dinnertime. She usually stayed awake and in good humor afterward, until seven thirty or eight o'clock. I lifted her from her bed and laid her down for a fresh nappie, making faces and saying nonsensical things, as women are wont to do with their babies. Quit thinking of her as yours, Mary, I told myself.

When that was done, I grabbed a rattle and made my way to the drawing room with Felicity. I could hear everyone just now rising from the table, and soon Mama, Lydia, and Kitty joined me.

"Mary, it would be nice to have some music tonight," Mama said.

"I am out of practice." The truth was, I hadn't felt much like playing since I'd been home. Although it reminded me of the happy times at High Tor, it also dredged up memories I'd sooner have forgotten, like the night at the ball when I deliberately set out to humiliate myself, only to be rescued by Mr. Walsh.

"Oh, Mary, you must. Andrew and Henry both enjoy your playing so much!" Kitty said.

"But I cannot neglect Felicity," I replied, trying to put them off.

"Nonsense!" Mama said. "There are plenty of people here to look after her, including her mother." She sent Lydia a pointed glance. "I insist. Come along, now, and find some music."

When the men entered the room, I was still sorting through the sheets of music. Mr. Walsh said nothing but took a seat near the pianoforte. I began to play a piece by Beethoven, the Sonata in C Sharp Minor, because I recalled that it was one of his favorites. Since I was so rusty, I knew I would probably regret it, but I wanted to please him. Music was the first thing that had made Henry take notice of me; perhaps it would serve that purpose again.

The piece was melancholy and the first movement played pianissimo. I needn't have worried about my playing; all the sentiments I'd buried welled up and flowed from my fingers as they glided over the keys. My deepest feelings for both Henry and Felicity had become, in some mystifying way, intertwined. If I had accepted Henry's proposal, perhaps he and I could have raised Fee together! My fingers strayed where they didn't belong, jarring me out of my reverie. *Keep your mind on your playing. Don't think of him. And you are not Felicity's mother!*

I'd begun the second movement, the allegretto, and, since it was less familiar, forced myself to concentrate. The notes lifted, hung in the air, dissolved. I stole a glance at Henry. He was leaning back in the chair with his eyes closed.

I decided not to attempt the final movement. It was by far the most difficult and always intimidated me, with its many arpeggios. It required technical skill I lacked, and I couldn't do it justice. When I started to rise, Mama said, "You must keep on, Mary! Play some Scottish airs. Something jolly!"

So I continued to play until the tea arrived. When at last I rose, my small audience clapped politely. Lydia came in behind the tea tray, and I noticed immediately Fee was not with her. I walked over and asked where she was.

"I've put her to bed. You are not the only one who knows how."

"No, of course not." I resisted the urge to ask if she'd changed the baby's nappie and covered her in the softest blanket. Had she remembered her cap? Had she sung her a lullaby? I knew she would berate me in front of everybody if I mentioned any of these things, and I'd had my fill of that. I would simply check later to make sure everything was just as Felicity liked it.

I situated myself on the chaise, and Charles strolled over to converse with me. "Jane and I would very much like you to return with me to High Tor, Mary," he said, seating himself beside me.

Did I look as shocked as I felt? "Oh, I couldn't possibly," I said. "Felicity needs me. I couldn't leave her."

"Are you certain of that? When she must, Lydia seems perfectly capable of tending to her needs."

"I don't think so, Charles. She *could* do so, but . . ." I dropped my voice to a whisper. "But she doesn't seem to love the child. I couldn't bear to think of Felicity without someone to love her."

"Your mama shows her a great deal of affection, I've observed. Perhaps between the two of them, and Kitty will be here as well . . . I wish you would consider it, Mary. You must think of yourself sometimes, you know."

"You are too kind, Charles, and I will consider it, of course," I said, knowing full well I would not in a million years leave that baby to Lydia and Mama's ministrations. And Kitty would be completely preoccupied with her impending marriage.

Mr. Walsh had been speaking to my father but now made his way over to us. "I've been trying to persuade Mary to return with us to High Tor," Charles said. "Perhaps you will have more success than I. If you'll excuse me, I need to speak with my father-in-law." When he walked away, Henry took his seat.

"May I compliment your playing, Miss Bennet?"

My face grew warm. "Thank you. I'm afraid I wasn't brave enough to attempt the third movement."

"No matter. The first two were enchanting."

Feeling tongue-tied, I could only smile.

"Charles is right, you know. I believe your

sister would welcome your company at High Tor. Especially since Kitty won't be returning." He watched me over the rim of his cup.

"It would be impossible for me to leave Longbourn at present."

He merely nodded, and I was thankful he chose not to press me. "Did the news take you by surprise?"

Kitty's news, he meant. "Not entirely. Jane had written to me about her suspicions. They seem to be a good match. His lightheartedness will offset her more melancholy disposition."

"Just so. I can assure you of my cousin's honorable and respectful nature, and he loves your sister."

"Truly?"

"He told me so himself."

I gave him a skeptical look. "I didn't think men spoke of such things to each other."

His smile seemed awkward, and I thought maybe I'd embarrassed him. "Most do not. But Andrew and I are more like brothers than cousins, and we're in each other's confidence."

"Then I am doubly happy for them, that they have made a love match."

"Would you call it that, then?" he asked. "Andrew is tenderhearted. I hope your sister wouldn't willfully deceive him as to her true feelings."

As I had done to him. What else could he mean? He'd made it clear that was what he believed. But he had deceived me, too. The fault was not all mine. Despite my discomposure, I had to reply. "I believe Kitty to be quite sincere in her feelings for him." I straightened my shoulders and looked him in the eye for a moment. "And if he really loves her, and is always truthful with her, I expect them to be quite happy."

"Touché," he said softly, his eyes watching me until I was forced to drop my gaze. "How do you think she will get on as a clergyman's wife?"

I released a huge breath. "Given your cousin's amiability, I believe she will fit the role. Andrew will always be there to steady her. In fact, I've already noticed a change in her, and must assume it's due to his influence." I glanced over at the couple, deep in conversation. "They seem very much at ease with each other. Away from Lydia's influence, Kitty's natural tendency to goodness will assert itself."

He looked uncomfortable at the mention of Lydia. Perhaps I should not have spoken so of her to someone outside the family. "When does Mrs. Wickham return to Newcastle?" he asked.

"We don't know." I wondered if in the course of one of his talks with Charles, he'd learned the truth. I knew my brother-in-law was not prone to gossip, but he may have confided in the man he considered his closest friend, next to Mr. Darcy. "Things are as yet unsettled." That seemed suitably vague.

"I see."

Standing, I said, "If you'll excuse me, I must check on the baby."

He rose, too. We were nearly at eye level, as his height reached a mere few inches above my own. "You once told me you wished you were more proficient with children," Mr. Walsh said. "It appears now that you are." His expression had softened.

"Not according to Lydia," I said, attempting a feeble joke.

"Do you think anyone believed her? That it was negligent Aunt Mary's fault the child fell?"

I considered the question, relaxed a bit, and laughed. "I suppose not."

"I won't keep you. Just know your sister Jane has spoken in admiring tones of how well you care for the baby, and now I've seen it with my own eyes, I agree with her. It's no easy task."

"Thank you." I turned to go, but his voice stopped me.

"Miss Bennet, I wish you would . . ."

I stopped, turned. Waited. His gaze was fixed on me. He gave his head a shake. "It was nothing," he said. "Forgive me."

I made my way out of the room and up to the nursery. What had he been on the verge of saying, and why had he stopped in mid-sentence? It was maddening! How was I to know what he wished for? And now I'd be left to wonder what it was he had wanted to say, and what had prevented him from expressing his feelings.

I tiptoed into the nursery. Fee was sleeping on her belly, her legs drawn up like a frog's. I pulled the blanket up and tucked it securely about her. Lydia had remembered everything, even Felicity's cap.

But it was not really thoughts of Fee that drifted through my mind. Most of the evening, Henry Walsh had treated me with a cautious civility, with no particular regard in his manner or conversation. And there *was* that smartly directed barb. He didn't seem the kind of man to deliberately make vengeful remarks, but I had wounded him by refusing his proposal. He had hurt me too, though, and I was glad I'd reminded him of it.

After the way things had ended between us, that he spoke to me at all gave me reason to hope, although I remained not at all sure what I was hoping for. Some things were not to be denied, however. His mesmerizing blue eyes made me feel weak when he looked at me. His voice captivated me. Was I to blame if his person — his mere presence — caused little flutters that seemed to dip and rise around my heart?

CHAPTER 19

Our visitors were lodging at Netherfield Park. The present owner was an old friend of Charles's, with whom he had renewed his acquaintance in the past few years. It was an easy ride over each day to supervise the work of creating new underground drainage, as well as the repair of existing drains. More often than not, the men returned to Netherfield to wash and change, and then rode back to Longbourn to dine with us.

One evening at dinner, Charles again raised the question of my visiting High Tor.

"Oh, we could not spare Mary," my mother said. "She is Felicity's . . ." Since she couldn't quite bring herself to refer to her daughter as a nursemaid, she didn't finish her thought.

I wished Charles had made no mention of the idea, though I couldn't deny having given it serious consideration over the past several days, despite my initial refusal. In my mind, I pictured taking Felicity with me. Of course, that would mean Lydia would accompany us, too, and I didn't think that would be acceptable to anybody. With the possible exception of Lydia herself.

"Well, why couldn't we all go?" Lydia asked. "Mary, the baby, and me?"

Oh, sister, you are so predictable!

Papa chimed in. "I believe Mary deserves a respite from child care," he said. "Not that she is one to complain." He sent me an appraising look.

"Indeed, Mary," Kitty said, "Jane urged me to prevail upon you to come to her. She misses you."

"Well, I do not see why Jane's desires should outweigh all other considerations," Mama said. "We couldn't get on without Mary at present."

I had as yet made no response, simply allowing the discussion to flow around me. Now it seemed as though I must say something. "Perhaps a short visit," I said. "A few days." If my mother and Lydia had urged me to go, had said I deserved to go, without a doubt, I would have continued to refuse. I suppose that did not speak well of my character.

"It is too far by half to spend only a few

days," protested Charles. "You must come for a month, or a few weeks at the very least." Charles turned to his friend. "What do you say, Walsh?"

Henry smiled. "I believe it's up to Miss Bennet."

"I don't see why she should have all the fun," Lydia said petulantly. "It is I who have been cooped up here for months, with no entertainment whatsoever except Mary, and a fine lot of fun she is. It is I whom you should invite."

My father's eyes darkened with anger, and I thought he might deliver a reproach to Lydia in front of everybody. In the end, he thought better of it, and fortunately the subject was dropped. But I knew Charles, or maybe Papa, would not let it die.

After dinner, as I made my way toward the staircase to check on Felicity, I felt a tug on my sleeve. It was Mama, with Lydia in tow. "Mary, we shall tend to the baby. We insist that you have the evening to yourself." She flung her arm out for emphasis.

Since Lydia was scowling mightily, I inferred that she had no interest whatsoever in my pleasure, but had been forced by Mama to undertake her motherly duties. I didn't think spending time with Kitty while the men drank port would be much cause for enjoyment, but as my mother was trying to do me a good turn, I graciously acceded. "Very well. I'll find Kitty in the drawing room, then."

"No," Mama said. "Mr. Bennet and Charles are looking at some new plants your father is cultivating. The other men have decided to forgo their port and walk outside, since it is such a fine night. You must join them, and Kitty, of course."

"But —"

"No buts, Mary. Run along, now. It is a lovely summer evening."

Mama had an odd look on her face, and I had a dreadful hunch she was matchmaking. *God protect me.* All I needed were my mother's machinations to bring further ruin to my relationship with Henry Walsh. But it seemed I had little say in the matter.

The twilit evening was very warm, and I had no need of a wrap. As I neared the entryway, I glimpsed Kitty, Andrew, and Mr. Walsh lingering out front, obviously waiting for me. Something awakened inside, and I felt a lightness in my step. Perhaps it was not too late for us after all. For Henry and me.

"Ah, here she is," said Mr. Carstairs as I approached them. Kitty gave me a big smile; Mr. Walsh's face revealed nothing.

And at that moment, a shriek from Felicity pierced the calm summer night. We all looked up, toward the open window of the nursery. When the cries abated slightly, Lydia and Mama's bickering could be heard over the baby's wailing.

"You pinched her, Mama!"

"I did no such thing!"

"Now she'll never stop screaming." Pause. "Mary!"

"Come along," Kitty said. "She must learn to get on without you, Mary."

I hesitated, glancing upward, and then back at the three people scrutinizing me. After a moment, Mr. Walsh said, "I have an idea. Come with me, Miss Bennet." He strode toward the house and I followed. "Don't wait on us," he called over his shoulder. "We'll catch up to you."

Before I guessed his intent, he was up the stairs and entering the nursery.

"Mr. Walsh!" Mama said.

"Did you get the nappie on her?" he asked the baffled mother and grandmother.

Lydia nodded, looking askance at him.

"Miss Bennet, carry the child downstairs if you will. Once we are outside and on our way, I'll take her."

"But we can't —"

"Certainly, we can. A little fresh air before

263

her bedtime will make her sleepy."

Mama and Lydia didn't speak another word, completely cowed by Mr. Walsh's authoritative manner. I lifted Felicity into my arms, and we proceeded down the stairs and outside. By now she was smiling and gurgling, her recent misery apparently forgotten.

"Is she a good baby?" he asked.

"Oh, exceedingly."

"Give her to me, then."

Pompous man, giving me orders. I handed her over, since he was actually one of the few people to whom I would have entrusted her. He gripped her under her arms and held her out in front of him. "Now, Miss Fussy Britches, you are to be a good girl so that your aunt can enjoy her walk. Understood?"

I laughed, not only at his words, but at Fee's expression. She studied him intently, as though deciphering the puzzle of just who this man was. He tucked her into the crook of one arm. There it was again, that comfortable way of handling a child. Completely relaxed and at ease. "How do you do it?" I asked.

"What?"

"Charm her in that way. You have such a. easy manner with young children."

He glanced down at me, and I thought how his eyes perfectly blended with the color of twilight. "You forget, I have experience. When Amelia came to live with us, she was only three months old. I could not have expected my mother to take on the burden of rearing another child by herself."

"Many men would have."

"Perhaps. But I like children, you see. That makes all the difference." He stared straight ahead for a moment. "You must allow me to apologize, Mary," he said.

I was confused. Because he liked children? "For . . . ?"

"I should have told you about Amelia as soon as I knew you were someone I respected and trusted. It was cowardly of me to have kept it from you."

"Why did you?"

"I was afraid you would think less of me because of it. Indeed, perhaps you do."

"No, I do not. Think less of you, that is." I hadn't intended to apologize but now found myself doing just that. "I'm sorry if it seemed I was judging you. Only, it was a great shock . . . surprise, rather." I felt his gaze on me but couldn't bring myself to look back at him. I hoped the darkening sky hid my rising color.

"I understand," he said.

I didn't want anything to ruin the perfection of the evening, so I changed the subject. "Is it true what you said about fresh air making babies sleepy?"

He laughed. "It worked sometimes for Amelia. If she fussed at bedtime, I would often walk about the property with her, talk to her, sing to her, and afterward she went right off to sleep once she was in her bed."

What an enchanting picture that made. I could imagine how his voice could lull a baby to sleep. Add to that the joy I'd feel in standing at the tall casements at Linden Hall and watching my husband walk about with our child . . . *Oh, blast, stop it, Mary.*

"I don't wish to give offense, but your sister seems extraordinarily disinterested in her baby."

I felt shame for Lydia, and a flash of anger with him for mentioning it. But I could forgive him this. Lydia's behavior was too pronounced to miss, and for someone who liked children, in fact had a child of his own, it would be disturbing.

When I didn't answer, he said, "I should not have spoken. Forgive me."

"No matter," I said, glancing up at him. "It's true. Lydia hasn't formed an attachment with Felicity yet. Jane tells me this happens sometimes."

"You, I believe, are devoted to the little miss."

He was watching me again. "Yes. It happened quite by accident. The first time she smiled at me, I was enchanted." I bit my lip and thought how to find the right words. "I adore her. I-I've never known a feeling quite like it. I would lay down my life for her." I realized I'd stopped walking and my fingers had, of their own accord, gripped his arm. He covered them with his free hand, and we stood there like that for a long moment.

The light was nearly gone, but I could see the vague forms of Kitty and Andrew ahead of us. Insects hummed around us, and frogs had begun their nighttime chorus. But my only true awareness was of his flesh pressing against mine. My smaller hand completely enveloped in his, so sensitive to his touch. It was sending an unaccustomed tingling through my body. "Do you understand?" I said at last. "About Felicity?"

"Yes."

And then I felt like a fool. "Of course you do. You have Amelia! Tell me about her." I wriggled my hand out from under his; he seemed reluctant to let mine go. We resumed walking.

"She's still living with my sister, and I'm still longing for the day she can live with me. The time is not yet right."

"Being separated from her must cause you pain. For the first time in my life, I think I can understand that. I cannot imagine being parted from Felicity for more than a short time."

"It's been hard on both of us, and my mother as well. Amelia is a very affectionate child, and while I know my sister and her family love her dearly, she still weeps when I leave her, or when she must leave me and Mother."

"I'm sorry," I said. A very inadequate comment, but I truly meant it.

"Thank you."

Felicity began to squirm and fuss a little. "Perhaps we should turn back," I said. "She must be fed before she goes to sleep."

Mr. Walsh called to Andrew and Kitty, and we strolled back toward the house. "Have you had a chance to read *Clarissa* yet?" he asked.

"I'm not quite done. One cannot help feeling a great deal of sympathy for her. Her family — they're despicable, heartless! Their social aspirations do them no credit. And Lovelace is the worst sort of rogue."

"And yet he has some redeeming qualities, I think."

"Oh, sir, you are mistaken! I see no

redeeming qualities in the man."

"No? You must admit, he's very clever."

"Devious, you mean. A scoundrel of the first order." I glared at him archly.

"There are moments when he shows true love, even devotion to Clarissa."

"In a most unnatural way!"

He laughed. "I surrender to your better judgment, Miss Bennet. You, being a lady, are much more likely to understand the matter from Clarissa's point of view."

"Shall I tell you a secret? She is a little too good for my tastes. I actually prefer her friend Anna, who seems more human by her faults."

"Which is precisely why I find Clarissa somewhat — dare I say it — tiresome." We both laughed. "Should you like to read *Sir Charles Grandison*? If you come to High Tor, I'll give you my copy."

"You are too kind. I'm embarrassed about having kept *Clarissa* for so long. I may be able to finish it before you leave." Fee had begun wriggling and crying, so I held out my arms for her. "There, there, little one. Don't cry."

"Try holding her so that she's facing out," he advised. "Sometimes that distracts them."

I turned her about, and she was happy for

a few minutes. But by the time we reached the house, she'd begun to cry again, her little fists flying up to rub her eyes. She wanted her bed. "I'll take her to Lydia."

He gave a slight bow. "Good night, Miss Bennet. We must be on our way back to Netherfield."

"Of course." The light was too dim for me to judge his expression, but he made no move to leave. On impulse, I held out my hand. He grasped it immediately.

"Thank you for your apology, Mr. Walsh."

He nodded. "Until tomorrow, then," he said, rubbing his thumb over my fingers in what seemed like a caress.

Later, when I found it impossible to sleep, I lit a candle and made my way to the upstairs sitting room. I leaned into the windows overlooking the front of the house. The moon had risen, spilling a luminescence over the avenue. One of the tall casements stood open, and a gentle breeze grazed my skin. I could see the front steps, where I had so recently stood with Mr. Walsh. Witʰ his voice echoing in my head, I recalled every word of our conversation. I wished I could see into his mind . . . his heart. This evening, I had sensed a change in him. Compared to his manner during the first days of the visit, there seemed a distinct softening in his behavior toward me.

For my part, although I would not admit it to anybody but myself, I felt a deep attraction to him. In fact, I loved him. His apology made it a certainty. *I was in love with him.* If that made me vulnerable, it would also make me happier, if only for a short while. If he could never love me in return, I would suffer for it, I knew. But I could no longer deny what my heart was telling me.

Tomorrow, I would inform Charles and the rest of the family of my decision to visit High Tor.

CHAPTER 20

I was the first one in the breakfast room the next morning. Papa and Kitty joined me soon afterward. As was their custom, Mama and Lydia were still abed. Kitty and I nibbled at toast and sipped tea, while our father drank coffee and studied his newspaper. Since I didn't have long before Felicity awoke, I said, "I've decided to go back to High Tor with Charles."

Papa lowered his paper and peered at me over his spectacles. A slow grin broke over his face. "Well, well, Mary. I am delighted to hear it."

Kitty squealed. "Oh, that is wonderful news! Jane, among others, will be so pleased." Her voice was smug, and she cast me a look. I knew that look.

"Please do not read into this more than I intend. You are correct in thinking I need a respite from my duties. And I do miss Jane. Perhaps I shall see Lizzy, too. That is all." I felt my face color and wondered why I was bothering to deny my true motivation.

"Yes, of course!" Kitty said, laughing. "A respite from your duties."

"What are you talking about?" said Lydia, who stepped into the room carrying Fee. "Take her, Mary, so I can eat."

I took the little wiggly bundle and kissed the top of her head. "You fed her already?"

"Yes, I got her up and fed her. And changed her, too. I am her mother, you know."

I ignored the sarcasm but now understood why I hadn't heard Fee crying.

Lydia piled her plate with two rolls, ham, and eggs. "I wish we had chocolate," she said. "What were you talking about when I came in?" She looked suspicious.

"Mary has decided to accept Charles's invitation to visit High Tor," Kitty said in a somewhat subdued tone.

"What? And leave me here to look after Felicity by myself? Papa, you cannot allow it!" She banged her plate down and threw herself onto a chair.

"It is not for me, or you, to allow or disallow it. Mary is a grown woman and is perfectly able to make her own decisions. I for one am happy to see her decide to please herself for once."

"Thank you, sir," I said, smiling at my father.

"This is outrageous! I am the one who has had no diversion for months, even before coming to Longbourn." She bit into a roll but continued her tirade anyway. "Mary's company doesn't entertain —"

"You much mistake the matter if you think my purpose has ever been to entertain you. My only aim has been to attend to Felicity's needs. To love her and take care of her. For your amusement I care nothing at all." Now that only family was present, I thought it was a fine opportunity to tell Lydia exactly how I felt. I'd finally lost patience with keeping my tongue. A wide-eyed Kitty stared at me, and my father looked on as though highly diverted.

"Well," Lydia said, "this will not do. I shall speak to Mama. She will take my part, you know she will." She paused to chew a bite of ham. "Why can't I go to High Tor? I could have some fun there, especially with that handsome Mr. Walsh a regular visitor."

Kitty nudged my ankle with her foot, and I had to bite my lip to keep from laughing. At the same time, the thought of Lydia attempting a flirtation with Henry made me cringe.

"Might I remind you, Lydia, that you are

a married woman?" asked Papa, no longer amused.

"There's no harm in a little innocent flirting," she said.

Papa leaped up from the table, as angry as I'd ever seen him. He threw the paper aside and slammed his glass of ale down so hard the contents splashed onto the tablecloth. "You dare to make such a statement when we can all see what kind of harm a 'little flirtation' has caused you? Indeed, Lydia, your first indiscretion — a polite way of putting it — with Wickham was bad enough. It was a miracle Jane and Lizzy found men who loved them enough to overlook the family scandal." He paused to draw in a breath. His face had grown quite red, and I feared his heart might give out.

"Papa, please do calm yourself. You don't look well," I said.

"No, Mary, I wish to have my say. It's been too long in coming." He dropped onto the chair but immediately took up where he'd left off. "You've disgraced our family a second time."

Lydia interrupted. "I have not, for nobody knows about what happened."

"How long do you think we can keep it a secret?" Papa asked, his voice rising in volume. "How much longer can we all pretend Wickham is still in the army and you are staying with us temporarily? And hide the fact that your husband is denying his fatherhood? Word will get out, Lydia, and the gossips will have their day with this latest imbroglio. Your shocking behavior reflects on your sisters and their families, as well."

Frightened by my father's shouting, Felicity began wailing. I stood and walked her about the room, rubbing my cheek against her sweet, soft scalp.

"I declare, Papa, you are being exceedingly mean to me. I daresay it is because your digestion is bothering you again. And Kitty didn't have any trouble getting a husband, despite my behavior. Mary is the only one left, and she'll never get a husband anyway."

"Sensible girl that she is, she'd never settle for the kind of husband you got." He rose once again and this time left the room, just as Mama entered. "Mr. Bennet, where are you going?" she asked. "Mr. Bennet?"

"He is upset, ma'am," Kitty said.

Lydia wasted no time. "Mama, Mary says she is going to High Tor, and Papa will not forbid it. You won't permit her to go, will you?"

The footman had brought in a fresh pot

of tea, and Mama poured herself some, taking her time before she answered. Lydia was deluding herself if she thought our mother would overrule Papa. She always bowed to his will, at least regarding anything about which he cared enough to express an opinion. "We shall manage without her."

"No!" Lydia said. "It's not fair that she should go and not me."

"You are a wife and mother, Lydia. You have responsibilities. Now I wish to break my fast in peace, and I have nothing more to say on the matter."

Lydia, after wresting Fee from my arms, ran from the room. "Take care!" I called.

Lydia kept to herself the rest of the day, remaining in her room for most of it. I assumed my usual duties with Felicity but kept out of my sister's way as much as was possible.

That evening, I told Charles of my decision.

"Well done, Mary!" he said. "After assuring Jane I would be able to lure you away, I'd have hated your proving me misguided in that belief."

"Lydia is none too happy about it," I said.

"She will adjust, although it may take time."

"I believe she is more vexed about being left out than she is about taking care of the baby. She's a fun-loving creature, and part of me pities her." I nearly retracted that statement when my eyes fixed on her across the room, shamelessly flirting with Henry Walsh. While I was watching, the nature of her talk with him changed. She began gesturing toward me, and I realized I was now the object of her conversation. God only knew what awful things she was saying about me.

"I neglected to tell you, Darcy and Elizabeth will be there, too."

I forced my attention back to Charles. "Oh, that is good news. I shall be very happy to see them. Are the children coming?"

"I believe so. Ah, here's Henry."

So he'd made his escape from my sister.

"You'll never believe it, Walsh! Mary has agreed to a visit."

"I'm glad to hear it," he said. "But I already knew. Mrs. Wickham told me."

Wincing, I looked at Charles. "When do we leave?"

"Within the week. The work here is nearly done, and we're eager to go home. Except Carstairs, of course," he said, chuckling.

"He will chafe at being separated from

your sister," Mr. Walsh said, "but it won't be long before they are wed."

The wedding had been fixed for two months from now. "I'm sure it seems an eternity to them," I said, laughing.

Charles's traveling chaise was quite comfortable, well sprung and fitted up with padded squabs. It was very warm, however, and I wished I could be outdoors riding with the men. An odd wish, since I didn't ride at all. I whiled away the hours by finishing *Clarissa,* at last. As I set it aside, I hoped I would have the opportunity to talk with Mr. Walsh about Clarissa's sad end and Lovelace's just deserts. Then I set to rereading *Paradise Lost.* I could never get enough of Milton's majestic poetry and the sheer bravado of Satan, who, now that I thought about it, had a few things in common with the villainous Mr. Lovelace.

Every so often I paused in my reading and reflected on my departure from Longbourn. My feelings confounded me, to say the least. While I looked forward to seeing Jane and Lizzy, and felt a bit short of breath when I thought about spending time with Henry Walsh, leaving Felicity had been most unsettling for me.

Just before we left, I'd carried her outside,

and we wound our way through the shrub-bery walk. Having left infancy behind, Fee was growing into babyhood. Who knew what she would look like before I saw her again? But it wouldn't be that long; a few weeks, a month at most, and I would be back with her. Assuredly I would, yet I could not account for the uneasiness weigh-ing on me.

I held her close, breathing in her baby smells, and talked to her as we walked, not wanting her to forget the sound of my voice or the feel of my body. "I will miss you, my little poppet. You must be the *best* girl while I am away. Your mama and grandmama and aunt will take good care of you." I held her so tightly she began to whimper, and I turned back, knowing the others were wait-ing for me.

Before handing her to Lydia, I kissed each of her plump cheeks. "Good-bye, little Fee. Don't forget me." To my great embarrass-ment, tears moistened my cheeks. I turned away hastily and accepted Mr. Walsh's hand up into the chaise. I could hear Lydia mut-tering.

" 'Little Fee,' " she said. "Whoever heard of such a ridiculous name? And I don't know why you are decamping if you are so vastly grieved about it."

I'd ignored her and waved to my parents and Kitty, trying to smile through my tears.

This would not do. Every time I thought of Fee, tears threatened again. Swollen, reddened eyes would never recommend me to . . . a certain gentleman.

After we stopped at a coaching inn to change horses and eat a light meal, Mr. Walsh, instead of mounting his horse, climbed into the chaise with me. Was it proper for the two of us to be alone together? *Don't be ridiculous, Mary. He's not wicked Lovelace, for heaven's sake.*

"May I ride with you for a while?" he asked.

I looked down but managed to stammer out my assent. "What about your horse?"

"One of the grooms will ride him. How are you bearing up?"

"Because of leaving Fee?" I gave him an embarrassed grin. "I confess to shedding a few tears every time I think of her."

"It's to be expected," he said. "Only natural. And I wanted to tell you, I think 'little Fee' is a perfect endearment for your niece."

"You heard what Lydia said, then? I think she meant only for me to hear, but no matter. It's of small consequence to me what

281

she thinks about it. It's just for me and Fee."

He chuckled. "Your missing her — it won't spoil your visit, I hope."

"No. I confess I feel as if I'm embarking on a holiday. While I admit to a certain reluctance to leave Felicity, I don't think it will spoil anything."

"Excellent." Pausing, Henry appeared to be gathering his thoughts. "Miss Bennet, I would very much like to introduce you to Amelia during your stay at High Tor, if you will allow me to do so."

I brightened. "I would be delighted to meet your daughter. I've been wondering — that is, I'm curious as to whether or not Charles and Jane know of her."

"I told Charles some time ago, and I'm quite sure he told your sister. Who by now has probably told both Kitty and Mrs. Darcy," he said, smiling. "I don't believe there is much you sisters do not tell each other."

I laughed. "It depends on which sisters. May I ask Charles's reaction to the news?"

"What you might expect from such a sanguine man. I believe he is — and your sister, too — incapable of judging anyone harshly."

"You are correct on that head. They have a tendency to be rather too forgiving at times." I colored fiercely. "I did not mean in your case," I said hastily. "And please believe I love them both very much."

"I know you do. I would never question that. Because we love someone, it does not blind us to their faults."

Was he thinking of his own faults again? Or possibly mine? I racked my brain for something to say. "Will Amelia wish to meet me?"

Henry sat back and eyed me thoughtfully. He didn't say anything for the longest time. I smoothed my skirts. I studied my hands and watched the passing scenery. When he spoke, it was so softly I almost missed it.

"Of that I have no doubt."

He said nothing more, because we were interrupted by Charles drawing alongside and tapping his whip on the door of the chaise. "The driver thinks something is amiss with one of the team," he said.

Henry left me to confer with Charles. I could not deny being more than a little pleased that he wanted me to meet his daughter and believed she would like me. If he didn't care for me, would that matter to him? But I knew I must not assume anything. After I had rejected him soundly only a few months ago, would he try again so soon to gain my affections? And I wasn't sure if caring for me was enough. I wanted his love.

CHAPTER 21

Unfortunately, one of the horses had gone lame. We limped into another coaching inn, delaying our arrival at High Tor by a few additional hours. When we drove in at last, Jane and David, and Elizabeth, with her twins, were all outside to greet us.

After giving Jane a kiss, Charles excused himself to wash and change.

"Won't you stay and dine with us?" Jane asked Andrew and Mr. Walsh.

"You are too kind, ma'am. My mother will be impatient for my arrival. Andrew, are you coming with me?"

"Much as I would enjoy spending the evening with all of you," Andrew said, "I'm afraid I am stuck with my cousin tonight. You'll be seeing enough of me in the days to come."

"You'll join us for dinner soon? You and your mother, too, of course, Mr. Walsh." Jane said she would send an invitation over, and after bidding us all good-bye, the two men rode off.

Lizzy's twins, Fanny and Jane, pulled at my skirts, demanding my attention. I stooped down and kissed them both. They were two years old now, and I imagined what Felicity might look like when she was their age.

"Leave your aunt be, dears," Lizzy said. "She's tired after her long journey."

"It's all right. I've been so eager to see them. To see all of you. Where is Mr. Darcy?" I took a little hand in each of mine and allowed the girls to lead me into the house.

"Riding about the estate. Charles asked him to keep an eye on things while he was at Longbourn," Elizabeth answered.

"We're keen to hear all the news," Jane said, eyeing me pointedly. "Aren't we, Lizzy?"

Lizzy laughed her irrepressible laugh. "We are indeed, but only after you've had a chance to rest and wash up. You must be very tired, Mary."

True enough. I was tired and aching from bouncing around in the coach for so long.

After refreshing myself, I wandered downstairs and found Jane and Elizabeth strolling around the back garden, examining the borders. Bright yellow phlox, purple penstemon, and white helenium bloomed in bursts of color.

"What do you think, Mary?" Jane asked. "What does this border need? Besides cutting back?"

"Something red, perhaps? You know I am not good with color or design."

"I believe she is right, Jane. About the red, I mean," Lizzy said. She linked her arm with mine and steered me toward a bench. "Tell us, Mary, how did you find Kitty?"

"Very much changed, just as Jane said. She even stood up to Lydia on occasion, although tentatively. And she apologized for her part in separating me from Mr. Walsh."

Jane ambled toward us. "I *am* curious . . . what was Lydia's reaction to Kitty's news?"

"To say the truth, I was sorry for Kitty. Lydia didn't wish her happy until Kitty rather pitifully asked her to do so. And then her felicitations were barely civil. I daresay she's been out of spirits ever since hearing the news."

"We may rest easy, I think, in believing Andrew's influence will outweigh Lydia's," Jane said. "But do we need to worry about Kitty and Lydia being thrown together these few months before the wedding?"

"I saw nothing to make me believe they were taking up their former ways with each other. Kitty is already preoccupied with wedding plans, and I don't think she would do anything to make herself look bad in Andrew's eyes."

"We shall have to trust in your judgment," Jane said.

Both my sisters continued to stare at me, so pointedly I could not help laughing. "Why do you look at me that way?"

Lizzy tipped her head and flashed a devious smile. "I'm quite sure there is something else that needs telling."

I feigned lack of understanding. "What is it you wish to know?"

"Everything about you and Mr. Walsh," Lizzy said, making a sweeping motion with her hand. "For heaven's sake, isn't it obvious?"

"He was as gentlemanly and polite as ever," I said, foolishly hoping that would be the end of it.

"Mary!" Jane said. "You can't leave it at that. We want the details."

So I gave them an abbreviated version of Mr. Walsh's visit to Longbourn. "He was noticeably cool to me upon his arrival. In fact, he seemed indifferent. It was what I expected."

"And then?"

"And then, after our being in each other's company for more than a fortnight, he assumed a more tender manner toward me. He complimented me on my playing and on my care of Felicity. And brace yourselves . . . Mama even did a bit of matchmaking."

"Good heaven, no!" Lizzy said.

"Only with me, not him, thank goodness. One evening she insisted I walk out with him, Kitty, and Andrew while she and Lydia put Felicity to bed. I did, and it was lovely. I nearly didn't go, because we could hear Fee screaming from the open windows. Henry — uh, that is, Mr. Walsh, marched into the house and snatched her away from Mama and Lydia. If you could have seen their expressions!"

Jane laughed, covering her mouth genteelly. "You can call him Henry with us, Mary."

"He's very good with children. I think you both know he has a daughter?"

They nodded, looking a bit embarrassed.

"On the trip here, he rode in the chaise with me for a short while. He said he wanted me to meet her."

My sisters were listening closely. "What are your feelings on that, Mary?" asked Jane.

"I'll be happy to make her acquaintance, but I'm trying not to read too much into it."

"I understand," Lizzy said. "But there's a reason behind his desire for you to meet her. He wouldn't introduce her to just anybody."

"Oh, Mary," Jane said. "That can only mean one thing."

"That he wants me to be her governess?"

That caused us all to crow with laughter.

"Mary is right to be cautious," Lizzy said.

Don't say that. It was no more than I myself believed, but hearing someone give voice to it only served to bolster my own doubts. "Because of this . . . Miss Bellcourt?" I asked. I decided that if they knew something, I might as well hear about it now. "You mentioned her in a letter, Jane. She sounds like the ideal wife for him."

"Oh, no!" Jane said. "I was only trying to goad you into coming back here."

"But they danced together, and he called on her —"

"I may have invented the part about his calling on her," she said sheepishly.

"Jane!"

"I do beg your pardon, Mary. I shouldn't have said anything. I've heard nothing more about any meetings between them. If I were better acquainted with her, I'd be more capable of judging whether she's the kind of woman he would like."

"I would think any man would like her fortune well enough," I said, which broke the tension. "Has he spoken of her to you or Charles?"

"Not to me," Jane said. "That would hardly be likely. Maybe to Charles. I'll ask him."

"No, don't," I said, mortified. "He might tell Henry I was inquiring."

"It would be me doing the inquiring, but I won't say a word if you'd rather I did not."

Lizzy looked at me thoughtfully. "If Henry were to offer for you again, would you accept him?"

Would I? I hardly knew. "If I thought he loved me . . . but it seems unlikely that his feelings have changed over such a short time. I can't bear the thought of marrying him only for Amelia's sake. Knowing he only *liked* me."

"Love can surprise you," Elizabeth said. "Some people wed without thought of love, and it sneaks up on them."

"And others remain in loveless marriages their whole lives. I don't want that. Both of you married for love; should I be satisfied with anything less?"

Jane smiled mischievously. "I might settle for less with such a man as Henry Walsh."

Lizzy interrupted. "Of course not, if such a union would bring you pain."

"Think of our parents," I said. "What if I married Henry and in the end, instead of eventually loving me, he had nothing but contempt for me?" We were silent for a long moment, and I knew we were all thinking about the same thing: the sarcastic and contemptuous way in which Papa invariably addressed our mother. The fact that he spent every day taking refuge in his library. There was no joy in their union, and it had been so as far back as I could remember. I felt tears gathering and blinked them away.

Sniffing a little, I said, "I have Fee now. She loves me completely. Unconditionally. I can live without Henry's love if I must, because I'll always have her."

An odd look lasting only a few seconds passed between Jane and Lizzy. Perhaps they didn't believe I could be happy without Henry.

"Just one more question, Mary. Do you love *him*?" Jane asked.

Confiding this would make me susceptible to their pity if nothing further happened between Henry and me. If he had absolutely no intention of offering for me again, if he were only the earnest, friendly neighbor, ready to find love with someone else, they would know I'd given him my heart in vain. But I wanted to tell them. "Yes. I believe I do," I said, smiling shyly. "But I cannot be certain that his feelings toward me have changed."

My sisters dissolved into squeals of happiness. They giggled and looked at me with tender expressions. To them, it was already settled. As I lay awake in bed that night, I thought about being Henry's wife. My skin prickled at the memory of his hand enfolding mine, how it had sent tingles through me. What would it be like to kiss him? To share a marriage bed with him? My stomach jumped. *Oh my,* I thought. *Oh my.*

A proned and wearing old shoes and gloves, Jane, Lizzy, and I worked on the borders. The gardener could have done this job, but Jane desired it to be her particular responsibility. She was pruning and pulling up dead foliage, while Lizzy and I planted crimson pelargonium, cultivated in High Tor's greenhouse. We had spent the better part of two weeks planning and working on this project.

"Mary," Lizzy said, in such a way that it made me think I would not like what followed.

I peered at her from under my bonnet brim and waited.

"Jane and I are worried that you've become too attached to Felicity." My stomach lurched, spiraling downward. Did she know something I was not privy to? I noticed Jane sidling her way toward us.

"Have you received a letter? Do you have news? To own the truth, I have been wondering why we've not heard from any of the family," I said, my voice shaky.

I must have turned pale, because both my sisters looked concerned. "Come, sit in the shade, dear," Jane said. She poured me glass of water from a jug we'd carried outside with us. "No letters. You know neither Mama nor Papa, and certainly not Lydia, spends any time in that occupation. And Kitty will be too busy with wedding plans."

"Why did you say that about Felicity?" I asked. "Is there something you're not telling me?" Removing my gloves, I felt beads of perspiration popping up on my skin, and I wiped at them with the back of my hand.

"Oh, no!" Lizzy said. "Only, when Lydia leaves Longbourn, Felicity will go with her, that is all. We worry about your being hurt if that should come to pass."

I thought a moment before replying. "It is true I am much devoted to her. I love her like a mother would, I think. But I'm not worried. There's little chance of Lydia ever leaving Longbourn again."

"In that belief, I think you are mistaken," Lizzy said. "Lydia will chafe at confinement with only our parents for company. Who knows what scheme she will work up to make her escape?"

"But Wickham doesn't want her," I said. "And once people learn the truth . . . she will not be welcomed in society." That this should please me made me feel the worst kind of sister imaginable.

"If I know Mama, she will see to it that the truth is never fully known," Jane said. "She will place all the blame on Wickham and deny Lydia's indiscretions. And who's to say she will not be believed? After all, it would be her word against Wickham's, a known liar and villain."

"I can't imagine what would be the means of her escape," I said. "And even if she managed it, there would be no place for Fee in it. Lydia has shown so little interest —"

"While you are away, she must be tending to Felicity," Jane said. "You know Mama will do the barest minimum possible, so Lydia will be forced to do so."

An unladylike sound escaped my lips. "She's probably found a way to get one of the servants to do it."

"Mary," Lizzy said, turning to me with a sober expression, "what do you envision for Felicity's future? And your involvement in her life?"

The question made me uncomfortable, because I had only a vague, shadowy notion of what the future might bring. I couldn't imagine life without her. Should I confess I'd imagined marriage to Henry and our raising Fee together? No. They might think I was unhinged.

"I don't think about it." It was true, for the most part. Being separated from her simply didn't enter my mind, perhaps because the idea was entirely unbearable. Even this conversation made me want to flee back to Longbourn.

Partly to change the subject, but also because I truly wished to know, I asked them a question. "I've been wondering if Henry knows the truth of Lydia's situation. Has Charles told him?"

Jane looked shocked. "No! We decided it was best not to speak of it to anybody."

A thought occurred to me. "It seems as if Kitty would have told Andrew by now. And he may have told Henry."

"I suppose it's possible. Why do you ask? Did Henry mention it?"

"A couple of times, Lydia's name has come up. In a perfectly innocent manner. Not at all like Amanda Ashton's nosy questions. But I've avoided any direct explanations." With a pang of guilt, I realized I'd kept Lydia's predicament from Henry, just as he'd kept Amelia's existence from me. How could I be angry with him for misleading me when I was guilty of the same thing?

"I don't think he knows the whole story, Mary. I'm convinced Kitty would be embarrassed to speak of it to Andrew, other than to tell him Lydia and her husband are living apart," Jane said.

"Madam," said a quiet voice behind us. "You have callers."

"Oh!" Jane said. "And here we are in our gardening attire, sweaty and dirty! Who is it, Simms?"

"Mr. Henry Walsh and Miss Walsh," he answered. "I've put them in the downstairs drawing room."

"Miss Walsh?" Jane said, looking perplexed. "You don't mean Mrs. Walsh?"

Simms smiled. "Young Miss Walsh."

Jane flashed a glance at me. "Of course. Amelia! Thank you, Simms. Please ask Cook to prepare a light meal, and tell our guests we will be with them shortly."

"Where are Charles and Mr. Darcy?" I

asked Jane as we hurried upstairs.

"Off riding about the property, as usual," Elizabeth said. "Unavailable. Are you all right, Mary?"

"Yes, yes, I'm fine. I just wish he hadn't chosen the morning we were gardening to visit." And that my sisters hadn't stirred up all sorts of disturbing thoughts about Felicity.

"You will meet Amelia," Jane said.

"As will you," I replied.

"Oh, I do not think it is Jane or I he wishes to meet his daughter," Lizzy said as we parted into our separate chambers.

CHAPTER 22

Henry introduced us to Amelia, who smiled and made perfect little curtsies to each of us in turn. He watched her closely, revealing with a soft glow in his eyes his pride in her manners. After being introduced to us, she sat with her hands folded in her lap and spoke only when spoken to.

After the food had been served, I turned to her. "Your papa told me he is teaching you to ride. How do you like it?"

Her eyes lit up. "I have my own pony," she said.

"And what is his name?"

"King George, but I call him Georgie Boy."

We all laughed. Henry's eyes were dancing, but he'd covered his mouth with the back of his hand to hide his smile. "Did you name him after the prince regent, then?"

"Papa often says he is comical, so that's why I named him that."

"So your pony makes you laugh?"

"Yes, except for when he won't do what I want. He's improving now, though, isn't he, Papa?" She grinned at her father, and he nodded his agreement.

"Perhaps you're becoming more adept at handling him."

The fact that she was missing a few front teeth made her smile not only charming but also sweetly innocent. "Papa thinks I'm coming along. Would you like to see my pony, Miss Bennet?"

"Very much. Did you ride him here?"

Her face fell. "No. It was too far. But if you will visit us at Linden Hall, you may meet him."

Lizzy leaned forward. "I have twin girls, Amelia. They are only two years old, but already they are clamoring for a pony. They love to ride up in front of their father."

"That's what I do, but I'm getting too big for that." She smiled at Elizabeth and said, "Maybe I could play with your twins. What are their names?"

Lizzy told her and said she was sure her girls would love to play another day. After a while, my sisters excused themselves to check on their children, leaving the three of us alone.

"Would you like to see me ride Papa's

horse, Miss Bennet?" said Amelia.

I glanced quickly at her father. "I think we'd better ask him about that."

"She likes to sit in the saddle while I hold the reins and walk her about," he explained. "It's a lovely day. Shall we?"

"By all means," I said. "Give me one moment to fetch my bonnet."

"Amelia and I will ask the groom to bring Guinevere around and meet you out front."

When I joined them outside, Mr. Walsh had already hoisted his daughter into the saddle. She sat astride the handsome bay mare with her skirts hiked up. Her skinny little legs dangled down but were not nearly long enough to reach the stirrups. We set off down the avenue.

"Any news from Longbourn?" Mr. Walsh asked.

"None. I am trying to take that as a good sign," I said, laughing. "No crises with Fee. I do hope they are managing."

"And Kitty will be making preparations for her wedding."

"Having her bride clothes made, I imagine. Lydia adores anything to do with fashion, so that may be diverting for her, too."

"Papa, stop talking to Miss Bennet. I want her to watch me!"

"I'm sorry, Amelia," I said. "How rude of me to not pay you any attention. You look fine in the saddle. Does it not scare you a little to be up so high?"

"Well . . . if my father did not have hold of the reins, maybe I would be a little scared. Can you ride a horse, Miss Bennet?"

"No, I confess I have never learned. We didn't have the opportunity when we were growing up. Two of my married sisters are learning now, though. Their husbands insisted."

Henry laughed. "Of course, since they are both accomplished riders."

"I think it would be fun to drive a curricle," I said. "Or a phaeton."

He looked at me in disbelief. "You do? I have a curricle. I'd be happy to teach you. There's a certain amount of skill involved, you know." He arched an eyebrow.

"And I can see you think it would be beyond me. I admit I don't have the first notion of how it's done. You would probably be sorry if you took me on as your pupil."

"Maybe you'll turn out to be a fearsome whip."

"Ha! I know when I'm being laughed at."

"Not at all," he said, although a smile pulled at the corners of his mouth. "But you must first feel comfortable around horses, and I don't think you do. Not yet." He looked up at his daughter. "Amelia, what would you say to giving up your place to Miss Bennet? This can be her first riding lesson."

"Riding lesson?"

Amelia's eyes sparkled. "Yes! Help me down, Papa."

"No!" I said. "I cannot mount that beast, and I'm too heavy for you to lift. Besides, I never said I wanted riding lessons."

"Nonsense. I can easily lift you. And you must learn to ride before you try driving a curricle." He said this as if it had been settled between us, that he would teach me to drive his curricle.

He swung Amelia down and motioned to me with his hand. "Sir, it's not a sidesaddle. I can't sit astride as Amelia did."

"No more excuses, Miss Bennet," he said. "This saddle will do well enough for the short time you'll be in it."

True, because I'll probably tumble right off as soon as the horse takes its first step.

Before I could stop him, he put his hands at my waist and lifted me into the saddle. I perched on it as if it were a sidesaddle. Henry adjusted the stirrup, so I'd have someplace to rest one foot. "Hold on to the pommel. I'll lead you, as I did with Amelia."

"All right," I said, wondering how Amelia had sat on the horse with such assurance. "Go slowly," I said, my voice trembling.

"You're riding, Miss Bennet!" Amelia said, clapping her hands.

"I'd hardly call it that." But I was in fact surprised I hadn't yet fallen off.

"Oh, Papa, your horse just did a big poop!" Amelia said.

I looked away and bit my lip.

"What have I told you about that, Amelia?" her father asked. "That is not proper language for a young lady. Nor is it a fit topic for polite company."

"I'm sorry, Papa. John and Richard always say it whenever their horses —"

"That's enough. Please apologize to Miss Bennet."

"I beg your pardon, Miss Bennet. I should not have spoken as I did." She hung her pretty head.

"Thank you, Amelia," I said with as much gravity as I could muster.

"Papa, may I walk along the stream for a while?"

"Only if you give me your solemn promise you won't get too close to the water."

"I promise," she said before dashing off.

He gave me an apologetic glance. "She's

very influenced by her male cousins, who run a bit wild. I hope she didn't offend you."

"Not at all. She seems like such a happy child."

He chuckled, his expression shining with pride. "Do you think so? But she must learn not to say the first thing that jumps into her head."

"Indeed, I had to bite back a laugh more than once. Honesty is a wonderful quality of children. They always tell you exactly what they think."

"I'm glad you resisted the urge to laugh. At times it is hard not to."

I glanced down at him. "Would you mind if I dismounted? I don't like talking to you from way up here."

"Of course. Let me assist you. You're going to have to slide partway down, and I'll catch you."

"Oh, no. I'm afraid I'll knock you over."

"Come, now." Henry held out his arms, and I simply stared at him. In truth, I was more afraid of being caught up in those arms than of looking stupid, although I was afraid of that, too.

I let myself slip down gradually toward the ground and landed within the safety of his embrace. His hands settled at my waist. Our faces were only inches apart, and for a moment I thought he meant to kiss me. My senses heightened, and I felt his breath brushing my skin, heard my own soft sigh, felt a sweet pleasure well up inside. We were standing far closer than propriety allowed.

After a long moment he released me. "I'd better find Amelia." Before he walked away, his soft gaze never left my face. "Stay here by Guinevere," he said.

"Guinevere," I repeated stupidly. He could have said, "I'm going to spear frogs," "I must relieve myself in the bushes," or "I spotted a new species of butterfly and must retrieve my net." His words had barely registered. Something about Amelia. After a minute, when I began to come out of the trance I'd been in, I heard him calling her name, and her laughing voice answering.

It was clear that Henry had wanted to kiss me. I certainly had wanted him to and would not have stopped him. I knew it was for the best, then, that he had demonstrated a gentlemanly self-control. I walked to Guinevere's fine-looking head and put my hand out for her to smell. Her head bobbed around a bit, and she huffed a few breaths. When I thought she trusted me, I reached out and stroked her and scratched behind her ears.

By the time my two companions returned,

Gwen and I had made friends. Henry lifted Amelia into the saddle, and we walked in comfortable silence back to the house.

Lizzy, Jane, and I sat in a patch of shade in the garden. Having finally completed the replanting of the borders, we'd whiled away most of the afternoon playing outside with the children and had just returned them to the care of their nursemaids. For the last several minutes, my sisters had been attempting to pry out of me whatever they could in regard to Henry Walsh's visit of the previous day. Never had I met with such relentless questioners.

"Did you like Amelia?" Jane had begun.

"Oh, yes. She's quite delightful."

"She seems very well behaved," Lizzy said.

"Oh, most definitely."

"What did you talk about? You were gone quite a long time."

I rose and made my way over to a flower bed, plucking out some weeds the gardener had missed. "Nothing in particular."

"Mary!" Jane said. "You're teasing us. You must remember your conversation."

I needn't have bothered suppressing my smile, since my back was to them. It was fun, evading their questions. I supposed I should reveal a little, or they would badger me to death. I surely wouldn't tell them Henry had almost kissed me, though, or that I was sorry he hadn't. Had they allowed their husbands a kiss before they were betrothed? I didn't think so, and I couldn't have borne it if they disapproved of my behavior. Besides, I wanted to keep the memory just for myself. And what if it had only been a figment of my overwrought imagination?

I meandered back over, resumed my seat, and told them about his offer to teach me to ride and drive his curricle. In the middle of it, Simms interrupted to announce the arrival of Amanda and John Ashton.

CHAPTER 23

"Oh no!" Jane said, sounding none too pleased. "What are they doing here? Did you put them in the drawing room, Simms?"

"Yes, madam."

It was late for a morning call, nearly time for us to attend to our evening toilettes. Amanda Ashton and her dour husband stood waiting as we entered the room. "Please, be seated," Jane said.

Casting away all decorum, Mrs. Ashton said, "This is not a social call."

"You have me at a disadvantage, Amanda. What else could it be?" Jane tried to smile, but her eyes held an uneasy expression.

Just then, Charles and Mr. Darcy, still attired in riding britches and Hessian boots, entered the room. Charles, ever the ebullient host, greeted his guests with his usual enthusiasm. "Ashton! How good to see you again. Amanda," he said, bowing in that lady's direction. "You remember my friend

Darcy?"

"Mrs. Ashton was just explaining the reason for their visit," Lizzy told her husband and brother-in-law. Something in her tone alerted the two men that all was not well.

Charles's smile slipped a little. Mr. Darcy, who barely knew the Ashtons, stood off to one side observing.

No one seemed inclined to sit down. The tension in the room grew, until finally Charles said, "Well, then. To what do we owe the honor of this call?"

"I've come to demand you do something about Mr. Wickham!" Amanda Ashton said at last. Her husband tugged at his cravat as if it were choking him.

Charles appeared baffled; we all did. No longer was she the foolish lady we had known before. Having now dropped all pretense of raptures and transports, she had transformed herself into a virago. "I beg you to explain," he said. "What is your connection to the man?"

"It seems impossible you could not know this, but Wickham's . . . mistress, Susan Bradford, is my sister. He seeks to divorce his wife in order to marry her. She is in possession of a fortune, you see."

My sisters and I looked at each other.

"Wickham is trying to divorce Lydia?" asked Jane. "We didn't know."

"Ah," Charles said. "I see. But what do you suppose we can do?"

"Pay him off! His interest in Susan is purely for his own gain. He has her in his power. She believes everything he tells her, including the pretense of a connection to the Darcy family and a share in their wealth."

Suddenly, the reason behind all the lady's questions about Lydia and Wickham became clear. "Mrs. Ashton, I told you the truth about Wickham's connection to Mr. Darcy," I said.

Jane and Elizabeth both cast me questioning glances. "You did?" they asked simultaneously.

I nodded in their direction and continued. "Did you not inform your sister? You posted a large number of letters when you were here." The eyes of my family were trained on me, in some surprise.

"Susan will not be swayed. She is entirely smitten with the scoundrel and will hear nothing from me on the matter."

Mr. Darcy stepped in. With his imposing manner, he perhaps was best suited for the task. "We have already done everything within our grasp. Did it not occur to you it was in the interest of my wife's family, especially her unwed sisters, to have this matter settled?"

"This is not to be borne!" Mrs. Ashton said. "You must do more. Surely you, sir, with your grand estate and your vast wealth, have some influence over him. You can convince him to see reason and return to his wife."

"Madam, I assure you, I cannot. And might not the same be said regarding you and your sister? You are in the best position to persuade her of her poor judgment in placing herself in the hands of such a man."

At last, she lowered herself onto a chair, and my sisters and I followed suit. The men remained standing. "Unfortunately, Susan is quite willful and headstrong."

Like Lydia.

"She's fallen head over ears in love with the man and truly believes he will divorce Mrs. Wickham."

"Does she not know how difficult it is to procure a divorce?" Charles asked.

Mr. Darcy situated himself directly i front of Mrs. Ashton. "This is another of Wickham's habitual lies," he said, looking down at her. "Please believe me, madam, when I tell you I have done all in *my* power to persuade him to return to his wife, including inducements monetary in nature. All to no avail. Your sister is naïve if she believes he seeks a divorce. If all else fails, Wickham needs Lydia and our family to fall back on."

Mrs. Ashton turned pale. Extracting a fan from her reticule, she furiously waved it about. "I feel a bit faint. May I have a brandy?"

Charles walked over to the drinks table and poured a brandy for Mr. Ashton and his lady. "It is an unfortunate situation, but we believe we have done all in our power to rectify matters," he said.

Mrs. Ashton spoke. "You must try again! Since money is what he wants, I can hardly believe he would not be swayed by a large sum. Perhaps if you increased the amount offered."

"Amanda, that is enough!" said her husband. "For all you know, Mr. Darcy offered him a sum larger than Susan's fortune."

"What has that to say to anything? Whatever he offered, it didn't do the trick." She tossed back the brandy like a desperate man about to lose his fortune at a gaming table.

Mr. Darcy spoke again. "I am afraid we cannot help you. It now remains in your hands to sway your sister."

Mrs. Ashton slammed her glass down on

the nearest table and leaped to her feet. "You will be sorry. All of you," she said, swiveling to gaze at each of us in turn. "The facts, if they become generally known, will cause a scandal and bring ruin on your family. Believe me, I have no qualms about spreading the truth around."

"The truth is generally known by anybody we care about," Charles said.

"Not the whole truth," Amanda said. "The fact that Wickham is not the father of your sister's child is not yet known by the gossips."

Jane gasped and Lizzy looked defiant. I stood my ground but wished my stays hadn't been laced quite so tightly this morning. I wanted to ask her how she knew, but wasn't it obvious? Wickham had told his mistress, and Amanda learned it from her.

"This sounds very much like blackmail," said Mr. Darcy.

"Call it what you will. Gossip is the fodder we live on; it's hardly a crime to repeat the latest *on-dits.*" She slid her eyes toward me. "There is a certain gentleman who may be interested in learning of this. One who would surely change his mind about offering for one of the two unmarried Bennet girls if he were to find out."

I went very still. What would Mr. Walsh

think of me if he knew the whole sordid story? I, who had denounced *him* for keeping a secret? I couldn't allow the woman to think I was afraid of her threats, though, so I glared boldly back.

"Miss Kitty Bennet has lately become engaged," Charles said, "and Miss Bennet has no plans to wed the man to whom you refer." Sadness tore at my heart when I heard those words. He sounded so certain.

Nodding decisively, Charles said, "In any case, I'll tell Walsh myself. I'm sure he's pieced some of it together on his own."

A voice spoke from the open doorway. "What have I pieced together?" It was Henry, standing there looking questioningly at all of us. He removed his hat and gloves and set them on a chest along with his whip.

"Amanda, we are leaving," said her husband. "Come along." He grabbed her arm and coaxed her unwilling form toward the door. Henry stood there looking perplexed.

"This is not the end of the matter," Mrs. Ashton said. "You have no choice but to pursue this further. If you do not, the consequences for your family will be dire."

"Enough, wife!" Mr. Ashton said, now practically dragging her out of the room. "My apologies, Bingley. Walsh." He nodded at Henry, who sidestepped to get out of the way.

Never had silence sounded so loud. We all simply stood there, faces pale, expressions somber. Henry gave me a fleeting glance and must have noticed my dismay. "I've obviously stopped at an inconvenient time," he said. "I'll return another day."

"No, that will not do," Charles said. "Will you come into the library with me? I must tell you something."

"Of course. If you're sure . . ."

"I'm afraid it must be now. Darcy, will you join us?"

The men strode out of the room, while we three sisters collapsed onto the chairs. It was a long while before anybody spoke. Eventually Lizzy said, "Mr. Walsh is an uncommonly generous man. I don't think Lydia's troubles will discredit us in his eyes."

"I agree with Lizzy," Jane said. "Henry is exceedingly kind. He will not judge you, Mary, or any of us, by our poor sister's faults."

I barely trusted myself to speak. "Perhaps not. But one could hardly blame him if he did."

After a while, Simms stepped in and went away again with Henry's hat, gloves, and riding crop. The burning heaviness in my chest increased when Charles and Mr. Darcy at last entered the room without him.

"Walsh's mother was expecting him for dinner. He only stopped in on his way home," Charles explained.

"How did he take the news?" asked Jane.

Charles shrugged. "He was sorry for our troubles. Aside from needing to be on his way, he wished to allow us time to deal with this matter in private."

Jane and Lizzy seemed content with that explanation of why he'd hurried away. But not me. If he was so understanding, why couldn't he have stayed, even just for a few moments? Apparently, he didn't wish to see me as much as I'd been longing to see him. Was he so shocked by what Charles had told him that he wanted to sever all connections with us? *Oh, what must he think of me now?*

After a few moments I excused myself. Ascending the stairs, I wondered how long it would take Mrs. Ashton to do her dirty work. Would she wait until she was sure we'd done nothing further to force Wickham to return to the fold? Or given what we had told her today, would she get right to work?

CHAPTER 24

Days passed. Nobody turned us away on our morning calls or ceased calling on us. We continued to receive invitations to dinners, soirees, and garden parties. Indeed, nobody of our acquaintance treated us ill in any way whatsoever, or differently than they had in the past. We began to believe that Mrs. Ashton had abandoned her plan, or that her husband had forbidden it.

Mr. Walsh did not call on us, and whenever my thoughts drifted to him, I busied myself with the children, who were completely entranced with a new litter of spaniel puppies. The twins had to be closely watched when they played with the pups, as they were wont to think of them as toys. I was certain one or more of them would be smuggled into the house before long.

Otherwise, I was occupied with flower arranging and gossiping with my sisters while we worked. Jane was painting a fireplace screen, while Elizabeth applied herself to decorating a tea caddy. I didn't walk unless in the company of one of them, and I'd curtailed my reading. To protect my heart, I did not engage in anything that would allow me, in an unguarded moment, to imagine a life with Henry Walsh.

I continued to feel a nagging worry about the lack of news from Longbourn.

One evening on my way to join Jane and Elizabeth after dinner, I wheeled around the corner and nearly stumbled right into a tall, disheveled man. He looked up and removed his beaver hat.

"Mr. Wickham!" I said, narrowing my eyes. I was none too happy to see the man whose conduct was the cause of so much pain for my family. "What are you doing here?"

"Why, Mary! You've grown up since I last had the pleasure of seeing you." His eyes roved up and down my body in an exceptionally rude way, and I felt myself coloring. Unfortunately, he had turned into a rather dissolute-looking ne'er-do-well. What had formerly been a handsome countenance had hardened, especially around his eyes and mouth.

When I didn't reply, he went on. "Would you be so kind as to take me to Bingley? I have a matter of some importance to discuss with him."

"How did you get in? Why were you not announced?"

"Please, my dear Mary, let's not quibble. I simply walked in. I am part of the family, am I not?"

As much as the old mare, but we don't let her in the house. I looked askance at my brother-in-law, turned on my heel, and bade him to follow me. He would be surprised — and put out — to find Mr. Darcy here to greet him as well.

I led him to the dining room, where the men were drinking their port and smoking cheroots. After knocking lightly at the door, I stuck my head in and said, "Charles. Please forgive me for interrupting you, but we . . . you have a visitor."

"Oh," Charles said. "Is it Walsh?"

I shook my head and swung the door wide. Wickham stepped through. I backed quickly out of the room, but not before I heard Mr. Darcy utter a curse, and Charles say more directly, "Good God! You!"

Leaving the door slightly ajar, I raced down the hallway toward the sitting room and my sisters. Breathlessly, I stood at the threshold and said, "Jane, Lizzy, come."

I must have looked frightened, or perhaps

frightening, because they both jumped to their feet, Jane with a cry of "What is wrong, Mary?"

"Hurry! Wickham is here. I took him to the dining room. If we make haste, we can hear some of the conversation."

"Wickham?" Jane said, looking confused. "Lydia's Wickham?"

"Of course. What other Wickham is there? Now come, or we shall miss the whole business."

None of us had any compunction about listening in. We were often not privy to discussions among the men. But I believe we all felt this one in particular was as much our business as theirs.

"Are you not even going to ask me to sit?" I heard Wickham say as we stepped gingerly toward the door.

"By God, man, we should by rights have you thrown out of here!" That was Mr. Darcy. Elizabeth gaped at us. I felt sure her husband seldom lost his temper.

"It's all right, Darcy," Charles said. "Perhaps it will be enlightening to hear what the man has to say. By all means, Wickham, be seated and pour yourself a glass of port."

"Do you know I've been over half of England looking for you?" Mr. Darcy said.

I heard the clink of glass before Wickham

answered. "I-I apologize for that. It could not be helped. You would only have demanded I return to my wife, and I was not willing to do that."

Charles spoke now. "Have you changed your mind, then? Is that why you're here?"

A forced laugh from Wickham. "No. I'm afraid it's too late for that."

"Do you not even ask after your wife and child?" Mr. Darcy asked.

On cue, Wickham said, "How do they get on?"

"Tolerably well. You have a daughter."

"So I heard. But the child is not mine, you know."

"How can you be sure?" Charles asked.

"Because Lydia and I stopped having relations soon after we were married. Oh, she wanted me badly enough before, but after we were wed, she denied me at the least provocation. I was forced to seek my pleasure elsewhere."

Lizzy's eyes widened and Jane's face flushed with mortification. And me? It was difficult not to laugh. I knew they were both thinking how dreadful it was for their unmarried, innocent sister, that she had to hear about Wickham and Lydia's intimate dealings, as well as his affairs. But it was only what we already knew, or had guessed, and it no longer embarrassed me. Besides, one heard things by the time she had reached two-and-twenty years.

"Even if you and your wife wished to live apart eventually," Mr. Darcy was saying, "it would be no hardship to remain together for a year or more, to quiet the gossip now circulating. It would be cruel to allow things to stand as they do at present."

"Announce to the world I am the child's father," Wickham said, "it makes no difference to me. But I will never live with Lydia again. Indeed, one of the reasons I came here tonight was to tell you of my plans. I depart for the Continent tomorrow morning."

A silence ensued, during which my sisters and I gaped at one another in astonishment.

"I have creditors, you see. More than I could ever hope to settle with, and I do not think debtor's prison would suit me."

"If you think —"

"Never mind, Darcy, even I would not be so crass as to ask you for more cash. But I did hope I might have a loan from Bingley, just enough to help me settle in France."

"If we may be rid of you once and for all, I shall gladly loan — give — you the money," Charles said. "But before you leave here tonight, I would have you sign a document attesting to your paternity of Felicity."

"Gladly."

Fearing the men were about to make their way to Charles's study, Jane, Lizzy, and I began tiptoeing down the hall. But Wickham resumed speaking.

"I regret everything, you know," he said in a voice so low I had to strain to hear him. "I never meant for things with Lydia to end in such a way. She is not the easiest of women to live with."

"We heard you were seeking a divorce," Charles said.

"No longer. Miss Bradford, the lady I left my wife for, has cast me off." A bitter laugh tore out of him. "Her sister, a shrew of the first order, somehow learned about some of my more blatant sins and revealed all."

Jane, Lizzy, and I widened our eyes at one another. We were all thinking the same thing: *Amanda Ashton.*

"Perhaps the fact that you lied about being related to me entered into her decision," Mr. Darcy said. "One can understand why she would not be so taken with a man who has the wealth of a pauper."

Wickham made no response.

"As matters stand," said Charles, "you have hurt the whole Bennet family, our wives included. And this scandal has lessened the chance for Mary to make a decent match."

Jane tugged on my hand, and in silent agreement, the three of us hurried back to the sitting room before we could be caught eavesdropping. As on another night when we had all been uncommonly vexed, Jane poured a glass of sherry for each of us. We sipped in silence, at last hearing the low rumble of male voices, hurried boot steps, and the door opening and closing. In another minute, the men were with us.

We contrived to appear innocent, but they were not fooled. When Charles had poured each of them a finger of brandy, he and Mr. Darcy stood silently watching us. Lizzy sipped her sherry; I had placed mine on a table and now rested with my hands folded in my lap, eyes cast down. But Jane allowed a small giggle to burst out. She tried to pretend it was a cough, but to no avail.

"You are incorrigible," Charles said, staring at us. "Did you truly believe we did not hear you lurking about in the hall, and glimpse you through the crack in the door?"

Mr. Darcy shook his head. "Just like their mother."

He must have known this was the one comment to raise the ire of all three of us. While Jane and I merely glared at him, Elizabeth spoke up. "Husband, you wound us. When Mary told us Wickham was here, we could hardly be expected to sit quietly by! It is our sister the man has treated so ill."

"Apologies, my dear," he said, "but some of that conversation was not fit for a lady's ears. Especially not an unmarried lady." He directed his gaze toward me.

"Sir, everything Wickham discussed we already knew. The chief of it, anyway. And although I appreciate your concern for my tender sensibilities, I am no schoolgirl," I said.

Mr. Darcy snorted, a sound I had never heard from him before.

"What about the document?" Jane asked, easing the tension somewhat.

"I wrote it, Wickham signed it, and Darcy witnessed it," Charles said.

Nobody mentioned the money, or asked how much Charles had given him, although I was sure Jane would pry the information out of him later.

"At least now, if needed, we can quash the doubts about whether or not he is Fee's father," Jane said. "And Amanda Ashton, having succeeded in separating her sister from Wickham, will have no cause to spread her stories around."

"Legally, I believe the document he signed

will hold up," Mr. Darcy said. "Unfortunately, the man has no money and will never be in a position to offer any pecuniary assistance to your sister."

"One never knows about Mr. Wickham," Elizabeth said. "He may turn up wealthy one day. In the event, Lydia will have her proof of his paternity."

Mr. Darcy's eyes sought Elizabeth's. I noticed she would not return his gaze. I had the feeling he would pay for his remark about our being like Mama, even though in her heart she could not believe he truly meant it.

CHAPTER 25

During breakfast the next morning, disaster struck. At least, I would always think of it that way. We all heard a rider approaching, and I couldn't have been the only one wondering what else could befall us.

Simms came to Charles and handed him a white folded paper, discreetly withdrawing.

"What is it?" Jane asked. "I recognize Papa's hand."

So had I. My stomach immediately protested any further ingestion of food, and I grasped Elizabeth's hand.

"Allow me a moment, my dear." Charles studied the missive, then said, "This is bad news indeed. If you're all agreed, I shall read it to you."

We nodded our assent, and he began.

22 August
Longbourn

Dear Charles,

I am sorry to have to impart shocking and disturbing news for all of you. Lydia has run off with her lover. Her note says they are taking ship to America, where no one will know them and they can pose as a married couple.

She begs us not to try to stop her. But for Felicity, I would be inclined to let her go. Lydia's lot here is bleak, since her husband shows no sign of wishing to reunite with her. When news of her situation gets out, as these things always do, it will be the ruin of her and may prevent Mary making a match. Perhaps we should let her go and be done with it. It is said about America, nobody takes much note of one's social standing, nor inquires too closely as to one's identity.

She did not tell us by what route they will travel to the coast, nor from which port they intend to embark. It would be Portsmouth or Bristol.

Since Mary left us for High Tor, Lydia has shown a marked improvement in her care of little Felicity, even seeming to have grown quite attached to the child.

Another reason to let matters lie.

Please inform me immediately as to your opinion on the matter. Mrs. Bennet is inconsolable, as you must imagine, and desires us to go after Lydia and Felicity. I will await your instructions.

Charles frowned. "That's the end of it."

A hush prevailed. Then everybody began to talk at once. Except for me. I had no words, and even if I had, I couldn't have spoken over the ache in my throat. I rose, felt the room swirl about me, and dropped back into my chair.

"We must go after them!" That was Jane.

"I agree with your father," said Mr. Darcy. "This may be the most favorable conclusion to Lydia's problems."

Lizzy glanced at her husband, then at me. "But Felicity . . ." she said, and now everybody's eyes swung toward me. "Oh, Mary, you are so pale!"

"Get her some wine!" someone said.

Jane had grasped my hands and was massaging my fingers furiously. Lizzy ran toward me waving a fan, with Charles close behind brandishing a glass of claret. If the situation hadn't been so exceedingly dreadful, I would have laughed.

I found my voice at last. "No! I don't want

the wine, or anything else, thank you." Lizzy began to wave the fan before my face. "I am not going to swoon," I said. "Do stop." My voice, though shaky, sounded calm and reasonable. "I think we must make an attempt to go after them." Apparently I shocked them all with the expression of my opinion. It seemed a long while before anyone broke the silence.

"Let's go into the drawing room," Jane said. This time I rose more slowly and somehow moved myself from one place to the other. It helped that Mr. Darcy's reassuring hand held my elbow.

As soon as I was seated, Charles came over and knelt beside me. "We must ask ourselves what we would accomplish by tracking them down. What good would come of it?"

"I fancy she took Fee with her because she had no choice. Because I wasn't there. We must make certain she and — blast! Doesn't the man have a name? — her friend truly want Felicity, wish to raise her and be everything a parent should." I rubbed the heel of my hand over my forehead and squeezed my eyes shut momentarily.

Charles remained where he was for a minute longer, pressed my hand gently, then moved to stand by Mr. Darcy.

Jane said, "Mary, there is no way to determine whether someone will make a good job of parenthood. We would only have their word, at best."

"In any case, we can't force Lydia to give up her child," Mr. Darcy said. "Captain Mason may claim paternity, which would complicate matters."

"But we have Wickham's sworn statement that he is the father," I said. "Couldn't we use that in some way?"

"Wickham would not fight for custody of Felicity, Mary. You know he would not," Lizzy said softly.

I couldn't argue with that. So Captain Mason was the name of Lydia's friend. Mr. Darcy would know, since he had met with the man when he was in Newcastle trying to locate Wickham. "I cannot disagree with what you are saying." I swept my eyes over all of them. "And yet I can't help believing one of us should look Lydia in the eye and demand to know if this is what she truly desires. We must convince her nobody would judge her harshly if she decided to leave Fee with us."

"Mary has a point," Elizabeth said. "Lydia may be having second thoughts, especially if the captain isn't particularly interested in raising a child. We should let her know we're willing to keep Felicity with us."

"Was there no warning, nothing in Lydia's behavior that would have made you suspicious, Mary?" asked Mr. Darcy.

"I was aware she'd had letters — she even told me to mind my own business when I inquired about one. But nothing led me to suspect she was planning something like this." *But it should have.* I remembered the letter she'd hidden in the folds of her dress in the breakfast room, and the one she'd stuffed inside the pages of *The Lady's Magazine* when I entered her chamber. And a few other letters. I should have confronted her, demanded she reveal who the sender was. Papa knew, too, but chose to do nothing, despite his threats to Lydia that he would confiscate further communication from the man. We had both been remiss in not pursuing the matter.

Charles and Mr. Darcy spoke in muted tones to each other for a few minutes while Jane, Lizzy, and I pondered the circumstances.

"How could she?" asked Jane. "After all her other misdeeds . . ."

"I don't blame her for wanting to escape her situation," I said. My sisters looked at me in surprise. "What hope had she for the future, after all? Exile from polite society, living at Longbourn until Papa dies. And then what? That kind of life would not suit Lydia. No, I don't blame her for wanting something more. But I cannot forgive her for taking Felicity with her."

Elizabeth lifted a brow at me.

"I know, you warned me something like this could happen. Your prescience is impressive, Lizzy, but hardly comforting."

"Oh, dearest, forgive me," she said, immediately contrite. "Perhaps we should look on the good side. Papa mentioned Lydia had shown a much greater interest in Felicity after you left."

"How could she have changed so radically in only a month?" I asked, skeptical.

"Ladies, we have a plan," Charles said, interrupting our discussion. "Darcy and I will take the post road to Bristol. We'll enlist Walsh and Carstairs to ride to Portsmouth. If we set out immediately, we have a fair chance of catching up with them before their departure for America."

"Wait," I said. "Each of you should ride with one of the other gentlemen. Someone who knows Lydia well must be the one to confront her. She would be much less inclined to hand Felicity over to two men she barely knows."

"I agree," Lizzy said.

Mr. Darcy nodded. "You're right. And we must make haste. If we ride through the night, we can make up a good deal of time. With the baby, Lydia and Captain Mason will be forced to stop."

"Are you sure Henry and Andrew will agree to this plan?" asked Jane.

"I'm sure of Henry," Charles said. "He'll do whatever he can with no questions asked, as I would for him. Andrew, because of his duties as vicar, may not be able to. If that is the case, either Darcy or I will ride alone."

Jane said she would write to Papa and inform him of our decision. In due course, the men bade us good-bye and set off on their journey. Since I knew they were acting only for my sake, and Felicity's, I thanked both my brothers most heartily for the loving concern which had guided their decision.

"I think I should return to Longbourn," I told Jane and Elizabeth the next morning. We were taking a turn in the shrubbery walk. Anything to distract ourselves.

"Whatever for?" Jane asked. "Mama at her worst, Kitty preoccupied with planning her nuptials. I think you would run mad!"

"Because if Charles and Mr. Darcy are able to persuade Lydia to give up Felicity, wouldn't they take her to Longbourn? Surely they wouldn't make the long journey all the way here with the baby?"

"I don't believe they know what they will do. Felicity is not yet weaned, and that could present a problem," Jane said.

Lizzy's brows drew together. "There are feeding bottles. On occasion, I've seen them used when the mother has died and there is no one to put the babe to breast. But I've no idea where they would get one."

"We should have talked about all of this before they left!" I said.

"Mary, I beg you not to place too much hope in Felicity's return," Jane said, gently squeezing my arm. "However, if Lydia does give her up, they will find a way to feed her."

I breathed out a long exhalation. "I suppose so."

When we returned to the house, we had a letter from Kitty.

23 August
Longbourn

Dear Sisters,

As I am certain you must be curious about what has transpired, I am writing to tell you what little I know. I'm afraid it is not much more than Papa has already told you.

Lydia made her escape in the middle of the night, so quietly as not to have awakened anybody. We found her note late the next morning, when by eleven of the clock she had not appeared for breakfast and we had heard not a peep from Felicity.

The note contained nothing more than Papa has already imparted. It was quite serious in its tone; I would go so far as to say it was commanding. None of us here had any inkling of what she had planned, although Papa suspected she'd received some letters from the man with whom she had her liaison.

Mary, if it is of any comfort to you, Lydia, in the weeks since you left, seemed to fill her role as Fee's mother with growing confidence and even satisfaction. Lydia and Mama spent many afternoons playing with her, laying her on the floor with some toys, and watching her with squeals of delight until she would grow sleepy.

Mama is bereft. She refuses to come out of her chamber. Even Lady Lucas and Aunt Philips cannot persuade her. Mary, she wishes you to return to Longbourn, but my advice is to prolong your visit to High Tor as long as possible. You all may be wondering what we are telling people. Unbelievable as it seems, we are telling the truth, for the most part. Laying the blame at Wickham's door perhaps a bit more than is strictly fair, but since he has not claimed the child nor made any attempt to see Lydia and the baby, I don't think it will matter. We are saying Lydia and Felicity have gone to America with a friend. People will think what they like; there is little we can do.

As for me, I miss all of you exceedingly. Especially a certain gentleman whose warm smile and laugh won my heart! The seamstress in Meryton is making my bride clothes, and I'm working mainly on embroidery of handkerchiefs, pillowcases, and the like. I am grateful I have only a month left before my wedding, as I do not know how much longer I can abide my mother's complaints and Papa's silent retreats to his library.

Yours,
Kitty

Jane looked at us, eyes sparkling. "That is undoubtedly the longest letter Kitty has ever written to any of us!"

Elizabeth laughed. "Yes, and she's taking this all in her stride. They do not know about Wickham. We should inform them."

Their words flowed around me, but I wasn't listening. I snatched the letter from Jane's hand and reread it. Tears stung my eyes because of all the things I'd missed. I'd chosen to come here, to High Tor, in the unfounded hope of making Henry Walsh love me. It should have been me sitting on the floor playing with Felicity. Not Lydia. Not Mama and Kitty. I was more her mother than anybody else. I brushed away the tears trickling down my cheeks. It wouldn't do for Jane and Lizzy to see me crying.

And now that Henry would be further exposed to Lydia's indiscretions, I had not the smallest hope of his affection. Indeed, since the day of the Ashtons' visit, when Charles had told him everything, he'd kept his distance. Even though he had his own somewhat tarnished history, it was one thing for a man to father illegitimate offspring, quite another for a woman to commit adultery.

Lydia's disgrace would have its most direct effect on me. I would be left with nothing. Kitty had mere weeks left at Longbourn, and Lydia had managed to flee as well. As for me, I would soon be returning home, taking up my role as spinster daughter caring for her aging parents, and doing her duty toward her sisters and their families whenever called upon.

I excused myself to wallow in hopelessness. Self-pity is a shameful thing.

CHAPTER 26

Later in the day I paced along the avenue alone. I had tried to take a nap, as everybody else was doing, but something had been plaguing me. Now that I was up and moving about, it began to take shape in my mind. If I had any hope of getting Felicity back, *I* must be the one to confront Lydia. *It had to be me.* Only I, who truly cared for Fee, could do so and expect to sway my headstrong sister. Could she deny me Felicity, when she must have known in her heart I'd been more of a mother to the child than she ever had?

I had to inform my sisters right away and beg Jane to let me use the chaise. Though I was at a disadvantage in making such a late start, surely a baby would have slowed the progress of the errant couple. Whether to set out for Bristol or Portsmouth I could not answer on my own. My sisters would have to help me decide. I was sure they would oppose my plan. Best to rouse them immediately and have done with the arguments.

I asked their maids to wake them, and although they were none too happy about it, they agreed to do so. "Say I have an urgent need to talk with them," I said as they hurried off. When Jane and Lizzy swept into the sitting room wearing dressing gowns and in dishabille, I realized I'd frightened them. They both thought I had bad news.

"What is it?" Jane asked, a worried look marring her face as she hurried in.

I'd asked for tea, and now filled my sisters' cups while I gathered my thoughts.

"Forgive me, dear sisters," I began. "I own I have no news. Indeed, what I have to say will startle you, and in all likelihood make you angry."

"You wish to go after Lydia," Elizabeth said in a calm voice.

"What?" I said, blinking. "How did you —"

"Frankly, Mary," she said, "I was surprised you did not insist upon it yesterday."

"Jane? Did you guess, too?"

"I confess the thought crossed my mind earlier, but when you didn't mention it, I forgot about the idea."

I leaned across the table. "I beg you, Jane, to allow me to use the chaise. I must be the one to deal with Lydia. I'm the only person who could make her see reason. When it comes to Felicity, that is."

Lizzy sipped her tea, took a bite of blackberry tart, and rubbed a few crumbs off her hands. "Have you considered the difficulties of such a journey? To begin, which way will you go? They have, now, a two-day advantage. I doubt you would reach them in time."

The fact that she did not oppose it outright gave me hope.

"Mary, dearest, I do not think this is a good idea at all," Jane said. "To set out by yourself, not even sure which way to travel. And knowing they may already have set sail before you could catch up to them. It seems a fool's errand to me."

"I could go with her," Elizabeth said.

"Lizzy! The children —"

"They have nursemaids, Jane, and you would remain here to ensure their well-being. I believe Mary is right. If Lydia is to be persuaded, it's she who is best qualified for the job."

Reaching for my hands, Jane said, "*If*. If she is to be persuaded. We all know what a willful, selfish creature she is! Are you prepared for the worst outcome, Mary? I fear you are deluding yourself."

She had such sadness in her eyes, I wanted to weep. Maybe I *was* deluding myself. "I have to try, Jane. Don't you see?"

"Jane, you are overruled," Elizabeth said. "We can take our chaise and leave in the morning."

"Oh, thank you, Lizzy! Shall it be Bristol or Portsmouth?"

"Bristol," she said without hesitation. "Fitzwilliam thought it the more likely route, and I agree. Portsmouth is closer, but if Lydia and the captain had wanted to mislead us, it would make more sense to go to Bristol."

Acknowledging defeat, Jane said, "I'll speak to Cook about food for your journey."

"And I'll talk to our driver and footmen," Lizzy said. "We shall be on the road at dawn."

I hugged them both and hurried to my chamber to pack my things.

"How many days, Donald?" I asked the Darcys' coachman before we set out.

"Two, and half of another, ma'am. Longest day today."

I nodded and cursed under my breath. *Blast! Three days.* We would be lucky to wave farewell to Lydia and Felicity as their ship sailed away at this rate. I tamped down my impatience, as there was absolutely nothing to be done about the distance.

We spent the first night at a coaching inn near Worcester. It was nothing fancy, yet provided clean bed linens and decent food, both welcome after rattling around in the Darcy conveyance all day. Not that it wasn't the epitome of such vehicles, fitted up with velvet squabs and exceedingly well sprung. After an early breakfast, we were on the road again.

Elizabeth and I talked of everything except the reason for our journey. Kitty's wedding, the relative merits of village versus city life, her horse-riding lessons, dealing with Mama during a crisis. And then she surprised me by announcing she was again with child.

"Oh, Lizzy, that's wonderful news. And I've dragged you off on this arduous journey. Are you feeling well?"

She smiled. "Yes, never better. Remember, it was Jane who was sick during much of her pregnancy, not I. And this time seems much the same. You're the first to know, Mary, except for Fitzwilliam, of course."

"Jane would never have allowed you to come if she'd known," I said, laughing.

"No, indeed. My husband may not be

pleased, either, but he will understand." She paused to plump up the cushion at her back. "How are you feeling about this situation? Are you content with the decision to pursue the matter yourself?"

"I am. I only wish I were more certain of the outcome."

"One never knows with Lydia. She could be eager to be rid of her daughter, or —"

"She may have taken a liking to her. I've never known a sweeter baby, Lizzy, nor one easier to love. Fanny, Jane, and David excepted, of course."

"Would it be so bad if she did love Felicity and wanted to raise her? You will marry someday and have your own children, you know."

I snorted. "I collect you're referring to Mr. Walsh? I've no hope of that at present. As to the other matter, if I could only believe Lydia truly loved Fee, I could accept parting from her forever. Though it would not be easy, I know."

On the second day we stopped early, which was good planning on Donald's part. It gave us a chance to rest before undertaking the remaining distance to Bristol the next morning. Donald thought if we left early, we would arrive by afternoon. In the morning, anticipation roiled in my belly. I couldn't eat, could barely swallow a few sips of tea. I waited impatiently while Elizabeth devoured eggs, bacon, toast, and fruit compote, washed down with two cups of chocolate.

Once we were under way, I wondered what would come next. Would we run into our quarry along the road? Or would we be forced to journey into Bristol to find them? What about Henry and Mr. Darcy? Wherever Lydia, Fee, and Captain Mason were, we were certain to find them as well.

I was apprehensive about entering Bristol. Mr. Darcy owned a town home in London, and he and Elizabeth took up residence there during part of the season each year. But she was the only one of us to have visited a large city. I knew Bristol was a bustling port and thus home to all manner of people, including unsavory types who loitered around the quay. Thieves, prostitutes, and con men. It was known, though nobody talked of it, that at one time Bristol had profited greatly from the slave trade with the Americas. Indeed, it had comprised the major part of their shipping industry. Although this was no longer the case, the possibility of Felicity ending up on such a ship didn't bear thinking about.

The day dragged on, and after a stop for

refreshments, the driver told us we would soon see the outskirts of the city. I watched out the window, and after an hour or so spotted tall church spires and the towers of what must have been the Bristol Cathedral. Not knowing how else to proceed, we instructed the coachman to take us straight to Bristol Harbour. He was disinclined to do so.

"Ma'am, Mr. Darcy will have my hide if I take you anywhere near there. Let me go on my own, ask around, and come back and tell you what I found out. You can wait at an inn, have a nice cup of tea." He gazed imploringly at us. He was right about his master, who probably would have his hide, or at least relieve him of his duties.

Lizzy and I looked at each other, neither of us knowing what to do. I knew she hesitated only on my account. "I think it's a good idea," I said. "Donald is bound to have more success than we ever could, two ladies completely out of their customary milieu." My sister sighed with relief.

After negotiating narrow streets, we arrived at a bridge swarming with people, animals, and all manner of vehicles. Wagons, sledges, drays, and carts, all jostling for position. Donald judged it unsafe to drive over. He left one footman with the carriage, while he and a second footman carried our bags and delivered us to a reputable-looking inn. He saw us installed in a private parlor before taking his leave. The innkeeper brought us cold meat, bread, and ale. We hadn't taken but a few bites when the door burst open and Mr. Darcy and Henry Walsh rushed in.

"Fitzwilliam!" Lizzy said.

He strode forward and clasped Elizabeth to his chest. "Whatever possessed you to come to Bristol? It's not a safe place for you." I'd never seen Mr. Darcy display such emotion toward Lizzy in public. Feeling my face flush, I turned toward Henry and held out my hand in greeting.

"I am only surprised we did not see you sooner," he said, smiling and shaking hands with me.

"How did you find us?"

"We ran smack into Darcy's coachman walking down the street. He told us where you were."

"I suppose I have you to thank, Mary, for dragging my wife here," Mr. Darcy said. He stepped away from Elizabeth and swiveled in my direction, watching me coldly.

I grimaced but stood my ground. "Yes and no. When I said I was determined to find Lydia, Elizabeth insisted she would accompany me. She was most adamant."

"Yes, I'm sure she was. We will have a talk about that," he said.

"Please, let's all be seated," Lizzy said, obviously wishing to deflect some of her husband's displeasure.

Mr. Walsh called for the innkeeper to bring more food and ale. While we waited, they told us what they'd found out so far.

"Unfortunately, we haven't tracked them down," Mr. Darcy said. "But we have found which ships will be sailing in the coming days. If Bristol was their destination, they're bound to have booked passage on one of them."

Henry continued the story. "Although they would not allow us to see the manifests, we asked around the docks. No one remembered anybody in the last several days who fit their description."

"Did you ask them to check for specific names on the manifest? For the upcoming crossings?"

"Of course," Mr. Darcy said. "They refused to do it." He paused in his recitation of the tale while a serving girl placed more food on the table. The two men filled their plates, and my brother-in-law again took up the story.

"I even offered money at one of the offices, but the clerk took offense. We had planned to spend the remainder of the day checking around at some of the inns," Mr. Darcy said. He turned toward Elizabeth. "But you, wife, and your sister, will be resting while Walsh and I take on that task."

"Oh, no," Lizzy said. "I didn't come all this way to be relegated to a room in an inn while you men do the investigating. Mary and I shall accompany you."

"Elizabeth . . ." His voice sounded ominous.

"We've been sitting in a coach for three days! I've done nothing *but* rest. Please, Fitzwilliam. I am not at all tired."

Mr. Darcy sighed, glared at all of us, but finally agreed.

"What if we don't find them at one of the inns?" I asked.

"Then I'm afraid our only hope is to lie in wait for them and accost them when they embark. Or pray that Charles has found them in Portsmouth."

It was decided we would split up. Henry and I would take charge of the two streets closest to the quay, while Lizzy and Mr. Darcy would search two blocks up. Limiting ourselves to the part of town nearest the port would be the most likely way to corner our fugitives.

Surprised there was no objection to my going off unchaperoned with Mr. Walsh, I leaped to my feet as soon as we'd finished our meal, before Mr. Darcy or Elizabeth could change their mind. "I'm ready. Like Lizzy, I am exceedingly bored with inaction. Mr. Walsh?" We had taken rooms for the night at the inn and agreed to meet there later to share any news.

Henry and I set off down the street, having decided to walk to the far end and work our way back. Unsettled by the hordes streaming along on all sides, I clung to his arm. What a far cry from Longbourn or Meryton. I didn't think this suited me, all these people massed together, pushing rudely past, and shoving anybody aside who did not give way.

A large number of inns awaited us, but we only stopped to inquire at those we thought would be acceptable to a couple with a child. After the sixth time an innkeeper swore he did not recognize the small family by name or description, I felt defeated. "I fear they've already sailed," I said to Mr. Walsh on the way out the door.

"Darcy and I must have arrived right on their heels," he said. "I can hardly believe we could have missed them, if they came here and not to Portsmouth. Don't forget, we have another street to investigate, as well as a few more establishments on this one."

"I can see you're an optimist, and I am quite the opposite."

"Come, there's a small park across the street. Let's rest for a moment." When there was an opening in the traffic, we rushed across and seated ourselves on a wooden bench with a view of the harbor. I was shocked to see that the ships, of which there were too many to count, rested on mud flats, their sails furled.

"I don't understand," I said, looking at Henry.

He laughed. "You mean, where is the water?"

"Well . . . yes."

"The quay is on the Avon River, and when the tide is out, the ships must wait. Sometimes for days." He lifted a brow at me. "Another reason to be optimistic."

"My goodness, I had no idea."

A tall crane was in operation, unloading cargo from some of the ships onto a wharf. Stout-looking men then moved it onto wagons or one of the many other vehicles we'd noticed on our way into the city. It was an impressive sight, and looked like a hard day's work. We watched in silence for a while. Before he spoke, I felt Henry's eyes studying me.

"I am sorry for all this," he said. "The thought of parting with Felicity must grieve you."

I turned to meet his gaze. "Yes. It has been difficult to remain hopeful." Tears pricked my eyes and my throat thickened. *Don't weep. You'll never stop, and what will he think of you then?*

Unexpectedly, a screechlike laugh rent the air. A very familiar laugh. I jumped up and whirled around, craning my neck. It only took a moment to spot Lydia and her Captain Mason, just entering the park. He was holding Fee.

Instead of waiting for their approach, which would have been a more calm and measured reaction, I rushed to them. "Lydia! We have been searching all over for you!" Perhaps not the ideal greeting in the circumstance.

She looked stunned, and for an instant I thought she might bolt. She remained standing just where she was, however, looking resolute. I walked over to her, and while I longed to reach out for Felicity, I knew that would not sit well with Lydia. I tried to look as unthreatening as possible.

"Oh, lud. I might have known. Didn't

Papa tell you I asked not to be followed?"

I ignored the question. "Will you introduce us to your friend?"

She seemed rattled by my request. "Oh, very well. This is Captain Robert Mason. Robert, this is my sister Mary and Mr. Henry Walsh." The captain bowed to me and shook hands with Henry, smiling most cordially.

"Thank you for taking such good care of my sister and niece, sir," I said. I looked at Fee. It was difficult to tell if she recognized me or not. She waved one arm up and down excitedly, while the other wrapped around Captain Mason's neck. Her dark hair had grown longer, curling around her face.

"My pleasure, ma'am."

I turned back to Lydia. "We did not come to try to stop you. Only to ascertain whether or not you and Captain Mason truly wanted Felicity with you."

Anger glinted in Lydia's eyes, and she strode over to the bench. "Robert, bring Felicity to me," she said, sitting down. He did as she asked, and Henry and I walked over, too.

He leaned down and whispered to me. "I am here if you need me. Otherwise I shall leave things to you." I nodded and whispered my thanks.

Lydia took the child onto her lap. "Today she is five months old! I'd wager you forgot, Mary. Doesn't she look well?"

I winced, because indeed I had not remembered Fee's birthday. I couldn't believe how she'd changed in a mere month. Upon closer scrutiny, I could see she'd grown chubbier, and a few milk teeth had sprouted on the bottom. I had to admit she looked contented and well cared for.

"Do you think me an unfit mother, Mary? And you have come to rescue Felicity?"

"Of course not —"

Lydia's face took on an indignant expression. "From the very first, you wanted her for your own. You wanted to be her mother, because you knew you would never marry and have a child."

That was too close to the truth for me to deny outright. "I only wanted to help you care for Felicity. You will recall having some difficulties adjusting to motherhood."

"You're right, I did have trouble at first. But when I was finally ready to be a mother, you wouldn't let me. You took every opportunity to shove me aside so you could change her, dress her, play with her. Even Mama noticed."

"What Mama noticed was that you had formed no attachment to your child."

"That's not what she told me after you left for High Tor. She said if you hadn't been so possessive and interfering, I would have been a proper mother to Fee a lot sooner."

I was certain Lydia was exaggerating. However, I wouldn't put it past my mother to have said something of that nature, even though she had expressed the opposite view to me. I felt desperation gripping me, but I knew I must control myself. "Just tell me one thing, Lydia. Do you love Fee? Swear to me that you love her, and I will acknowledge you've changed and are ready to be a good mother to her."

"I don't have to swear anything to you," Lydia said. "But if it makes you feel better, I do love her with all my heart, don't I, poppet?" She plopped a kiss on Fee's cheek. "And so does the captain."

I glanced at him. "Is that true, sir?"

"I've grown to care for her, yes." He was an ordinary-looking man, lacking the dark good looks of Wickham, and perhaps the sophistication. But his expression seemed sincere, and despite everything, I believed him.

It was over. My hopes of reclaiming Felicity were dashed. I had no choice but to believe my sister, and there was an honesty about Captain Mason that made me trust him. I gave a brusque nod. "I didn't come here to demand you give up your daughter, only to let you know we were prepared to raise her if you felt unable to do so."

"What do you mean by 'we'? You and Mr. Walsh?"

Heat flooded my face and neck, and I shook my head vehemently. "No, of course not. The family. Jane and Lizzy and I."

"Good God, are they all here, too?"

"Only Elizabeth and Mr. Darcy. They're looking for you as well."

"Well, now you've found us, and you know the truth. Let's have dinner together tonight! Lud, this is all a monstrous good joke! I can't wait to see the look on Lizzy's face."

Determined to remain civil, I said, "I'm sure she'll want to see you before you set sail. We're at the Twin Anchors, just up the street from here."

"I know where it is," said the captain.

"We shall see you there tonight, then." I barely got the words out, my mind jumping ahead to the nightmarish experience of sharing a meal with Lydia and her captain. And with Felicity close by, but entirely out of my reach.

CHAPTER 27

When Lydia and her little family arrived at the inn, Lizzy at once spirited our sister away while Mr. Darcy and Mr. Walsh took Captain Mason in hand. Lydia had passed the baby to me after Elizabeth hugged and kissed the niece she'd never met, and I held her in my lap to play pat-a-cake and peeka-boo. Although Fee seemed perfectly happy with me, there was nothing in her behavior to suggest she remembered me. Every so often, I glanced toward my sisters. Lydia's countenance had grown flushed, and she seemed agitated. Lizzy's face bore a stern expression, and her hand gripped Lydia's arm firmly. I had no doubt she was telling her how I had suffered and demanding she behave with decorum.

On the whole, she did. Such was the state of my emotions, I took no note of what she said, but only wished to observe her with Felicity, to try to judge if she truly had developed those motherly qualities which she previously had lacked. As the evening wore on, however, Lydia couldn't resist a few unkind remarks. "Mary is not in spirits," she said, and later, "I declare, Mary, you are duller than usual tonight." To my astonishment, I heard Captain Mason say softly, "Lydia, that is unkind." She quickly lowered her head, so I couldn't see her expression.

With that, Mr. Darcy scooted his chair back and rose. "It has been a long and trying day, especially for Elizabeth and Mary. Perhaps it is time to say good-bye."

Lizzy was staring pointedly at Lydia, whose face bore a petulant look. "May I have a private word with you, Mary?" she asked after a moment.

Startled, I nodded my assent and we moved to one corner of the room. Mr. Darcy and Henry had engaged Captain Mason in conversation, while Lizzy entertained Fee. I waited for Lydia to speak.

She wouldn't look at me. Her words were rushed and her color heightened. "I only wanted to say thank you, Mary, for all you did for me and Felicity. Even though I think it was horrid bad of you to try to take her away from me, I know I could never have managed without your help. So, I am grateful to you for it."

"Taking care of Fee was a privilege." I felt myself choking up but blinked back the tears. "She's a wonderful child, and I shall miss her very much." I was strongly tempted to dole out some advice regarding Felicity's care but concluded Lydia now knew more about that than I. "I wish you happy in your new life in America. You will write, of course." She kissed my cheek and, without giving me a chance to do likewise, scurried back to the others.

Lydia made as if to take Fee from Elizabeth, but before she could do so, I asked, "May I hold her a moment, just to say good-bye?" Lydia's lips thinned, but she stepped aside so I could take the baby from Lizzy's outstretched arms. I walked toward the far end of the room, rubbing my cheek against her dark curls.

I was not Felicity's mother, and yet my whole being cried out that I was. That it was not right for Lydia to separate me from her. When I had arrived at Longbourn after Fee's birth, broken and dispirited, it was Fee who made me whole again. She who, by the mere fact of her existence, showed me how I might get on with my life. Felicity had proved to me that no matter how low one's spirits may sink, life holds something in safekeeping to present at the most fortuitous moment. She had filled the emptiness in me with her innocent and trusting love, and I prayed I had given her that gift in return. I would give her up to Lydia, as indeed I must, but I would hold her in my heart forever.

Tears streamed down my face, dripping onto the bodice of my gown. I felt a gentle arm slide around my shoulders, and Lizzy was there, comforting me, her voice sounding a little wobbly. "Come, dearest, it is time to let go. Dry your tears." She blotted my face with a handkerchief.

I inhaled an audible breath and, with a supreme effort of will, regained my composure. I could not allow Lydia to see my anguish, the true depth of my sorrow. She was taking Fee to America, and there was nothing I could do but accept it. "I'm ready," I said, and placed Fee in Lizzy's arms.

Within moments they were gone. And there we sat, Elizabeth, Mr. Darcy, Henry, and I, in the private dining parlor of the Twin Anchors, drained and silent. The clatter of plates, glasses, and serving dishes being cleared by the servants barely penetrated my fog. Certain the others were worried about me, concerned for my feelings, I thought perhaps I should be the one to speak first.

I glanced up, catching Elizabeth's eyes. "It's true, what Papa and Kitty said about Lydia. She has settled into motherhood, and in a most natural way. She can even eat while Fee bounces about on her lap or falls asleep on her shoulder! Instead of depending on someone else to see to her daughter's needs, she takes care of them herself. One can tell Felicity trusts her, loves her." A throbbing ache in my throat stopped me for a moment. "Lydia must be given credit for making such strides." I rose and walked over to the windows, staring into darkness. I wanted to hide the pain I knew must have shown in my eyes.

"I suppose we must give credit where it is due," Elizabeth said. "She is a different person with Felicity than what Jane had described. But overall, Lydia's behavior, her manners, continues to be wanting."

"I thought her not as uncontrolled in her behavior as in the past," Mr. Darcy said.

"Perhaps the influence of Captain Mason had something to do with that," I said, returning to the table.

Henry, who had remained quiet during this exchange, now said, "She is so unlike the rest of you." He spoke so softly, he almost seemed to be talking to himself.

Then he looked at us squarely. "My pardon, but I can hardly credit that she is from the same family."

Mr. Darcy chuckled, but Elizabeth and I glanced at each other, unable to hide our chagrin.

"Forgive me," Henry said when he noticed our unease. "I should not have spoken."

"Please, say no more. We understand." I turned to Elizabeth. "If you wouldn't mind telling me, Lizzy, I should like to know what was said between you and Lydia."

"Oh, Mary, are you sure? She made some quite unjust accusations against you."

"I expect I heard some of them already, when we met them in the park, so it should not be too shocking."

"Mary has a right to know," Mr. Darcy said, a gentle prompt to his wife.

"The chief of it was that you had tried to make yourself into Felicity's mother, pushing Lydia aside whenever you could, never allowing her to perform any care of the baby except feedings."

She paused, no doubt considering if I could bear hearing the rest.

"Go on."

"When I reminded her of her seeming indifference to the child, she agreed it was true at first, but said that long after she had gotten over it, you continued in the same manner."

"That is nearly word for word what she said to me in the park," I said, looking toward Henry, who nodded his agreement. I supposed I needed not own to the truth. I could let them believe I was the injured party, completely innocent of the charges laid against me by Lydia. Instead, I shocked them all by saying, "There are some parts of her account with which I cannot take exception."

Elizabeth furrowed her brows. "But Mary —"

I held up a staying hand. "Hear me out. I must make a clean breast of it." Now they were all silent attention, three sets of eyes fixed on me. "As you know, Lydia did not take easily to motherhood." I laughed a little at the memory. "When I look back, I wonder how we survived those first few months, with Lydia so completely withdrawn and myself so ignorant. If Jane had not been there for the first weeks, I don't know how we would have managed.

"For the longest time, I did everything in my power to force Lydia to be a mother to Fee, but nothing worked. In the end, it was simpler to do everything myself. After a time, I began to believe I *was* her rightful mother. When at last Lydia started to show an interest in Felicity, I was immediately resentful and jealous. I wasn't proud of those feelings but couldn't seem to overcome them."

"That was only natural —" my sister broke in.

"Let me finish, Lizzy." Thank God nobody knew I'd put the baby to my breast. That was surely *not* natural, and I'd never tell another living soul. I hesitated about saying what I had to say next with Henry present, but there was really no point in hiding anything else from him. "At the time, I was desperate for love, and Felicity loved me! We loved each other." I glanced up, catching Lizzy's eyes. They shone with tears.

"I harbored dreams of raising her myself. I'm afraid I did not encourage Lydia's efforts, so she reverted back to her coldness toward Felicity. I blame myself for that."

"Given the situation, I believe you take too much blame upon yourself, Mary," Elizabeth said.

"Perhaps. In all fairness, however, I was at least partly to blame for Lydia's poor mothering and her disinterest in Felicity. The fact that she has grown to love her daughter, and taken full responsibility for her care, proves my point. She may have done so sooner if not for me."

An awkward silence prevailed. I risked a quick glance at Henry. He was looking back at me with eyes full of sadness and something more. Pity, I thought. That was probably the only emotion he felt toward me now, or was ever likely to in the future.

"I know what I did was wrong, and I apologize to all of you for allowing you to think the fault was Lydia's alone. At the time I deceived myself into believing I was the better person to be a mother to Felicity." I dipped my head, unable to look at any of them directly. It was not an easy thing to admit one's failings to others, especially those so well loved. Looking up, I said, "It is only since this latest crisis that I've had time to reflect upon my actions, and I now see I was wrong. Lydia seems to love Fee, and that is a great comfort to me."

"I think we all believed her sincere in that regard," Mr. Darcy said.

"Will you be all right, Mary?" Elizabeth asked.

"She will in time," Henry Walsh said, quite unexpectedly, with the same blend of sorrow and pity in his gaze, evoking in me the feeling that he understood better than anyone else what I was suffering. He'd had to endure long separations from Amelia, after all. He was the only one present who knew what that was like.

My lower lip trembled. I glanced at him before I answered. "Yes, in time I will be all right. And it is one thing I have a great deal of." I rose. "If you will excuse me, I must retire before I collapse." I managed a smile, to let them know I was joking.

Elizabeth jumped up. "I'll help you prepare for bed."

"Thank you, but no. I'm quite all right on my own."

I made my way out of the now-suffocating parlor and began climbing the steps to my chamber. I could hear the others speaking in low voices. At least they weren't talking about me. Mr. Darcy said, "We must get word to Bingley."

"Jane too," Lizzy said. "And Papa."

After that, they were out of earshot. When I finally crawled into bed, one thought, one horrifying truth, filled my mind.

I would never see Felicity again.

On the way home, Elizabeth and I rode in the chaise, while the men, who had traveled to Bristol on horseback, rode alongside. After an hour or so of desultory conversation, Lizzy nodded off. In her condition, she was probably exhausted. She and Mr.

Darcy had been so kind during this ordeal. How could I ever repay them?

I thought of a line from *Macbeth,* "Sleep that knits up the raveled sleeve of care," and acknowledged the truth of it. I didn't feel as sad as I had expected. I had slept well and deeply. Although I knew the pain of losing Felicity would always be with me, I was not torn asunder by it. With time, as Henry had pointed out, I would be all right.

And what was I to do with my time? That was a conundrum. Even worse than losing Fee was the prospect of returning to Longbourn and living out my life with my parents, with periodic visits to my married sisters to help at births, nurse the sick, and stay with the children while their parents journeyed to interesting places. It wasn't that I didn't love my sisters and their husbands and children. It was simply that I wanted more from my life. If I was not to be married and have a family of my own, what else could I do? I felt very keenly the desire to earn some money of my own, to not be dependent on my father for the remainder of his life, and my sisters after he was gone.

Opportunities of employment for genteel women were extremely limited. Companion to elderly widows, or to young girls who, for a variety of reasons, needed a chaperone. Teacher at a private girls' school, or governess in someone's home. Granted, there were some women in trade — dressmakers, milliners, shopkeepers — but I had no skills for anything in that realm, never mind the disgrace my family would feel.

In a school, I could get by with teaching only the subjects in which I was well versed, such as literature and music. None of us had ever learned to draw, nor did I know French or Latin. This would be a drawback for a governess position, although in well-heeled families, masters often provided tutoring to supplement what the governess taught.

How did one go about finding such a position? The only way open to me was to approach my aunt Gardiner. She and my uncle had young children, and no doubt counted other families with children of a similar age among their friends. I was sure my aunt would be sympathetic to my plight and willing to advise me. Her own children had a governess, but I recollected her speaking of sending her eldest daughter to a school one day.

My family would be the biggest obstacle, possibly insurmountable. If my mother and father raised strong objections, my aunt might feel it would be ill advised to help me. And I wasn't sure what Jane, Elizabeth, and Kitty would think. Would it be embarrassing for them to have a sister employed as a governess? I sighed. In all likelihood, it would. Jane and Lizzy would probably wish me to come and live with one of them and tutor their children. Considering the generosity of Charles and Mr. Darcy, they would most likely insist on paying me, but I could never accept their money.

Elizabeth finally stirred, and after a minute or so came fully awake. "Oh, my shoulders and neck!" she moaned. "They are so stiff."

I knelt on the seat beside her and gently worked my hands into the flesh of the affected areas. "That feels wonderful, Mary! How long was I asleep?"

"A few hours, no more," I said, giving her a final pat.

"I expect we will try to make it to Gloucester tonight."

"Yes," I said. "But we're slowing now. It seems too soon for a change of horses, though. I hope nothing is wrong."

We pulled into the yard of a coaching inn, and when I peeked out the window, I saw the men dismounting. Mr. Darcy came over and lowered the steps for us. "I thought you might need to stop, my dear," he said to

Lizzy, who laughed. She took his arm and they disappeared inside. When Henry offered me his arm, I slid my hand into the crook of his elbow. Once inside, we asked for the private parlor and made our way to the table, situated before a welcoming fire. The innkeeper's wife brought wine, cheese, and rolls. Until that moment, I hadn't felt hungry, but the sight of the food whetted my appetite. I reached for a roll and bit into it hungrily.

"How do you feel today?" Henry asked me.

I dropped the roll like a hot coal. He thought I should feel worse, perhaps. Not like eating. But in truth, I'd eaten nothing for dinner last night, and very little for breakfast. I was ravenous. "I feel better than I expected to," I admitted. "There's an empty place here," I said, pressing my hand against my chest, "but that may be from hunger. I've hardly eaten the past few days."

"You're looking far better today. Last night you looked terribly wan and disheartened, and there was nothing to be done for it."

I was suddenly struck by his kindness in helping us find Lydia and Felicity. Although I doubted he would deny Charles any good turn, this went beyond the scope of the usual favors one asked of a friend. In some small measure, I suspected he had done it for me as well.

"Please allow me to tell you now how much I appreciate all you've done, Mr. Walsh. Journeying so far for what must have seemed like a useless endeavor. It's the nicest gesture anybody has ever made on my behalf."

He watched me intently. "I know too well what it means to be separated from a child one loves so dearly."

I struggled to gain control of my emotions, and he paused a moment as if sensing what a fragile state I was in. When he did speak, he said something entirely unexpected.

"Could you not bring yourself to call me Henry? We have been friends many months now."

I laughed a little, nodding my assent. "Henry. You were aware of how things stood when you were at Longbourn."

"I couldn't help observing Lydia's disinterest in her child. It was you who cared for Felicity with all the love and tenderness one would expect from her mother."

I choked up, and my voice sounded shaky. "Thank you. You understand better than anybody, because of Amelia." And with that thought, my composure crumbled. Tears rolled down my cheeks, and I lowered my face into my free hand. Henry was beside me in an instant, placing an arm about my shoulder. I laid my head against him and allowed myself to weep without restraint.

I was dimly aware of Elizabeth and Mr. Darcy entering the room and quickly withdrawing. I raised my head, and Henry offered me his handkerchief. After blotting my face I said, "I have lately wept more than ever before in my life. Please forgive me —"

"Nonsense! Don't dare apologize to me. Indeed, you have every reason to cry. You lost a beloved child! I perfectly understand."

I gave him a quavering smile. "Thank you." I held out the handkerchief, but he pushed my hand away.

"Keep it. You may have need of it still."

We did not stay at Gloucester that night. Mr. Darcy wanted to travel as far as possible, so we would need to spend only one night on the road. Elizabeth vowed she felt quite well, so we traveled late into the evening. Although my sister watched me closely, her gaze a silent plea to enlighten her, I was silent. Emotionally, I felt too brittle. After dinner, Henry said he would be departing quite early in the morning and would take his leave of us tonight.

I offered him my hand, and his voice seemed thick with emotion when he spoke. "You have behaved throughout this ordeal with remarkable fortitude, Mary. I admire your courage."

Stunned, I could only stammer out a thank-you. That he would think so well of me, the woman who had refused his offer of marriage, was too generous of him.

"We will have the pleasure of seeing you at the nuptials, will we not?" Elizabeth asked.

"Of course. I look forward to being in your company again soon."

A quick bow, and he was off. I would not see him again until the occasion of Kitty's wedding.

We had only been en route a short time the next morning when Lizzy demanded to know what had transpired between Henry and me the previous day.

"He most kindly lent me his shoulder to cry upon, as well as his handkerchief when I fell to pieces in the parlor. I tried to apologize, but he wouldn't hear of it."

"And last night?"

"He — he said he admired my courage."

My sister's eyes glowed. "Oh, Mary. You would be a fool to believe his feelings for you stop at admiration!"

"I believe he cares for me in the same way he always has. We are friends, and a friend is a good thing to have."

"Oh, yes, do try to convince me you wish for nothing more than friendship from him! What if he loves you?"

I gave her a disparaging look. "He doesn't love me. He admires my character and has compassion for me because of Fee."

"Indulge me. For the sake of argument, if he said he loved you and he offered for you again, would you accept him?"

"Oh, Lizzy, you have asked me this before. I wish you would not harass me so."

She cocked her head at me. "Do you think he came all the way to Bristol because of his friendship with Charles?"

"I do," I said stubbornly. The temperature in the chaise seemed unbearably hot. I dug in my reticule for a fan, then remembered I never bothered with one. "Even if he did so for my sake, can you honestly think, after learning the worst about Lydia, that he would wish to be connected to the Bennet family?"

"And yet Charles, his closest friend, wed one of us disreputable Bennets," she said, laughing.

"May I remind you, that was before we

knew about Lydia and Wickham's latest peccadilloes?" I smiled, though, because I truly believed Charles would have married Jane no matter what scandals had befallen our family, and the same held true for Mr. Darcy.

"You are purposely avoiding the question I asked, so I shall repeat it. If Henry said he loved you, and offered for you, would you marry him?"

I dodged it again. Leaning forward, I said, "Lizzy. Does it seem strange to say I feel at peace with all that has happened?"

She seemed taken aback. "With Mr. Walsh? Or Felicity?"

"Both, I think. I'll always feel a yearning for Fee. I have a hollow space inside, where loving her filled me up. I imagine it will diminish with time. But when I view the matter objectively, without considering my own feelings, I know being raised by her parents is best for Fee."

"And Henry Walsh?"

"Friendship doesn't equate with love. Not romantic love, anyway. I can accept that."

Elizabeth sighed, a look of frustration shadowing her face. "What exactly did Kitty say to you that caused you to doubt both your own and Henry's feelings? You made a vague reference to it when we talked the night of the ball, and Jane and I wondered what you were speaking of."

I shrugged. The pain of it had abated, and I didn't wish to recall Kitty's words. But my sister was staring at me, her eyes insistent, demanding an answer.

"She said I had no looks or fashion. That I was too serious, and men didn't want to marry girls like me."

"But that's ridiculous!"

"I insisted Henry wasn't that sort of man. Unfortunately, at the ball, it seemed he was indeed that sort of man. I realized there was some truth to what she'd said, and it stung."

"And that was when your anger got the better of you?"

I nodded. "I'm sorry about acting like such a simpleton. I shudder to think how I must have appeared."

Elizabeth raised a hand to stop me. "It was short-lived. I doubt anybody gave it a thought by the next morning. You do know, Mary, our love and esteem for you have been growing. I speak for Jane and Charles and Fitzwilliam and myself. If only we had shown you how much we valued you —"

"You are not to blame, Lizzy. I was a foolish girl for many years. It's no surprise my family had difficulty seeing me in any other way. I'm happy to have your respect and affection, but I doubt if it would have changed anything with Henry."

She smiled. "You cannot deny that he recognized your best qualities. He liked you for your quick mind, your candor, your sweetness."

"Oh, you cannot apply the word 'sweet' to me, Elizabeth. You know I am far from it. And I would remind you that because he admires my character does not mean he loves me. His primary emotion regarding me at present is pity."

She groaned and eyed me irritably. "You realize you're being irrational?"

"Perhaps. Isn't that a characteristic of love?"

Elizabeth tilted her head and studied me. "So you admit to loving him?"

"I have never denied it. Now, may we please talk of something else?"

And even though we did, I could not get the memory of Henry's face when he'd expressed his admiration for me out of my mind. Nor the sweetly tender sound of his voice. I wished I did not have to wait an entire month before I would see him again, although a reunion was likely only to bring me pain.

CHAPTER 28

Home to Longbourn, at last, after a few days' respite at High Tor. I was glad wedding preparations were in full swing. They distracted me from thoughts of Felicity. Her absence was palpable. I tiptoed into the small chamber we'd used as her nursery, and to my surprise, someone had cleared it of all vestiges of her. Lydia couldn't have taken everything, since she'd sneaked away in the night. Perhaps Mrs. Hill and Kitty packed up the rest, since the room had to be made ready for wedding guests.

Only one object remained. The silhouette I'd made of her, intact in its frame and still adorning the wall. As poor as it was, it resembled her to some degree, enough so that I had to hastily quit the room.

Mama had finally emerged from seclusion, persuaded no doubt by the pending nuptials. After I told the family about the meeting with Lydia, I think she felt comforted.

"Captain Mason seems a good man," I said, "and wields some influence over Lydia. And we could see she'd formed an attachment to Felicity."

"I shall never see my darling girl again!" wailed my mother. "Or my granddaughter."

"Perhaps not," I said. "But she will write as soon as they're settled, and you may write to her."

With Kitty, I was more forthcoming, describing Lydia's demeanor in more detail. She inhaled sharply when I told her of Lydia's halfhearted expression of thanks.

"Was she cruel to you, Mary?"

"Not precisely. She accused me of committing all manner of injustices in regard to herself and Felicity. Of some, I was guilty, I freely admit. Captain Mason admonished her when she said something nasty about me while we were eating."

"Well done of him! Exactly what she needs. Do you think he will be a good father to Felicity?"

"Of course there is no way to judge for a certainty, but he seemed affectionate with her and told me himself he'd become fond of her." Wishing to change the subject, I said, "How have you managed here? This should be a time of great joy for you, yet you have been forced to deal with this crisis and Mama's resulting hysterics. I am sorry for that."

"Never mind. It was nothing compared to what you suffered." She stopped to squeeze my hand. "My greatest pleasure of the past few weeks has been corresponding with Andrew. I cannot wait to remove from here to my own home." And then she looked a little ashamed, upon realizing, I supposed, I was doomed to life at Longbourn.

"Are you happy, Kitty? Do you love Andrew?"

Her face glowed. "I do. I didn't love him at the beginning. He grew on me! When I was fixed on attaching . . . a certain other gentleman, I viewed Andrew in an altogether different way. Not as handsome or as fine-figured a man as Henry Walsh. Now I think him the finest and handsomest man I have ever known!"

This statement sent us into whoops of laughter and caused Mama to peek her head in the door to see what we were up to. "I declare, it is good to hear laughter again in this house! We have all been in poor spirits since Lydia left us. Kitty, do show Mary all you have accomplished since she's been from home."

And so I was obliged, for an hour or so, to look at embroidered bed hangings, counterpanes, pillowslips, handkerchiefs, and the like. I did not mind, though, because my sister's face shone with a quiet happiness and something very like contentment, which I'd rarely seen there before.

After many days had passed, I felt courageous enough to broach the subject of my future with my father. The library door was closed, so I rapped softly before entering.

"May I speak to you, Papa?" I said, thrusting my head around the door.

"Yes, of course, Mary. Come and be seated."

He waited until I was settled, and then, to my surprise, started the conversation himself. "Tell me, what is your opinion of Andrew Carstairs?"

"I like him very much, sir. He is all that is amiable and has a good living in Steadly, which will allow Kitty to live quite close to Jane. I imagine they'll see each other often."

"Excellent. She seems happier than I've ever seen her before."

I nodded. "I think so too. More than anyone else, Mr. Carstairs seems to have the ability to make her laugh. To banish that melancholy part of her nature."

"Hmm. And I thought she was determined to catch Mr. Walsh. But I understand from

Kitty and Mrs. Bennet it is you, Mary, who has an interest there."

The familiar flush heated my neck and traced a path up to my face. *What should I say? "Yes, Papa, your stupidest daughter had a chance to marry a wonderful man and ruined it"?* "Perhaps at one time we had an interest in each other, but now we are merely friends. I wanted to speak to you about something else, Papa."

He watched me closely for a moment before signaling for me to go on. "I would like a chance to do something with myself besides remain here at Longbourn. I have been contemplating asking my aunt and uncle Gardiner to help me find a governess position in town."

I thought a look of shock flashed across his face, but it happened so fast I couldn't be sure. "What brought this about?"

"I have given it much thought, sir. I don't wish to be dependent on you — or my sisters — for the rest of my life. Therefore, I must earn some money of my own."

"By all means, go on, Mary." Now he seemed amused.

"Please understand I am serious about this, Papa! It is most likely I shall never marry, and I must plan for my future. When I think about remaining here at Longbourn,

I feel a sense of . . . hopelessness. Of simply surrendering all control over my life to the wishes and needs of others."

My father's face seemed to droop before my very eyes, the whole of it slowly sliding downward. The deep grooves at each side of his mouth became more pronounced, and his chin tucked in and down. Even though I'd thought his expression one of amusement mere moments ago, now he looked as sad as I'd ever seen him, and it frightened me. The idea of my not wishing to stay at home must have wounded him.

"Papa! Are you all right?"

He recovered himself enough to insist he was quite well. "The family will oppose it, you know."

I nodded. "Yes. I abhor the idea of causing them pain, but I think this is something I must do." I reached my hand across the desk and he grasped it. "And you, Papa. What do you think?"

He let out a burst of laughter. "My dear child, I would much prefer you to find a good man to marry. I think you give up too easily. Even if Walsh is not up to it, you may meet other fellows. Burying yourself in town and spending most of your waking hours with children will not afford you much opportunity to meet eligible men." He patted my hand before releasing it.

"Not all of us are meant to be married, sir."

"That may be true, but I do not believe you are one of those. That view notwithstanding, if this is what would make you happy, by all means write to your aunt and seek her help. I cannot think of anybody in a better position to aid you in this."

"Thank you, Papa! I shall do so directly. Perhaps she will have some news for me when she comes for the wedding."

"I would caution you, my dear, to say nothing to either your mother or sisters until after the wedding. No reason to upset the whole household before the big day."

"No, of course not. I would want Aunt Gardiner's reassurance first, in any case. For all I know, she may decide helping me in this venture would not be in the best interests of the rest of the family."

"Being a governess is no easy life, Mary. If in the future it seems assured you will never marry, I intend to give you your marriage portion. If teaching children is not all you hoped, you can depend on a little money, anyway."

"Thank you, Papa. That is very generous of you. But only if you and my mother have no need of it."

"It is yours by right, Mary. The other girls have gotten theirs. Why should you be deprived simply because you haven't got a husband? In any case, you will have a greater need of it than they ever will."

A corner of my mouth curved up. "True enough."

We chatted of other things for a few minutes, and when a break in the conversation came, I rose and headed for my chamber, where I began a letter to my aunt.

Upon completion of my letter, I decided to walk to Meryton and post it. I stopped by Kitty's chamber to see if she wanted to come with me. She was not there. Bandboxes filled with all the linens she'd been embroidering lay about the room, and a trunk with its lid flung back sat ready to receive her bride clothes. On her bed rested a piece of parchment, a letter from the looks of it, probably from Andrew. But no. Even from a distance, I could see the penmanship was Jane's. Curious, I walked over and picked it up. An unwelcome dread took hold of me, but like a fool, I read it anyway.

High Tor
13 September

Kitty dear,

I need your advice — and possibly your intervention with Andrew — on a matter of some concern. It has recently come to our attention that Henry Walsh is showing serious interest in Miss Bellcourt, who resides not far from us. Tongues are wagging, and the gossips have it that he is soon to offer for her. Henry doesn't speak of her, and Charles feels it would be the height of poor manners to pry into his personal life.

I have mentioned Miss B. to Mary before, but at that time, I believe they had only a passing acquaintance. I did so only to encourage Mary to come back to High Tor! I admitted as much to her upon her return. But this is different.

We saw him at a private dinner, where he was seated next to the lady at table. She's quite lovely, has a great delicacy of behavior, and of course her fortune of £20,000 doesn't hurt. The two seemed quite intent on their conversation, and spoke but little to others seated near them. But it is, of course, difficult to judge what two people feel for each other.

Lizzy says Mary confided a great deal to her on the ride from Bristol to High Tor. She does not believe HW loves her, and insists he has no intention of offering for her again. But there is a vast deal of difference between what one will share with a sister and what is in her own heart. Have you and Mary talked of this since she has been home?

Will you ask Andrew what he knows? Perhaps I ask too much. I am trying to decide what we should tell our sister. If there is no hope, if indeed HW has settled on Miss Bellcourt, I believe we should tell Mary before the wedding. However, if Andrew feels this is all rumor and innuendo, it is perhaps best to say nothing.

I await your response.

Yours, etc.,
Jane

Blindly, I stood, swaying a bit, my legs feeling as if they might give way. I replaced the letter approximately where I'd found it and fled the room. Ignoring the stabbing hurt in my chest, I decided to walk to Meryton alone, stopping only long enough to tell Mrs. Hill where I was going. I thought about asking if she knew where Kitty and my mother were, but what did it really matter?

So much for bragging to Elizabeth about my calm acceptance of a mere friendship with Henry. I felt a deep, wrenching pain, but to everybody else, I intended to appear unfazed. This outcome was, after all, what I had expected. Miss Bellcourt — even her name sounded elegant — no doubt encompassed all a man would want in a wife. Beauty, manners, fashion, and wealth. And all these attributes would make her an ideal mother to Amelia. I hoped she was kind and affectionate, and possessed a modicum of intelligence, too.

You had your chance with Henry Walsh, Mary, and you recklessly cast it aside. Now I would never have him. In truth, I didn't deserve him. I walked faster, the sooner to post what now seemed a very urgent letter to my aunt.

CHAPTER 29

The week of the wedding came at last, and guests began arriving. Among them were my two elder sisters and their families, all of whom were lodging at Netherfield. Nobody took me aside to inform me of the imminent nuptials of Mr. Walsh and Miss Bellcourt, or even to warn me of the serious nature of their attachment. Perhaps my sisters were desirous of protecting my feelings, or maybe they'd learned nothing from Andrew. It seemed pointless to speculate.

About my aunt Gardiner's actions on my behalf I had no need to conjecture. I'd received a response from her only a few days after she would have been in receipt of my letter. It was short and to the point. She had two families in mind, both unexceptionable, whom she believed were in need of governesses. Although she didn't discourage me, she urged me to use all caution and prudence in choosing this life for myself.

She ended by saying she knew my parents and sisters would not wish me to rush into anything, and we would speak about this when she arrived for the wedding. That suited me well, because when the celebration was over, the newlyweds off to their new life, and the guests gone home, I was most eager to inform my family of my plans. I desired no delays; in fact, it would please me to return with my aunt and uncle Gardiner to London if possible.

Andrew, Henry, and Mrs. Walsh were lodging at a coaching inn in Meryton. Andrew wasted no time in visiting his bride, but of Mr. Walsh we saw nothing. I tried to put him from my thoughts.

When my aunt reached us, she begged my indulgence in delaying our conversation regarding the secret matter. "My dear, your mother is quite unable to exert herself to accomplish anything. May our discussion wait until after the wedding?"

Of course she was right. Mama had thrown herself into a state of agitation equal to what she had experienced prior to Jane and Elizabeth's wedding. My aunt, indeed all of us, had to assume her duties. We organized the servants, designated chambers for guests who would be lodging with us, planned the menu for the wedding breakfast, and ensured that our guests would have excellent fare at table and all the comforts a good host would provide. None of us truly minded, because it was an exciting time. Another sister to be wed! And Kitty went about in a cloud of joy, especially after Andrew's arrival.

The day before the wedding, she hovered near the windows watching for him. Jane and I were upstairs discussing my wedding finery. She had brought several gowns with her from which I could choose. My gaze lingered on the apricot crape dress, the one I wore to the Pennington ball. "I should like to wear this one again, if you think it would suit," I said.

"It's perfect, Mary," my sister said. By the crooked little smile she gave me, I knew she also remembered when I'd last worn it. "We shall have to make a few adjustments, since the wedding is in the morning. Add a lace tucker, perhaps remove the flounce."

Suddenly I heard Kitty cry out. "Andrew is come. And Henry too!"

I glanced at myself in the pier glass, not pleased with what I saw. A silent understanding passed between Jane and me. She dropped the crape gown, rifled through the other clothes she'd brought, and offered something entirely different. "Change into this frock, dear." She held out a white muslin dress with a rose band under the bosom.

"But that's not exactly a day dress, is it? I don't want him to think . . ." I felt my cheeks flush. What didn't I want him to think? That I was trying to impress him?

"Yes, it is a day dress, only a little fancier than your usual ones. You can wear a tucker at the neckline. Perfectly proper." She bit her bottom lip. If I was not mistaken, my eldest sister was trying very hard to quell a grin. But I was beyond caring what she thought, or what she might tell Elizabeth or Charles, or even Mr. Darcy.

I quickly disrobed and changed into Jane's dress, and in a moment I was seated at the dressing table while Jane repinned my hair. She let a few ringlets dangle at the neckline, which I thought a bit daring for daytime, but I allowed it.

"You look quite pretty, Mary. Are you ready?"

I nodded, even though my stomach was fidgeting about. Downstairs, the men were just making their entrance. I shook hands with Andrew, and then with Henry. "You look well, Miss Bennet," he said.

"Thank you." He looked so handsome in a blue morning coat and buckskin britches, he quite startled me out of my senses. *Quit staring, Mary, and say something, for the Lord's sake.*

"Please, do come in and take some refreshments," Jane said. Thank heaven someone could speak.

We gathered in the downstairs sitting room, and not long after, my mother, and even my father, joined us. A footman carried in a meal of cold meats, cheese, rolls, and cakes. Mr. Walsh walked over to speak to Papa. Owing to my position on the sofa, I caught only a little of their conversation, but it seemed field drainage was the subject. No doubt Henry was asking about the work that had been done for the tenants, and if it had proved to be effective. Mama was teasing Kitty and Andrew about wedding jitters. Jane whispered in my ear, "You and Mr. Walsh need some privacy. Why not ask him if he would care for a walk?"

"What? No! That would be too forward."

Jane heaved a sigh. She leaned back in her chair and a scheming look spread over her face. Before I could stop her, she was on her feet and walking toward Papa.

"I do beg your pardon, Mr. Walsh, but I must speak with my father on an urgent matter." She took a firm hold of Papa's arm and began guiding him away. Her voice had carried so that we all heard, and Mama immediately responded as might have been expected.

"Jane! What could be so urgent as to interrupt a conversation between your papa and Mr. Walsh?" Jane gave a quick wink in our mother's direction. Kitty and Andrew smiled at each other in a knowing way, while I wished to sink into the floor.

But her ploy worked. Henry was suddenly at my side. "Would you care to walk out with me, Miss Bennet? The weather is fine."

"I would enjoy that. Do I need a wrap?"

"There's a slight chill in the air. I'll wait for you at the entryway while you fetch one."

We set off down the lane, both of us quiet at first. It was a clear, shining autumn day, and I hoped tomorrow would be the same, for the nuptials. "Do you recall our discussion regarding which was our favorite season?" I asked.

"Of course."

"This is exactly the kind of day I had in mind when I told you I loved autumn above all the others."

"You said the air 'shimmers.' " He made a show of looking about, and then, chuckling, he said, "I must agree with you. I believe it does. However, I still love spring best."

"We shall continue to disagree, then. Your

mother is well?" I asked, feeling remiss that I hadn't asked after her sooner.

"Oh, yes. She is most eager to see you again. I quite like your father, Mary," he said, rather unexpectedly.

"He can be very affable, when he troubles himself to emerge from his library. I suppose with the burden of six females in the house for so many years, he needed a retreat."

Henry laughed. "Some men would not view that as a burden." He looked down at me, his eyes teasing. "He seems affectionate with all of you."

"He is, in his way. My father has always been especially fond of Jane and Elizabeth. You see, my parents . . . have not had the happiest of unions." I felt my cheeks warm. Why was I confiding such a thing? "I believe he transferred his affections to my eldest sisters, the most sensible and engaging of all of us."

"I would take exception to that." He drew my arm through his, pulling me closer in so doing. I smiled, not daring to look at him directly. "Neither were my parents happy in their marriage. My own father was gruff and distant. I often wonder why my mother married him."

"Will you tell me, if it's not too intrusive a

question, did you ever reconcile with your father after Amelia came to live with you?"

"No." He glanced at me, his expression sad. But there was a hard set to his jaw, as well. "He was ashamed, I believe. Until the day he died, he was ashamed of Amelia, and most certainly of me. He withdrew from society, and eventually from life."

"I'm sorry. A rift such as that must be heartbreaking."

"I hope to overcome my bitterness toward him someday. With the years, the memories are fading. Of course his actions made my mother very unhappy, too, which I find hard to forgive. She's the most generous of women."

"I thought her a most kind and warm person," I said. "For the sake of my parents, I'm hoping, no doubt foolishly, that once all of us are gone my father and mother will grow closer, since they will only have each other."

Henry came to an abrupt halt. "Do you have plans, then, to leave Longbourn?"

"I-I am thinking of taking a governess position. In town." I stammered, not having anticipated that this subject would arise between us. Given the turn the conversation had taken, it seemed only natural to tell him about my plans.

"I see. You never said . . . I didn't know you were thinking of this."

"No. I haven't even told my family. I decided to wait until after the wedding, as I know it will cause an uproar."

"In London, you say?"

"Yes. My aunt and uncle live in Cheapside and know several families with young children. She — my aunt Gardiner — has suggested two in particular who may need a governess." He made no response, and I could only imagine what he must have been thinking. Another embarrassment for the Bennet family; a brash daughter running off to town to place herself on one of the lower rungs of society. Deliberately.

I could not keep silent. "You do not approve."

"If this is what you truly want, what would make you happy, it is not for me to question your decision."

I should not have told him. But some part of me had wanted him to know. Before he could announce his engagement to Miss Bellcourt, he would learn that I had plans of my own. If he didn't want me, there would be no cause for pity. I was not destined to waste away here at Longbourn.

What hopes I had held for a different outcome to this conversation vanished. In a few moments, Henry suggested we should be getting back. When we entered the drawing room, Jane looked at me expectantly. I couldn't meet her eyes. The two visitors remained for most of the day, but Henry and I did not speak privately again. In fact, I felt his aloofness like a rebuke.

CHAPTER 30

"Mr. Collins, please!" Charlotte Collins's voice intruded on her husband's recitation of the numerous ill-considered actions of the Bennet sisters. But it was as if she had not spoken. He went right on, seemingly unaware that some of those present might find his words offensive.

The ceremony having taken place earlier that morning, we were now enjoying the wedding breakfast. The vicar, the very one whom Kitty had poked fun at due to his advanced age, performed the ceremony, and my sister and her new husband had been casting adoring looks at each other ever since. I, too, basked in their glow, until Mr. Collins began his declarations. Could I slip unobtrusively from the room?

"The two eldest daughters, Mrs. Bingley and Mrs. Darcy, are exemplary in their behavior," he said in his pompous way. His listeners stood in a small cluster, and they were few — Charlotte; her parents, Sir William and Lady Lucas; and her sister, Maria. Several other small groups of guests were within earshot, however.

"Although Elizabeth . . . well, never mind. It shall go unsaid."

Excellent decision, since Mr. Darcy would probably call you out if you uttered one word against Lizzy.

"I cautioned my cousin Mr. Bennet on many occasions to end his overindulgence of the other girls." He ceased talking, but only long enough to draw breath and survey the room to see who was listening. Did he not notice Mr. Darcy standing not three feet away, in conversation with Henry Walsh?

"The family is fortunate, after the most recent scandal, that Kitty found a husband. I told Mrs. Bennet when we arrived, however, that any chance Mary may have had for a happy union now seems out of the question. Mrs. Wickham's actions have tainted the poor girl." He smirked, making his expression even more self-satisfied than usual. "Her own mother said there was not much chance to begin with. Mary, while a good enough girl, is bookish, and most men —"

This was the point at which Charlotte interjected. As I backed away on tiptoe, I heard Henry say to Mr. Darcy, "Who is this person?"

"Have you not had the pleasure, Walsh?" my brother-in-law asked. "Allow me to introduce you to my wife's relation, Mr. Collins."

The last thing I saw before I fled the room was Henry and Mr. Collins eyeing each other in an antagonistic way. My cousin nodded curtly; Henry did not acknowledge the introduction in any way and soon resumed his conversation with Mr. Darcy.

To think that my own mother had informed Mr. Collins that she thought I would never marry! And he repeated her words in the company of all the wedding guests. Could I hide until the celebration was over? Henry's refusal to acknowledge my tactless cousin, equivalent to a direct cut, warmed my heart. Blast! If only I hadn't ruined everything and thrown Henry into the arms of Miss Bellcourt.

Drawing my shawl around my shoulders more closely, I walked toward the avenue. The day had begun with a downpour, which most fortuitously had let up before the wedding. Now the mist had burned off, and the sun fought valiantly for dominance, warming my back and neck. The air felt fresh,

403

washed of any impurities by this morning's rain. I slowed, thinking I heard footsteps behind me. Turning, I glimpsed the very man who occupied my thoughts striding toward me, and I stopped to wait for him. It would have been rude to do otherwise.

"Mary," he said almost curtly.

"I —"

"My pardon, but I do not like listening to your boorish, idiotic cousin insulting you. Nor do I like it any better to hear of your own mother doing so." He walked ahead of me and spun abruptly to face me. "I did not care for it when Kitty and your sister Lydia made snide comments about you, either. What possesses these people?" He flung out his arms, as if beseeching me for an answer.

I wanted to laugh but held myself in check. For once it was not my face that was flushed, but his. Not from embarrassment, but from anger.

"Mr. Walsh —"

"Henry. You agreed."

A big smile broke out. "Henry, I thank you for your concern and your spirited defense of me. But you should know that in the not-too-distant past, I deserved their censure." He started to speak, but I held up a hand to forestall him. "Perhaps not to the degree it was heaped upon me, but I was . . . I used to be, well, somewhat foolish."

"I have never counted you as such." He took a step closer to me.

"You have a great deal of forbearance, sir. There was a time in our acquaintance during which I behaved very foolishly."

"Yes, you did. But I believe you are wiser now." Another step closer. "My own behavior had nothing to recommend it."

"I cannot disagree with you on that point."

"Are you determined to go through with this plan to become a governess, Mary?"

I laughed, and now he stood close enough for me to see the smoothness of his face, the strong line of his jaw, and the unusual blue eyes I'd come to love so well. "Yes, I suppose I am. Why do you ask?" I added.

"Because it would be most inconvenient. I would not like having a wife who lived at such a distance from me."

I staggered backward, nearly toppling over when my one of my slippers slid on the gravel. Henry put out a hand to steady me. "I beg your pardon?" I said.

"No indeed, that would not do at all. I think I would want you close by me at all times."

"But we heard — that is, I thought your betrothal to another lady was imminent."

"That rumor traveled all the way to Long-bourn, did it?" He chuckled. "Nonsense. There is only one woman I love."

"Who?" I asked, feeling ridiculous, since the answer was obvious. When I looked into his eyes, if I was not mistaken, it *was* love I saw there. But still, I wanted him to tell me.

Henry took my face in his hands, rubbing his thumbs across my cheeks. Tears pooled in my eyes and traced a path down my face. "You, my dearest girl. You have besieged my heart." He leaned in and kissed the tears away. "Will you accept me this time, Mary?"

I nodded, sniffling indelicately. "Oh, yes. I will. Of course I will."

"Amelia needs a mother, you know."

The breath rushed out of me. But when I looked at Henry, I realized he was teasing me.

"I can only say how fortunate I am that the woman I love will be — has shown herself to be — a most devoted mother."

I placed my hands on his chest. Most certainly this was too bold, but I didn't know where else to put them, and I had an overwhelming need to touch him. "Will this be all right with Amelia? Do you think she can love me someday?"

"She has already expressed the opinion that you are her favorite of any lady I have ever introduced to her."

"Does that include Miss Bellcourt?" I asked, arching a brow at him.

He scowled. "Amelia would have taken an instant dislike to her. She has no warmth about her. Let's not talk of her, please."

Before pulling me close, he said in a low, teasing voice, "You are lovely. Did you wear this gown just for me?"

And for a few moments, we did not talk at all. We found a much more pleasurable occupation for our lips and mouths and, to my surprise, tongues.

Before Henry and his mother departed, he took me aside. Since we did not wish to arouse suspicion, we had only a few moments to speak privately. Even though the newlyweds had left long before, we agreed it would be best to wait until the next day to make our announcement. The men had arranged a shooting party for the morning. Henry would speak to my father beforehand, while I told my mother and sisters the news. Afterward he would take himself off with Charles and Mr. Darcy for the sport.

"I think you should bring your mother to spend the morning with us," I said. "She must be part of our celebration."

"How kind of you to think of her. I can't wait until tomorrow to give her the news, however. I shall tell her tonight."

"You believe she will be pleased, then?"

"She has done nothing but sing your praises ever since the day we all spent together at Linden Hall."

"Even after . . ."

"Yes, even after you spurned me so cruelly."

I knew he was teasing me again, but the mere thought of that painful day by the river made me cringe with embarrassment. "Oh, don't mention that. I shall never get over my shame!"

He laughed. "Until tomorrow, my dearest Mary."

My knees felt weak.

When Henry and his mother arrived the following morning, and I saw him whisper to my father, I thought I might lose what little breakfast I'd been able to eat. Jane and Lizzy had been giving me inquisitive looks since last night, and they were no longer bothering to hide their smiles. My mother seemed to be the only one who had not an inkling that Henry Walsh, at this very moment, was asking for my hand in marriage.

"I am so pleased you could join us," I said

to Mrs. Walsh as we settled ourselves in the drawing room. She squeezed my hand, and, to my surprise, I noticed a gloss of tears in her eyes. But she was fully in command of herself.

She spoke in a low voice, since she knew I had not told my family yet. "I have waited so long for Henry to find just the right wife. My son deserves so much happiness, and I believe he will find it with you, Mary."

"Thank you, ma'am. And now I must not delay the news any longer." I took a steadying breath. "Mama, Jane, Lizzy. I have something to tell you."

My sisters could hardly contain their glee, while my mother simply looked perplexed. "Well, what is it, Mary?" she asked.

"Mr. Walsh — Henry — has asked for my hand and I have accepted. He is speaking to Papa right now."

"Oh!" Mama fell back onto the sofa. Nobody paid her the least attention. In the meantime, my sisters embraced me joyfully. Of course, they prodded me for the details, but I thought those would best be shared when we were alone. For now, a simple explanation would suffice.

"He asked me yesterday afternoon, but we thought the day should belong to Kitty and Andrew alone. This morning seemed the perfect time for him to speak to Papa, and for me to tell all of you."

My mother sprang up from her prostrate position, seemingly having recovered herself. "Upon my honor! All my daughters married. I thought you would remain a spinster, Mary, I must admit. And I was depending on you to care for your father and me in our decline." She sounded embarrassingly sad.

Jane leaped in. "Oh, Mama, you know we will all care for you and Papa. And that time is a long way off, in any case."

"But you will all be so far away from us, clear up in horrid Derbyshire."

"And you may spend as much time with each of us as you desire," Elizabeth said. "You will never lack for an invitation from one of us."

She visibly brightened. "I suppose you are right. Mary, you deceitful creature! How long have you known this was to be?"

"I knew nothing until yesterday, Mama."

Before she could pry further, Henry and my father entered the room. I caught Henry's eye, and he nodded imperceptibly. I felt relieved, although I'd hardly expected Papa to withhold his consent.

"I see you have all received the good news," Papa said. He turned to my mother.

"My dear, we are to lose another daughter. I console myself with the knowledge that Mr. Walsh is the best of men." He came over to me and kissed me on both cheeks.

"Thank you, Papa," I whispered.

"I shall miss you, Mary. You have brought me comfort these last few years."

Tears filled my eyes then. It was the closest my father had ever come to saying he cared for me. That my presence here since Lizzy and Jane left had meant something to him. If it had not been for the sudden entrance of Mr. Darcy and Charles, with their accompanying hounds making all kinds of racket, I would have wept. Instead, we swept them up in the news, setting off a new round of kisses and congratulations.

My father passed around glasses of wine for a toast, and Mama told Mrs. Hill to treat the servants to a bowl of punch.

"What a shame our aunt and uncle had to leave so early this morning," Jane said. "They will be so happy when they hear the news." Our uncle Gardiner had many business interests in town and could never be away for long.

"When is the wedding to be?" Charles asked.

Henry and I looked at each other. "I don't know," I said, at the same time he said,

411

"Soon." Everybody laughed.

"Will you be married from Longbourn?" Mama asked.

"We haven't discussed any of the particulars yet," I said.

"I have a splendid idea!" Jane said. "Why not be married from High Tor? I would guess you will want Andrew to marry you, so that would be perfect."

Mama fussed. "But —"

Jane cut her off. "It would give you and Papa a chance to meet Henry's family and see Mary's new home."

My mother did not yet know about Amelia, although Henry and I had agreed he should inform Papa. I hoped nobody would mention her now, as one could never be sure of my mother's reaction, or what ludicrously offensive statement she might come out with.

Mrs. Walsh looked at my mother. "I would be delighted to have your company at Linden Hall. And Mrs. Bingley is right — the rest of the family will wish to meet you."

Mama relented. "Well, I suppose I can be content that three of my girls married from here."

"What would please you, Mary?" Henry asked.

I did not really need to think about it at

all. I wanted to marry from High Tor, where we had met and fallen in love. But I didn't want to appear too eager, or there would be ruffled feathers to smooth. "I like the idea," I said. "If my parents are in agreement."

So it was decided. Henry and I would be married from High Tor, in a month's time. My mother protested at first. "I cannot possibly prepare for another wedding in such a short time!"

"But, Mama," Lizzy said, "we will all take part in the preparations." Casting me a mischievous glance, she added, "As we did for Kitty's wedding."

"I hope Henry will not change his mind when he hears the news, but I will not be embroidering pillowcases or handkerchiefs or anything else. So we need set aside no time for that." I turned to look at him. "I detest needlework," I said, pulling a face. "Do you wish to cry off?"

"I'm sure my mother would agree we have more than enough embroidered linens. Besides," he added, "you won't get rid of me that easily."

"When did you first know you liked me?" I asked Henry later that day. I'd lost some of my shyness around him and even could tease him a little. We were seated together on the sofa, the rest of the family having apparently decided to allow us a bit of privacy.

"When I first met you at High Tor. There was something in your manner, perhaps your reserve, I was attracted to. I liked hearing you play the pianoforte. But you took no notice of me. At least not then."

"Oh, but you're wrong. I was very conscious of your watching me, although at that time I never believed you could be interested in me."

He grinned. "Foolish girl. It was a long time before I had the pleasure of seeing you again, however."

"Indeed, I had no idea of returning. Jane forced me into it, after Lydia arrived at Longbourn with her shocking news."

"I am indebted to both your sisters, then. To Lydia for her indiscretions and Jane for her good sense. What about you, Mary? Did you like me at all then?"

I felt my cheeks warm but decided to tell the truth. "Oh, yes. The more I knew you the better I liked you. I believe it was after the picnic that I decided I was quite smitten."

"So I wasn't mistaken in thinking you cared for me! I felt it keenly at Linden Hall. What happened to turn you away from me,

Mary? Can you tell me now?"

"It wasn't just one thing, you know."

He sighed, only half serious. "Tell me all my sins."

"It started with Kitty. I must have your promise never to let on to her that I revealed this to you. She would die of mortification."

"I already suspected she was involved."

"After the day at Linden Hall, she told me you were meant for her, that you were her last chance to get a husband. She begged me to step aside. To leave High Tor, in fact."

"But you didn't."

"I refused, although I did give her some sisterly advice about how she might win you."

One corner of his mouth curled up and he said, "And what exactly was your advice?"

I smiled teasingly. "She didn't like the fact that you always talked to me instead of her, so I told her to read and behave with more decorum. I said in that way, she might transform herself into someone interesting."

He shook his head, puzzled. "I never noticed any difference in her manner toward me."

"That's because she abandoned any thought of changing when you didn't respond immediately. Ironically, looking back on it, I advised her to be more like me, while I endeavored to be more like her."

"Good God, no! In what way?"

I didn't know how much to tell him without embarrassing myself, but in for a penny, in for a pound. "She had said I wasn't pretty." He started to protest, but I stopped him. "I suppose I took her comments to heart, because I chose the apricot gown for the ball, and had my hair done in a more becoming fashion. I thought to please you."

"And nothing went according to plan that night, for either of us. I did notice how lovely you looked, though, which I believe I mentioned the following day."

"Yes, well, by then the damage was done, wasn't it? Oh, don't look that way — I can laugh about it now! After the ball, I convinced myself you liked me but would never *love* me. I was sure you would choose Kitty, or one of the other younger girls who were following you around that night."

His eyes were grave. "I didn't love you the first time I proposed. Oh, I cared for you a great deal, but I didn't love you yet. I'm sorry if I hurt you, Mary."

"It did hurt at the time, but I see now everything was for the best. I needed Felicity in my life. I needed her love, as she needed mine. Were you surprised when I declined your offer?"

"Yes, and confused. Because all our dealings with each other had been so harmonious. I thought we were well matched. But I see now that was rather a cold view of the matter. Not precisely the way a man should approach the woman he wishes to marry."

"I was so angry with you, for ignoring me at the ball and not telling us about Amelia. I couldn't believe you had the audacity to propose. Then I had that awful moment when I was convinced you wanted me only because you believed I would be a good mother."

"I hate thinking about that day. I was a fool."

I toyed with one of the sofa cushions. "I've been wondering, when exactly *did* you begin to love me?"

His eyes gleamed with amusement, but he answered without hesitation. "At Longbourn, when Charles and I were there. You had a new vitality, and more confidence than you'd ever shown before. And Bristol made me certain. You experienced the worst loss imaginable and bore it with grace. That was when I knew beyond a doubt that my heart belonged to you."

"Another reason I will always love Felicity. I thought you pitied me most of all."

"Never. I felt a deep sorrow for what you were suffering because of Fee. If you interpreted it as pity, well, you were wrong."

Henry reached for my hands. "Will it hurt you to know I *did* believe you would be a good mother to Amelia? Because I did . . . I do. But that was only *after* I loved you."

He drew me close. We were quiet for a moment, preoccupied with other things. He finally released me, but kept hold of my hand.

"Why did you help us find Lydia?"

"How could I not? I knew how strong your attachment to Felicity was. Although I believe my motives were unselfish, deep down I hoped my actions might give us a new beginning."

"And did you come here with the idea of offering for me?"

He laughed a little. "Oh, yes. I intended to propose the day before the wedding. But then you announced your plan to become a governess, and I thought perhaps I'd misread you once again."

"I still had unreasonable doubts about your intentions. In any case, I thought you were about to tell me you were engaged."

"I understand," he said. "But it did give

me a scare."

I reached up and touched his cheek. "Loving you has eased the sting of losing Fee." I laid my head upon his shoulder, and the soft wool of his coat pressed into my face. The feel of it reminded me of the day he'd picked me up and carried me out of the river. In a minute, I heard voices in the hall, most assuredly a warning from the family that they were about to enter the room.

I started to pull away, but he held me against him. As though he thought I might disappear if he let me go. "I love you, Mary Bennet," he said, and kissed my mouth sweetly.

We pulled apart when the door opened and our laughing relations poured into the room. "You must wait for the nuptials, Walsh!" Charles said.

"Oh, let them alone," Elizabeth countered.

I drew him down for another kiss, folding into his embrace. For once in my life, I didn't care what the family thought.

ACKNOWLEDGMENTS

My deepest gratitude to my agent, Steven Chudney, for believing in this book and delivering it into the hands of Rachel Kahan and Amanda Bergeron at William Morrow. Thank you, Amanda, for your editorial insights and gentle guidance. Thanks also to the behind-the-scenes professionals who had a hand in bringing *The Pursuit of Mary Bennet* to publication.

Five years ago I joined the Jane Austen Society of North America (JASNA) and began attending the meetings of the Denver/Boulder chapter. The members, with their comprehensive knowledge of all things Austen, rekindled my love of the six novels and greatly enhanced my understanding of Jane Austen and her time.

Among the numerous resources about Austen, I found David M. Shapard's *The Annotated Pride and Prejudice* the most essential. So many details, big and small, explained in one handy volume!

Thanks to my husband, Jim, and daughter, Katie, my loyal first readers. Katie in particular helped me find the heart of this story with her sure grasp of character. To my critique group, the Wild Folk, you nourish, encourage, and sustain my writing. I couldn't do without you.

I often wonder what Jane Austen would make of all the sequels featuring her characters. Perhaps she would say one thing in public, and something entirely different — with a little bite to it — in a letter to her sister Cassandra. Here's hoping she would be, if not kind in her criticism of my work, at least a bit amused.

P.S.
INSIGHTS, INTERVIEWS
& MORE . . .

■ ■ ■ ■

ABOUT THE BOOK

■ ■ ■ ■

WHY I WROTE
THE PURSUIT OF MARY BENNET
BY PAMELA MINGLE

An intense longing for more of Jane Austen is what compels the sequel writer and reader. More of Elizabeth and Mr. Darcy, more of Elinor and Edward, more of Emma and Mr. Knightly. When Jane Austen died, tragically, at the age of forty-one, she left her work unfinished and her readers unsatisfied. With great longing, we imagine eight novels, not six. If only she'd had a chance to complete *Sanditon* and *The Watsons.* And if she'd lived to be as old as her sister and mother, she might have written many other novels.

Pride and Prejudice and the five Bennet sisters stand at the head of the parade of Austen's memorable characters. About Elizabeth Bennet, Jane Austen said, "I must confess that I think her as delightful a character as ever appeared in print, and how I shall be able to tolerate those who do not like her, at least, I do not know."

But a story about Mary, the most ma-
ligned Bennet sister? Perhaps I did not
always like her as well as I do now. She grew
on me.

Mary, of course, is overshadowed by the
other sisters, as we lose ourselves in the
stories of Elizabeth and Jane and Lydia. In
the first few readings of *Pride and Prejudice*,
Mary barely registers with the reader.
Sometimes I wondered why Jane Austen
had included her in the story at all. Though
she provides a little comic relief, she's
nowhere near as fully drawn as Mr. Collins
or Lady Catherine. Nor is she sympathetic,
except in the Netherfield ball scene, when
Mr. Bennet dismisses her playing so cruelly.

Did there need to be five daughters to
prove how diligently the Bennet parents
were trying for an heir? David Shapard, editor of *The Annotated Pride and Prejudice*,
suggests that by including a fifth daughter,
Austen renders each individual daughter's
financial plight more dire, further limiting
their marriage prospects and giving the
heroines added obstacles to overcome.

In the novel, we find Mary mentioned
only about a dozen and a half times. Most
often, these are not actual scenes in which
she speaks. She isn't lively or beautiful, like
Elizabeth and Jane. Nor is she flirtatious or

outrageous, like Kitty and Lydia. Instead, like so many middle siblings, Mary is isolated, not really a part of the camaraderie shared by the pairings of her elder and younger sisters. Left to her own devices, she tries to find her niche, but her attempts make her seem more foolish than appealing.

Aside from the novel, the many adaptations of *Pride and Prejudice* for television and film color our perceptions of Mary. In the 1940 movie version, she is part of the sisterly circle, but still a caricature. In the iconic 1995 version of *Pride and Prejudice,* the family tolerates her because she is, after all, one of them. She spouts her platitudes, and the other characters roll their eyes. The 2005 film portrays her as a young girl who is afraid of society and is always the last one to know the latest gossip shared by her sisters. At least in this version, we see her in a more sympathetic light, especially after her father humiliates her. He finds her weeping and comforts her.

So as a character, Austen leaves Mary unformed, except in the most basic way. For an author who wanted to try her hand at a sequel, this was not a shortcoming, but an opportunity. Mary was rich with possibilities. With Mary, I could begin anew and develop her into a character readers would care about.

We know that Mary lacks common sense, like her mother, and is studious, like her father. Those qualities formed the jumping-off point for my book. In the beginning, Mary's worst traits still dominate, along with something new: a simmering anger regarding her prospects, her family's expectations of her, and her own perception of herself. When Henry Walsh enters the picture and begins to show an interest in her, she's thrown completely off-balance. She doesn't know how to accept a man's addresses, nor is she even sure she wants to.

This story, then, is about both the pursuit of Mary by Henry, and Mary's own pursuit of a future and an identity of her own.

Most of the Austen-inspired sequels are written in third person. I decided to write *The Pursuit of Mary Bennet* in first person, as the truest path to Mary's heart and mind, the best way to get close to her. Just as Mary knows she can never be Jane or Elizabeth, I knew I could never write in the voice of Jane Austen. Rather, in borrowing her characters and striving to stay true to their essential natures, I've tried to write in the spirit of Austen.

My best hope is that Mary, through my

imagining of her life after *Pride and Prejudice,* may turn out to be a delightful character in her own right.

DISCUSSION QUESTIONS

1. What are your impressions of Mary at the beginning of the story? How would you describe her?

2. What has changed for the Bennet family since the end of *Pride and Prejudice*? For Mary in particular?

3. Why does Mary say she "carries a degree of anger and resentment in her chest"? Why is she more relaxed at High Tor than at home?

4. How would you describe Mary's feelings toward Henry leading up to the Pennington ball? His toward her? Are her rash actions at the ball justified? Her anger and hurt feelings?

5. Elizabeth neatly sums up Mary's state of mind: Mary is afraid of love, because she

has always felt unloved. Do you agree with her opinion?

6. Henry's proposal to Mary has certain similarities to that of Mr. Darcy's to Elizabeth. What are they? Why does Mary refuse his offer of marriage?

7. After the birth of Lydia's child, Mary returns to Longbourn. How can you explain the fact that Mary, unwed and childless, almost immediately bonds with her new niece? How does Felicity make a difference in Mary's life?

8. Is Mary's assessment of her role in caring for Felicity accurate? Does her self-recrimination remind you of any Austen heroines? If so, explain.

9. What happens during the stay at High Tor and Bristol to persuade Mary that Henry thinks of her only as a friend?

10. Describe the circumstances that allowed Mary and Henry to slowly make their way back to each other. In what way(s) did each of them have to change?

11. Writer and editor James Collins says that

beneath the famous first line of *Pride and Prejudice* is this reflection: "It is a truth universally acknowledged that a single woman of small fortune must be in want of a husband." How is this relevant to *The Pursuit of Mary Bennet*? Does it have relevance for women today?

12. Did the author remain true to Jane Austen's portrayal of the *Pride and Prejudice* characters?

13. How does Mary's relationship with Henry compare to Elizabeth's with Mr. Darcy?

■ ■ ■ ■

READ ON

■ ■ ■ ■

PAMELA MINGLE'S FAVORITE REGENCY BOOKS

All of Jane Austen's novels, especially *Pride and Prejudice, Sense and Sensibility, Emma,* and *Persuasion*

Jane Austen Made Me Do It, edited by Laurel Ann Nattress

Bath Tangle, by Georgette Heyer

Arabella, by Georgette Heyer

The Bridgerton Novels, by Julia Quinn

An Assembly Such As This, by Pamela Aidan

The Emperor's Conspiracy, by Michelle Diener

ABOUT THE AUTHOR

Pamela Mingle, a former teacher and librarian, lives in Lakewood, Colorado. She is the author of *Kissing Shakespeare,* a time-travel romance for young adults set in Elizabethan England (Delacorte Press, 2012). Pamela is a member of the Society of Children's Book Writers and Illustrators, Pikes Peak Writers, Romance Writers of America, and the Jane Austen Society of North America. She and her husband are frequent visitors to the United Kingdom, where they enjoy walking and visiting historical sites.

CPSIA information can be obtained
at www.ICGtesting.com
Printed in the USA
FFOW02n0323021213
2522FF

9 781410 464552